The kiss was s   **lasting.**

When Ingrid didn't resist, Luke leaned into her, taking her fully into the heat that flared up between them.

He gathered her close, sinking into the pleasure as she made a soft sound in her throat. Surprise? Delight?

There was no time to wonder as a wave of desire, hot and swift, nearly swamped him.

One minute he was simply acting on a whim. The next he felt the pull of raw, sexual need taking over his mind, his will, his senses.

RAVES FOR R. C. RYAN'S NOVELS

MATT

"With tough, sexy cowboys set against the beautiful, rural landscape of Montana, Ryan's latest is a must-read."
—RT Book Reviews

"Touching and romantic...Readers will eagerly anticipate future installments."
—Publishers Weekly

THE LEGACY OF COPPER CREEK

"Solidly written romance. Rich, layered, vulnerable characters in Whit and Cara, coupled with strong chemistry and intense heat between them, proves Ryan does the contemporary Western love story well."
—RT Book Reviews

"What a perfect ending to a series...I love this story."
—SillyMelody.blogspot.com

"If you're looking to lose yourself in a fictional family that will steal your heart and pull you into the thick of things, this is the book for you. *Copper Creek* is where a wayward soul can find a home and have all their dreams come true."
—MommysaBookWhore.com

THE REBEL OF COPPER CREEK

"A winner. Ryan writes with a realism that brings readers deep into the world she's created. The characters all have an authenticity that touches the heart."
—*RT Book Reviews*

"An awesome story."
—NightOwlReviews.com

THE MAVERICK OF COPPER CREEK

"Ryan's storytelling is tinged with warmth and down-to-earth grit. Her authentic, distinctive characters will get to the heart of any reader. With a sweet plot infused with family love, a fiery romance, and a bit of mystery, Ryan does not disappoint."
—*RT Book Reviews*

"Full of sexy cowboys and a Western feel that is undeniable...A well-written, fun story that I really enjoyed."
—NightOwlReviews.com

JAKE

"A must-read...cozy enough to make you want to venture into the Wild West and find yourself a cowboy...And if you haven't read a Western romance before, R. C. Ryan is where you should start."
—ReviewsbyMolly.com

MONTANA GLORY

"These not-to-be-missed books are guaranteed to warm your heart!"
—FreshFiction.com

"Wonderful romantic suspense tale starring a courageous heroine who is a lioness protecting her cub and a reluctant knight in shining armor...a terrific taut thriller."
—GenreGoRoundReviews.blogspot.com

MONTANA DESTINY

"5 stars!...R. C. Ryan delivers an ongoing, tantalizing mystery suspense with heartwarming romance. Sinfully yummy!"
—HuntressReviews.com

"Ryan's amazing genius at creating characters with heartfelt emotions, wit, and passion is awe-inspiring."
—TheRomanceReadersConnection.com

MONTANA LEGACY

A *Cosmopolitan* "Red Hot Read"

"A captivating start to a new series."
—*BookPage*

"Heart-melting sensuality...this engaging story skillfully refreshes a classic trilogy pattern and sets the stage for the stories to come."
—*Library Journal*

LUKE

R. C. RYAN

FOREVER

NEW YORK BOSTON

Copyright © 2016 by Ruth Ryan Langan
Excerpt from *Reed* Copyright © 2016 by Ruth Ryan Langan
Excerpt from *A Cowboy's Christmas Eve* Copyright © 2016 by Ruth Ryan Langan

Cover photography by Claudio Marinesco. Cover design by Elizabeth Turner. Cover copyright © 2016 by Hachette Book Group, Inc.

Forever
Hachette Book Group
1290 Avenue of the Americas, New York, NY 10104
forever-romance.com
twitter.com/foreverromance

First Edition: November 2016

Forever is an imprint of Grand Central Publishing. The Forever name and logo are trademarks of Hachette Book Group, Inc.

The publisher is not responsible for websites (or their content) that are not owned by the publisher.

The Hachette Speakers Bureau provides a wide range of authors for speaking events. To find out more, go to www.hachettespeakersbureau.com or call (866) 376-6591.

ISBNs: 978-1-4555-9163-3 (mass market), 978-1-4555-9164-0 (ebook)

Printed in the United States of America

OPM

10 9 8 7 6 5 4 3 2 1

For my second son, Patrick

And as always, for Tom
With love

LUKE

Prologue

Glacier Ridge, Montana—Thirteen Years Ago

Carter Prevost, owner-manager of the Glacier Ridge fairgrounds, stopped his pacing when rancher Frank Malloy and his foreman, Burke Cowley, walked into his office.

Though Frank was owner of one of the state's largest ranches—several thousand acres and growing—he was still just a neighbor and friend to the folks in Glacier Ridge. A man still struggling to pay the bills required to maintain such an operation.

"Okay, Carter. Now why the frantic phone call, and why couldn't you just tell me what you wanted over the phone?"

"It's about Luke."

The old man let out a slow breath. "It's always about my middle grandson. What did he do this time?"

"Luke signed up to compete in the motorcycle challenge during rodeo weekend."

"He did what?" Frank removed his wide-brimmed hat and slapped it against his leg, sending up a cloud of dust. "He's only fifteen, Carter."

"Don't you think I know that?" The thickset man ran a hand through the rusty hair that was now more gray than red. "But he paid the entrance fee and signed all the forms. Since there's no age limit, I didn't want to be the one to face Luke's temper, so I figured I'd call you and let you deal with it."

"Oh, I'll deal with it, all right." Frank swore and turned away. "No grandson of mine is going to risk his life jumping his Harley over a line of trucks."

"Everybody knows Luke's capable of a trick like that. If jumping vehicles was all there was to it, I wouldn't be so worried."

At Carter's words, Frank turned back. "What's that supposed to mean?"

"Jumping a line of trucks is just the preliminary. This year we're building a ramp higher than anything ever tried before. At the end of that ramp, the biker will see nothing but air. We've issued a challenge to all the professional bikers who want to enter the final. They'll have to land in one piece—and to prove they're still able to function, they'll be expected to circle the stadium. If more than one succeeds, the finalists will have to do it again, until only one is left standing. The first prize is ten thousand dollars."

"If it was a million dollars, it wouldn't be enough." Frank Malloy turned to the door and stalked toward his truck.

Burke Cowley followed more slowly.

As they started toward the ranch, Burke held his silence while Frank gave vent to every rich, ripe curse he knew.

"Damned hotheaded kid will be the death of me."

Burke cleared his throat. "I know Luke's a handful."

"A handful?" Frank was fuming. "There's a devil inside that boy. I think he sits up nights dreaming of ways to challenge his grandmother and me. I swear, he's the most ornery, fearless boy I've ever known."

"He is that." Burke smiled. "But he has a way of getting under the skin. Despite all the trouble he causes, you know we can't help but love him. He has the greatest heart in the world. And as Miss Gracie likes to say, he has an old soul. Like his daddy, God rest him, Luke's a sucker for a sad story."

The mention of Frank's son, Patrick, who had been killed five years ago along with his wife, Bernadette, on a snowy stretch of Montana road, had Frank Malloy sucking in a painful breath. Their death had left a void that would never be filled. Not for the Malloy family, and especially not for Pat and Bernie's three sons, Matt, Luke, and Reed, who were left to figure out a world rocked by the sudden, shocking loss of their parents.

Burke stared straight ahead, his tone thoughtful. "Luke's the kind who will always stand and fight beside anybody who's down and out. That boy would give you the shirt off his back."

"I know what I'm about to give him." Frank's eyes narrowed with flinty determination. "God knows, I don't like coming down too hard on the boy, after all he and his brothers have suffered. But this time he's gone too far. If I have to, I'll lock him in his room until rodeo days are over."

"Pretty hard to keep a fifteen-year-old locked away."

Frank's head swiveled. "Are you on his side?"

Burke shrugged. "The boy's wild and reckless. But he's not stupid. If you forbid it, he'll find a way around you. But if he knows he has your blessing, he might look at this challenge with a clear eye. He might even be willing to back down if he sees that it's too dangerous."

"And if he breaks his fool neck?"

Burke squinted into the sunlight. "It's his neck. Like you said, there's a devil inside him. Maybe in time he'll learn to tame it. Or maybe, whenever he feels it taking over, he'll just ride that devil into the eye of the storm and see where it takes him. Either way, he's the sort who's willing to play the hand dealt him."

After a few more miles, Frank muttered, "I guess we'll see."

"You're going to give him your blessing?"

Frank shrugged. "Like you said, it's going to be impossible to keep him locked away during rodeo week."

A week later, when Luke proudly handed his grandfather a check for ten thousand dollars, the old man's eyes narrowed. "What's this about, sonny boy? It's your money. You're the one who risked your neck for it."

Luke shrugged. "I heard you telling Gram Gracie the bills were piling up, and you were going to have to hold off on buying that bull you've been itching to import from Calgary."

"Are you telling me you risked your neck for a damned bull?"

"It's my neck, Grandpop. And honestly, it wasn't much of a risk."

"You weren't scared?"

The boy grinned. "Yeah. But it was really cool. I felt like I was flying."

"Here." Frank held out the check. "You earned this, boy. I won't take it."

"You know you need that bull." Smiling, Luke ambled away, leaving Frank staring after him.

It was then that he recalled Burke's words.

Despite all the worries and sleepless nights spent on his middle grandson, there was no denying that Luke Malloy had the biggest heart in the world. That breathtaking daredevil...that defiant rebel...had the heart of a champion. And the soul of a hero.

CHAPTER ONE

Glacier Ridge, Montana—Current Day

Luke Malloy sat easily in the saddle as his roan gelding, Turnip, moved leisurely up a hill. Luke had spent the last three weeks in the hills that surrounded his family ranch, tending the herds, sleeping under the stars. It was something he never tired of. Though some of the wranglers complained about the solitary lifestyle, it was the very thing that fed Luke's soul. He planned to build a home up here someday, far enough from his family to listen to the whistle of the wind in the trees, yet near enough to visit when he craved their company.

The time spent alone was a soothing balm to his soul, though he had to admit that after weeks of solitude, he wouldn't mind a night in town. A night of good whiskey, loud country music, and lusty women in the smoky atmosphere of Clay Olmstead's Pig Sty. That wasn't the name on the sign above the saloon. But Clay had been a pig farmer before opening his saloon in Glacier Ridge, and everyone there referred to it as Clay's Pig Sty. Just the thought of it had Luke grinning.

Luke's body was lean and muscled from hard, physical ranch work. He was heavily bearded, his long hair tied in a ponytail beneath his wide-brimmed hat. He was hot and sweaty, and now he was thinking about a swim in the welcoming waters of Glacier Creek.

As he and his mount crested a ridge, all thought disappeared at the sight of a herd of mustangs feasting on the rich vegetation of a meadow spread out below him, between two steep mountain peaks. Their leader, the elusive white mustang his grandmother had been trailing in vain for the past two years, stood a little apart from the herd, keeping an eye out for intruders. With five of the mares nursing foals, the herd was especially vulnerable to predators.

Urging his mount forward, Luke kept to the cover of the trees, hoping to get close enough for a clear photograph. With Gram Gracie's birthday approaching, he couldn't think of anything that would please her more than a framed picture of the mustang stallion she'd named Blizzard, since she'd first spotted the animal years ago during one of Montana's worst winters.

Luke lifted the expensive camera he carried with him. It was a gift from his grandmother, who was widely acclaimed for her photographs of the herds of mustangs that roamed their ranchland. He focused the viewfinder and started clicking off shots, all the while urging his mount into a run. The mustang stallion's head came up sharply, scenting danger. But instead of facing Luke, the mustang turned and reared, just as a shot rang out, missing the animal by mere inches. At the sound of the gunshot, the entire herd scattered.

Luke's mount, caught in the midst of it, reacted instinctively, rearing up before bucking furiously, tossing its rider from the saddle.

In a single instant Luke felt himself flying through the air. His last conscious thought before he landed on his head and saw the most amazing display of fireworks going off in his brain was that once again Blizzard had managed to slip away without a trace. Damned if he hadn't just missed his best chance ever for Gram Gracie's precious birthday gift.

Ingrid Larsen came up over a rise and heard the gunshot, followed by the herd of mustangs dissolving like ghosts into the surrounding forest. One minute they were grazing; the next there was only flattened bear grass left to suggest they'd been there at all.

As she looked around, she was surprised to see one horse remaining. As she drew near, she could see the reins dangling. Not a mustang. A saddle horse. But where was its rider?

When she got close enough to see the wide eyes and hear the labored breathing, she dismounted and approached the animal cautiously.

"Here, now. Steady." She took hold of the reins and spoke soothingly as she ran a hand over its muzzle.

Within minutes the big red gelding began to settle down.

"I know you didn't come all this way alone. So let's find out where your owner is."

Leading the horse, she peered over the edge of a steep cliff and caught her breath when she saw the still form of a cowboy on a narrow shelf of rock below.

"Hello." She cupped her hands to her mouth. "Are you okay?"

There was no response. The body didn't move.

With a sigh of resignation, she whistled her own horse over and removed the lariat. Tying it securely to the saddle horn, she stepped over the ravine and began inching her way to the rocks below.

Once there, she touched a hand to the man's throat. Finding a pulse, she breathed a sigh of relief. Not dead.

She lifted a canteen from her pocket and held it to the man's lips. He moaned and choked before instinctively swallowing. After a few sips, he pushed her hand away and opened his eyes.

"Think you can sit up?" With her hands around him, she eased him to a sitting position.

He swayed slightly, before fixing her with a look of fury. "What the hell...shooting at...herd? You damn near killed me."

"Save your energy, cowboy." She didn't bother saying more. Seeing the blood oozing from his head, she realized he was much more injured than he realized. From the spasms shuddering through him, he was going into shock. "I'm going to try to get you out of here. I'll need your help."

She looped the lariat under his arms, around his chest, and gave a hard, quick tug on the rope.

The rope went taut, signaling that her horse had taken a step back from the edge, jerking the barely conscious man to his feet. Satisfied, Ingrid wrapped her arms around his limp body and gave a whistle.

Both figures were lifted from the narrow rock shelf and eased, inch by painful inch, up the ravine until they were on solid ground. At once Ingrid scrambled to remove the rope. That done, she wrapped her blanket around the still form of the man and began cutting and lashing tree branches together, covering them with the blanket she found tied behind his saddle. Within the hour she'd managed to roll the heavily muscled body onto the makeshift travois, which she'd secured behind her horse. From the amount of blood he'd lost and the swelling on the back of his head, there was a good chance this cowboy was suffering a very serious head injury. And then there were the bones he might have broken in that fall.

Catching up his mount's reins, she pulled herself onto her horse's back and began the slow journey toward the ranch in the distance.

Black clouds scudded across the sky. Thunder rumbled, and lightning sparked jagged flashes overhead. The wind picked up, sending trees dipping and swaying. Minutes later the sky opened up, and a summer storm began lashing the hills. By the time Ingrid's mount crested the last peak and caught the scent of home, they were drenched.

It took all of her strength to hold her horse to a walk, when the animal's instinct to run to food and shelter was so strong.

When they reached the barn, an old man was standing in the doorway, watching her. "What you got there, girl?"

"Not what, Mick. Who." She slid gratefully from her mount and looked down at the still figure. "Some cowboy shot at a herd of mustangs and got himself tossed from his horse. Landed halfway down the mountain on a pile of rock. He's out cold."

"Injuries?"

She nodded. "Pretty bad head wound. Lost a lot of blood. Wasn't making any sense."

"Going to call for a medevac?"

"In this storm?" She bent down and felt the pulse. "I guess, at least for tonight, we'll just get him inside, keep him quiet, and hope for the best."

The old man unsaddled the stranger's horse and settled it into a stall with fresh feed and water. Then he moved along beside her as she led her horse to the back door. The two of them struggled under the man's weight as they removed him from the makeshift travois and half dragged, half carried him up the back steps and into the house.

"This cowboy's all muscle." Mick pulled a handkerchief from his back pocket and wiped his face, damp from the workout. "We'll never get him upstairs to a bed."

"You're right." Breathing heavily, Ingrid shed her parka before once more taking hold of her burden. "Let's get him to the parlor."

They dragged him past the kitchen and managed to roll him onto a lumpy sofa in the big room.

Mick glanced around the cold, dark parlor. "I'll get Strawberry back to the barn and bring in an armload of logs. You'll want to get this guy out of those wet clothes and wrap him in dry blankets."

She shot him a sharp look. "I'm no good at playing nurse. I'll take care of my own horse, thank you. And I can handle the logs. You can get him out of his clothes."

The old cowboy was already halfway across the room. With a chuckle, he called over his shoulder, "Your stranger, your problem."

His laughter grew as her curses followed him out the door.

Left alone, Ingrid gathered whatever supplies she could. Several thick bath towels. A basin of warm water and soap. Then she set to work washing the blood from the back of his head. That done, she folded a dry towel and placed it under his head before moving on to his clothes. Her attempt at unbuttoning his flannel shirt, which was completely soaked, was a huge effort. Next, she turned to his boots, but because they were so wet, she could barely budge them. It took long minutes of pulling and tugging, while muttering curses through gritted teeth, before she got them off. Then, with much tugging, she finally managed to get him out of the last of his clothes.

By the time old Mick returned with an armload of firewood, the stranger was wrapped in a blanket, and his clothes lay in a heap on the floor.

Once the fire was blazing, Mick walked to the sofa to stand beside Ingrid. "I brought his saddlebags inside." He hooked a thumb toward the doorway. "Tossed 'em over a chair in the kitchen. They might give you a clue to just what kind of cowboy you dragged in from the storm."

"Good idea." She huffed out a breath. "I just hope the idiot who was shooting at mustangs isn't also an ax murderer."

"I doubt he'd carry that kind of information in his saddlebags."

She turned away and headed toward the kitchen. "You never know."

"He wasn't your shooter."

She paused. Turned. "And you know that because...?"

"His rifle was still in its boot. If he was trying to take down a mustang, the rifle would have been in his hands." Mick poked and prodded the flames, adding an-

other log to the fire before ambling back to the other
room, where Ingrid had spread out the contents of the
saddlebags across the kitchen table.

"Find anything interesting?"

She looked up. "Where'd you get this?" She held up
the camera.

"It was hooked to the saddle horn."

"German. Expensive. Not what I'd expect from a wan-
dering cowboy."

The old man shrugged. "Maybe he's a professional
photographer."

She opened a worn leather wallet and began sorting
through the cards stored inside. She picked up one. "Lu-
cas Malloy. Twenty-eight. Height six feet two inches.
Weight one hundred eighty-five pounds. Hair black. Eyes
blue. Doesn't need glasses." She looked over. "Ring a
bell?"

Mick shook his head. "The only Malloy I know is
Frank. Owns one of the biggest spreads in Montana.
Frank Malloy's my age. Got a famous wife. Some kind of
photographer."

"Now this makes sense." She pointed to the camera.
"Maybe he's their son?"

"What makes sense is he's probably a grandson. Unless she made medical history."

They grinned at each other.

"Okay. He's a long way from home. With a head injury, you never know what might happen. If I could find
his cell phone, I'd notify his family."

"It could be back there on the mountain."

She nodded. "And trampled by a herd of mustangs."

"I'm sure you can find a number for the Malloy

Ranch." Mick filled two mugs with steaming coffee. Handing one to her, he said, "Lily and Nadine have been asleep for hours. You going up to your room, or are you planning on keeping an eye on your guest?"

"He's not my guest, Mick." She picked up her mug and headed toward the parlor. "But since I was the one who brought him here, I guess it's my job to see him through the night."

"You got that right, girl." With a grin the old man shuffled off to his room next to the kitchen. "If you need me—"

"Yeah." She didn't wait for him to finish.

It took her several minutes to move an overstuffed chair beside the sofa. She draped an afghan over her lap and cradled the mug in both hands as she watched the steady rise and fall of the stranger's chest.

Her head nodded, and she felt the hot sting of coffee on her skin before setting aside the mug and snuggling deeper into the warmth of the cover.

After the day she'd put in, she was asleep before she could form a single thought.

CHAPTER TWO

Now that's what I call a hunk of burning love." The female voice was rough, fog shrouded, like someone who had consumed an entire pack of cigarettes in an hour while downing half a dozen whiskeys.

"Why am I not surprised?" A softer voice. One Luke had heard before, though he couldn't recall where or when. "He's more dead than alive, but all you can see is your next conquest."

"I'm seeing a killer body and the face of a devil. Honey, he can park his boots under my bed anytime. But for now, I'll wait 'til he has more fire in his chimney. I'm off to Wayside. Don't wait up."

"I never do."

As the door closed, a strobe light shot bursts of color across Luke's closed eyelids. A strange bell rang nearby. And his head ached with the worst hangover ever.

Had he been in Clay's Pig Sty in Glacier Ridge? He

couldn't recall. But since it was on his mind, he must have made it there. But where was he now?

He'd been in enough saloon brawls to know how the next day felt. He touched his face. No tender eye, no swollen cheek.

There was something sharp poking him in his back. He reached a hand around and located a metal coil of some sort, covered in cloth. He opened his eyes, as gritty as sandpaper, and saw the odd-colored lights flickering across the ceiling of a room, coming from a fire on the grate. And there was a terrible ringing in his ears. When he moved his head, he became aware of the pain throbbing in his temples.

He sucked in a breath and tried to remember what had happened. The herd of mustangs, the shot...

He'd been shot?

He felt around his body for fresh dressings. None. He touched a hand to the back of his head and felt the swollen mass. Not a bullet, he realized. He must have taken quite a fall. He could almost recall flying through the air and landing hard. Rocks. Yes, a solid rock ledge. Had he actually fallen off the edge of the cliff? But he wasn't there now. He was in a room, naked under a soft blanket.

How did he get here?

The shooter?

He struggled to sit up and felt the room spin at the same instant that a shaft of pain sliced through his head. Strong hands pressed him back against a springy cushion. The woman with the rusty voice? Or the one with the soft voice?

He tried to fight back but lost the battle. In his mind he was uttering a string of fierce oaths as the intense pain dragged him under.

* * *

"Good. You're awake. Try to drink this." It was the soft voice.

He struggled to focus. At first there were several blurred images swimming into his line of vision. Gradually they merged into a single woman perched beside him. She put a hand beneath the back of his head and gently lifted it high enough that he could drink from the cup she held in her other hand.

He liked her touch. Gentle. And he knew he wasn't dying when his body reacted instinctively.

At his first sip the mood was shattered. He gagged and pushed her hand aside. "You trying to poison me?"

She chuckled. A low, warm sound like the purr of a kitten. He would have taken the time to enjoy the sound, if it weren't for the fire sliding down his throat.

"Some crazy witch's brew Mick concocted. He swears it'll kill pain anywhere in the body."

"If it doesn't kill me first."

"You're angry. Good." She stood. "Sounds to me like you're feeling better than you did yesterday."

"Yester...?" His voice trailed off as he struggled with the implication of that. Had he been here overnight? "When...? How...?"

She held up a hand. "According to Mick, you'll be out in a matter of minutes. But you should wake next time in a lot less pain. When you're feeling up to it, we'll talk. For now"—she turned away—"sleep tight."

Luke tried to summon the energy to be angry at her patronizing tone. But in truth, he was already fading.

The world went soft and gray as he drifted off.

* * *

The room was in shadow. The only light came from the fireplace, where a log burned, giving off the comforting fragrance of wood smoke.

Luke had heard voices on and off during the day between his bouts of waking and sleeping. An old man's growl. A child's whisper. The two females, one soft, one rough as sandpaper, engaged in a slap-down of sorts, though he couldn't figure out what it was about. He only recognized the anger in their tones.

He was thirsty, but the thought of that vile drink he'd been given hours ago put him off. He could probably eat something, though at the moment nothing appealed to him. He felt vaguely restless, and he knew it was time to saddle up and head for home. But since he didn't know where he was or how badly he'd been injured in that fall, he figured he would just lie here a while longer.

"Mick said you'd be waking up soon."

The woman was little more than a shadow in the doorway, but he knew the soft voice now. As his memory cleared, he knew, too, that she was the one who'd offered him something to drink after his fall. The one who'd managed to get him to safety. The one who'd brought him here.

The shooter.

She switched on a light and he muttered an oath before lifting his hand to shade his eyes.

"Sorry. But I need to check your head wound." She eased down beside him on the sofa and gently lifted his head. "I'm Ingrid Larsen."

"Luke Malloy."

"Yes. I checked your saddlebags for ID and notified your family that you're recovering from a fall at my place." She seemed distracted as she poked and prodded. "Good. As Mick said, the bleeding stopped on its own, and the swelling's gone down by half. I guess we won't need a medevac after all."

"Is Mick a doctor?"

"Of sorts. He doctors the herd and for years kept all our wranglers in good condition."

She pulled a chair beside the sofa and sat facing him.

It was his first real look at her, and he couldn't look away.

Despite the faded denims and a plaid baggy shirt with the sleeves rolled to her elbows, she was stunning. Pale corn silk hair cropped close to her head. Eyes the color of a summer sky. A dimple in each cheek whenever she smiled, which he suspected she did rarely. There was something stiff and unyielding in her demeanor, as though his very presence here annoyed her.

Maybe it did. But this was all her fault. She was the one to shoot at the mustangs, sending them into a frenzied stampede.

She was studying him as closely as he was studying her.

"So. Why did you shoot at the mustangs?"

Her question caught him completely by surprise. "Me? *You're* the one who shot at them."

She shook her head, sending a lock of pale blond hair dipping over one eye. She brushed it back absently with her hand. "I heard the shot and came running. When the herd vanished, I saw your horse, reins dangling, and realized its rider was nearby. You're lucky I took the time to search or you'd still be out there. I doubt you'd have survived in that storm."

He remembered the rain falling on his face as he'd been transported across the meadow and, later, the sound of a furious storm howling in the night. The storm was still ongoing, though now there was just the steady tattoo of rain on the roof and the occasional flash of lightning, followed by a rumble of thunder that shook the house.

"If you didn't shoot, who did?"

She shrugged. "All this time, I thought it had been you, even though Mick disagreed. Now I haven't a clue."

He studied her slender frame, which she tried to camouflage beneath the baggy clothes. "How did you manage to get me here? Did you have help?"

"I made a travois out of tree limbs and tied it to my horse."

He thought about the effort it must have cost her to rescue him, bring him down from the mountain, and then get him to this place. "Sorry I caused you so much time and muscle."

She smiled, showing those dimples. "See that you don't try that again."

"This Mick. Is he your husband?"

"No."

"Is this Mick's ranch?"

She arched a brow. "It was my father's. I hope soon it will be mine."

"Oh. I thought..."

Her smile faded. "Yeah. I get it. What woman in her right mind would want to take on all the work of running a ranch without a man by her side?"

"I didn't mean that. It's just... you mentioned Mick a lot." Luke shrugged.

"When my dad was alive, Mick was in charge of the wranglers. I'm grateful he stayed on, even though he's doing triple duty for half the pay. He tends the herds, keeps all the buildings and equipment in repair, feeds me, and keeps me from ripping Nadine's head off."

"Nadine?"

"My mother. She's in town tonight. If you're lucky, maybe she'll stay there until you're well enough to leave. If not, you'd better be prepared..." She didn't finish her sentence as a girl of about six or seven rushed into the room.

"Mick says supper's ready. Oh." The girl skidded to a halt when she realized Luke was awake.

"This is my sister, Lily."

"Hi, Lily. I'm Luke." Luke managed a smile at the girl, who looked nothing like her older sister. Her hair, a wild tangle of thick, dark curls, fell nearly to her waist. Her eyes were the color of chocolate. She wore faded, patched denims and a shirt that was missing a sleeve.

"Hi, Luke. Are you going to eat with us?"

Ingrid got to her feet. "I think tonight I'll bring a plate for Luke in here. Maybe by tomorrow he'll feel strong enough to join us in the kitchen."

When her older sister walked away, the little girl remained, staring intently. "Are you a bad man?"

"Do I look like a bad man?"

She shrugged. "You look funny with all that hair."

He touched a hand to his heavily bearded face. "I guess I look more like a big old hairy bear."

"You do. Or a bad man. But if you say you're not..." She smiled, displaying the same dimples as her sister. "Do you like roast beef and potatoes?"

At the little girl's question, he winked at her. "It's my favorite."

"I'll tell Mick." As she started to scramble away, she paused and turned. "I believe you. I don't think you're a bad man."

"Any reason in particular?"

She shrugged. "I don't know. Maybe it's your smile."

"Thanks. I like yours, too."

He lay listening to the sounds of voices in the kitchen and found himself reliving the scene on the mountain, when the herd of mustangs had scattered at the sound of a gunshot. He was pretty sure he'd suffered a concussion. It was the only explanation for this feeling of malaise. It wasn't like him to willingly lie around doing nothing.

"Here's your supper." Ingrid shoved a scarred old coffee table close to the sofa and placed a plate on it before turning away.

"Thanks. And, Ingrid..."

She turned back.

"Thanks for saving my hide and for contacting my family."

She shot him a look of surprise mingled with pleasure. "You're welcome. That's not what you said when Mick and I dragged you in here."

"What did I say?"

"You condemned us both to..." Her smile was quick and brilliant. "I'd better not repeat it while Lily is apt to overhear. I believe there were a few amazingly inventive curses even I hadn't heard before."

"Yeah. That's me. Creative." Luke tried to remember. Bits and pieces of being half dragged, half carried across the room, leaving him feeling more dead than alive, played through his mind. His entire body had been on fire by the time they got him to this sofa. He could only imagine how many curses he'd lashed out with. Probably as many as he'd been able to think of before passing out cold.

Ingrid returned a little later with a cup of steaming coffee. She glanced at the plate and then at Luke. His eyes were half closed, the remains of most of his dinner still untouched.

Her sister, Lily, trailed behind her. "You didn't like Mick's roast beef?"

Luke struggled to rouse himself. "It was good. So were the mashed potatoes. But I didn't have the energy to finish."

Lily glanced at Ingrid. "That's how I felt when I fell off the hay wagon and hit my head. Remember?"

Her older sister's smile disappeared. "Yeah. You scared me half to death." She turned to Luke. "Mick wants to know if you want any more of his medicine."

"You mean his poison? Thanks, but I'll take my chances without it."

She bit the corner of her lip to keep from grinning. "I'll tell him not to bother mixing up another batch."

"Does he draw a skull and crossbones on it when he's through?"

Lily stepped closer. "What's a skull and crossbones?"

"A warning sign for dangerous, poisonous substances."

"Oh. Like paint thinner and stuff?"

"Yeah. In fact, my first taste of Mick's medicine reminded me of paint thinner."

She glanced at Ingrid. "He's making a joke, isn't he?"

"I'm glad you recognized that. Proof positive that he's

feeling much better." She shot a meaningful look at Luke. "Isn't that right?"

"Yeah. Feeling like a million dollars."

Ingrid stepped closer and picked up the plate. "Do you need anything?"

Enough energy to get off this lumpy sofa and head home.

Aloud he merely said, "No. I'm good. Thanks."

"All right. Good night, then."

"'Night."

Lily hung back, staring at him as though he had two heads.

He tried for a smile, though his energy was definitely at low ebb. "What's wrong, Lily?"

"Does your beard tickle?"

"Yeah."

"Why did you grow a beard?"

"I've been tending a herd in the hills for the past couple of weeks."

"I heard Nadine telling Ingrid that even with all that hair she could tell you were"—she struggled to think of the word—"hunkly...huntly. Hunky. What's *hunky*? Did she mean like the Incredible Hulk?"

He had to choke back the laughter that bubbled up. "Yeah. Something like that."

"Do you think Ingrid's pretty?"

Her question caught him off guard. "Yeah."

"Prettier than Nadine?"

"I don't know what Nadine looks like, but Ingrid's not as pretty as her little sister."

Lily giggled behind her hand. "I'm not pretty. I don't look at all like Ingrid. And she's pretty. I'm just..." She tried to think of a word. "Mick says I'm a tomboy. I guess he's right. I'd rather be with the horses or cows any time than with people."

"I bet Mick means that as a compliment. I happen to like tomboys."

As she started to leave, he asked, "Why do you call your mother Nadine?"

Her eyes rounded in thought. "'Cause that's her name."

"You don't call her Mom?"

She shrugged. "She said not to. She likes Nadine better. It makes her feel young." She danced out the doorway, closing the door behind her.

Whatever other questions Luke had dissolved in a fog of sleep.

CHAPTER THREE

Sunlight streamed through a crack in the curtains, shining a light in Luke's eyes. He awoke and lay still, listening to the morning sounds. A pair of doves cooed outside the window. Cattle lowed on a distant hill. Somewhere upstairs a door slammed.

The smell of bacon frying and bread toasting reminded him that he hadn't eaten anything substantial in days. His stomach was grumbling.

An old man ambled across the room and paused beside the sofa. "'Morning. I'm Mick Hinkley."

"Luke Malloy."

"You're looking more alive than dead today. Think you're up to taking a shower?"

Luke grinned. "That must mean I'm not smelling too good. You going to help me take that shower?"

The old man chuckled. "Not if I can help it. But Ingrid

asked me to follow you up the stairs to the bathroom, to see you don't keel over."

"You realize I'm naked?"

Mick's grin widened. "Nothing I haven't seen in my lifetime. But here." He handed Luke a bath towel. "This ought to cover your backside."

He offered a hand and Luke accepted, easing to his feet and waiting for a moment until the room stopped spinning. He used the time to fasten the bath towel around his hips.

With Mick leading the way, Luke followed him up the stairs and along a hallway to a bathroom. Inside, the old man pointed to an assortment of disposable pink razors and tubes of shaving cream.

"Yours?"

Mick shot him a foolish grin. "That's why I don't share this place with three females. I think they buy this stuff by the case. I've got my own bathroom downstairs."

He indicated Luke's clothes, freshly laundered and folded atop a basket of towels. He studied Luke, holding on to the edge of the sink. "You going to be okay by yourself?"

"I'll be fine."

The old cowboy turned away. "When you're done, come on down to breakfast."

"Thanks, Mick."

When he was alone, Luke began the tedious process of shaving a wild tangle of beard with several of the throwaway plastic razors he found in a beribboned basket of supplies. Using copious amounts of shaving cream and plenty of hot water, he managed to finish, cutting himself only four times.

When he stepped under the warm spray, he sighed with contentment as he shampooed his hair and soaped his body with some kind of girly body wash that smelled like a summer garden. And finally, when he was too weak to stand, he sat in the old-fashioned tub and allowed the water to run until it was nearly overflowing. With eyes closed, his head dropped back and he thought about just staying here all morning. The only thing that had him finally stepping out and toweling dry was the wonderful smell of food drifting up the stairs.

He dressed and tied his hair back, relieved to find a black ponytail clastic among the clutter of pink ones that littered the counter.

Gathering up his wet towels, he headed down the stairs, following the scent to the kitchen.

The chorus of voices stopped abruptly as he stepped into the room, but not before he caught the note of tension in the room.

He flashed Ingrid a smile and winked at Lily. "Thanks for the use of the bathroom." He held out the armload of towels. "I figured I'd save you a trip upstairs."

"Thanks."

As he handed over the towels, his fingers accidentally brushed the swell of her breast. Her head came up sharply as she took them from his hands, while her cheeks turned the most becoming shade of red. He couldn't stop the grin that spread across his face as she walked into a small alcove off the kitchen. When she returned, she avoided his eyes, while he studied her with a look of pure male appreciation.

Mick handed him a steaming mug of coffee. "You're looking better."

"Thanks." Luke took a sip. "I'm feeling like a new man."

"What a coincidence. So am I." The smoky voice behind him had him turning toward the doorway. A curvy woman with big hair dyed fire-engine red and enough makeup to start her own cosmetics company was looking him up and down. "I'm Nadine Larsen."

He extended his hand. "Luke—"

"Oh, I know. We met earlier, though you were out cold." She glanced at the others. "I see you've met my girls. I know it's hard to believe I'm old enough to have a twenty-three-year-old daughter, but like I tell everybody, I was a child bride."

She took his hand between both of hers, smiling up into his eyes. "While you were mending, you looked mighty tempting with all that facial hair, but now, with that naked face, I've got to say you're looking downright delicious."

The silence in the room was deafening.

"Hungry, Luke?" Mick held up a frying pan, where bacon sizzled.

"Yeah." Grateful to the old man, Luke extracted his hand and beat a hasty retreat to the table.

"Me too." Nadine settled herself beside him, nudging his knee with hers under the table. "A good-looking cowboy always makes me ravenous."

Mick circled the table, ladling scrambled eggs and crisp bacon onto each plate before returning to the stove.

While Ingrid and Lily ate in silence, Nadine kept up a running conversation.

"You know how to handle a rifle, Luke?"

"I grew up using one. Why?"

Nadine looked around at the others. "I always say you can't have too many men who know a thing or two about rifles willing to watch your back. Especially since we've become the Wild West way out here in the middle of nowhere."

Ingrid bristled. "This is none of Luke's business."

"What isn't?" Puzzled at the tone of the conversation, he looked from one to the other.

"Nothing." Ingrid clamped her jaw and shot her mother a warning look.

"Suit yourself. I think it's all in your twisted little minds anyway." Unfazed, Nadine went on as though she hadn't been interrupted. "You'll never believe who was in town yesterday."

When neither of her daughters responded, she continued on: "Alberta Crow. And believe me, she's looking more and more like an old crow. I can't believe she let her hair go gray. She was wearing one of her husband's cast-off shirts and the baggiest pair of jeans I ever saw."

"I heard they're losing their ranch," Mick muttered. "A crying shame. Three generations of blood, sweat, and tears going up for auction."

"That's no reason to look like something the cat dragged in." Nadine stared pointedly at her older daughter. "You know. The way you look when you're mucking stalls. Oh, I forgot." The sarcasm in her tone was thick enough to cut. "That's how you look all the time. You even wear the same tired clothes when you go to town."

"You spend enough on fancy duds for both of us." Ingrid pushed away from the table and set her empty dishes in the sink.

Nadine's eyes narrowed. "Where are you going?"

"To muck stalls. In my baggy work clothes. Unless you'd like to take a turn at ranch chores. Now, that would make headlines."

The two women stared at each other before Nadine picked up her mug and drank.

"Wait, Ingrid." Lily drained her glass of milk and carried her dishes, depositing them in the sink with a clatter. "I'll go with you."

The two sisters walked out, letting the back door slam behind them.

Mick stood up and began clearing the pots and pans from the stove before setting them in a sink filled with hot, soapy water.

Nadine turned to Luke with a satisfied smile. "Looks like it's just you and me now, cowboy." She strained toward him, showing plenty of cleavage in her low-necked tee as she put a hand over his. "Why don't you tell me all about yourself?"

"Some other time." He crossed the room and handed Mick his dishes. "Thanks for a great breakfast. I'm going to give the ladies a hand in the barn."

The old man's eyes went wide. "Think you're strong enough?"

He wasn't sure he could even walk to the barn, but he was willing to do whatever it took to get away from the shark at the table.

"I guess I'll find out." With a smile he ambled out of the room, pausing at the back door to retrieve his boots. He noted with surprise that they'd been polished. He removed his battered hat from a hook by the door before stepping outside.

As he made his way to the barn, he thought about the latest twist. So this was Mama Larsen. There was nothing subtle about her. She'd gone to a lot of trouble to try to look like a hot chick. The candy-apple-red hair, the heavy-handed makeup, and the skinny jeans and too-tight T-shirt were over the top. But nothing could hide the desperation in those eyes. She looked determined to hold on to her last vestiges of youth.

He thought of his grandmother, Gracie, at least twenty years older than Nadine but infinitely more beautiful. She had not only a physical beauty but also an inner light and peace that radiated from her, casting everyone around her in a golden glow.

Luke stepped into the barn and paused, allowing his eyes to adjust. In a far stall Ingrid forked straw and manure into a wagon. Lily worked beside her, spreading fresh straw.

Ingrid worked like the very devil himself was after her. It occurred to Luke that he always did the same, whenever he was working off a temper.

Though she'd remained mostly silent in the kitchen, Luke figured Ingrid had found a better way of expressing herself. He'd bet good money that she was not only angry but also embarrassed by her mother's behavior, and this was her way of getting past it.

He watched her for several silent minutes. Even the loose, faded work clothes couldn't hide a killer body like hers. And the unexpectedly short, tousled haircut that looked as though she'd taken scissors to it in a fit of anger only added to her cool, Nordic beauty.

She looked up in surprise when he helped himself to a pitchfork and walked to the adjoining stall.

Apparently she wasn't expecting a man to pass up the chance to be charmed by her mother.

Her tone expressed both surprise and anger. "What are you doing?"

"The same as you."

"You're not strong enough..."

He shrugged. "I'll quit when my body tells me to."

"Fine. It's your body." She bent to her work. "But don't ask me to pick you up if you fall on your face. Once was enough."

"I'll keep that in mind." He was chuckling as he turned away.

Lily climbed up to perch on the upper railing of a stall as Luke stepped into his horse's stall and was greeted by a friendly head-butt.

"Hello, Turnip." He ran a hand over the horse's forelock and was rewarded by a soft nickering. "How're you doing, old boy?"

"Why do you call your horse Turnip?"

"Because when he was just a foal, he wandered into Yancy's garden and started eating the turnip tops."

"Who's Yancy?"

"Yancy Martin is our ranch cook and all-around housekeeper."

"You have a cook and housekeeper?" The little girl turned to her sister with a look of amazement.

"The best cook in Montana. And when Yancy saw that animal chewing up his tender garden greens, he was ready to have him ground up into horsemeat. And ever since then, poor Turnip has had to endure that silly name."

"It is silly."

"But he likes it. Don't you, boy? Speaking of names..."

He studied her, perched on the top rail, looking like a tiny doll. "I think instead of Lily, I'm going to call you Li'l Bit."

The look on Lily's face was priceless. She couldn't hide her pleasure at having her very own nickname.

Luke began forking dung and straw into the wagon.

"Do you do this at home?"

"You bet."

"Do you own your own ranch?"

"I live on my family's ranch. My father and grandfather before him lived there, too."

"But if you can afford a cook and housekeeper, why not hire people to do your ranch chores?"

"I like doing my own, like my daddy."

"Is your daddy as big as you?"

He paused for a moment before saying, "My dad is dead. My mom, too. They died when I was little."

"My daddy's dead, too. But I've still got Nadine and Ingrid. Who do you live with now?"

"My two brothers. My uncle. My grandparents. And old Burke, who's tough as nails."

"He's . . . mean?"

Luke shook his head. "Never. Burke doesn't have a mean bone in his body. But he's tough. When he says he wants something done, it had better be done to his liking. And he's fair. He's as much a pa to me as my own. You'd like him. He's like Mick."

"Ingrid says Mick is like our grandfather. Except he isn't." She watched him for long, silent minutes before asking, "Do you and your brothers always look out for each other?"

"Yeah." He laughed. "That's what brothers do."

"Do you fight?"

He winked at her. "That's one of the first rules of being a guy. You have to know how to fight. Especially if you have brothers."

Her tone grew wistful. "I wish I had a brother."

"You have a sister."

"I know. But she's not big and strong like a man and sometimes I worry..."

"That's enough, Lily." Ingrid shot her sister a warning look.

Her head swiveled as a shadow fell over the doorway and a rough voice called, "Where is she?"

Ingrid stepped from a stall. "Nadine isn't here."

"I didn't ask if she's here." The man was well over six feet, with a thick midsection and the muscled shoulders of a rancher. His face was red with anger, or possibly sweat. "I asked where she is."

"You know Nadine." The soft voice was tinged with sarcasm. "She doesn't leave us her itinerary."

"Don't be funny with me, girl." The man's breathing was ragged, as though he'd been working up a fierce anger. His hands were fisted at his sides. "I told her I wanted an answer to my offer."

"And as you already know, I told her not to accept your offer until the cattle are sold at the end of summer."

"Yeah. She told me. What right do you—"

As he started toward Ingrid, Luke stepped out of the stall he'd been cleaning, the pitchfork resting casually over his shoulder. "If you have something to say to Ingrid, you'll stop where you are and say it. You take another step toward her and you'll answer to me."

The stranger gave a sneer. "Think you're big enough, cowboy?"

"Try me."

"You'd better bring an army if you decide to go up against me."

"I don't need anyone but myself." Luke kept the pitchfork resting lightly on his shoulder. Though he smiled, there was something about his voice that had the man blinking before reaching for the gun at his hip. As he withdrew it, he grinned. "I don't give your puny weapon much of a chance against mine."

Luke set aside the pitchfork and reached for the rifle in the boot of his saddle, which was hanging over the top rail of the stall. Taking aim, he drawled, "Now that the odds are even, how about it? Are you a gambling man?"

That had the stranger backing up a step. He turned to Ingrid with a scowl. "Tell your mother I'm not in the mood to wait until the cattle come down from the hills. She'd better give me an answer soon, or else."

Luke never raised his voice, but the thread of steel beneath his words was clear. "You've had your say. Now get off the lady's property."

The stranger shot him a killing look before stalking away. Minutes later they heard the sound of a horse's hooves pounding the earth. Lily scrambled down from the railing to stand beside her sister.

Luke studied the two of them. "Who was that?"

"A neighbor. He wants to buy our ranch."

"This neighbor have a name?"

"Bull Hammond." Ingrid spoke his name with contempt.

Luke saw the way Lily's small hand crept into Ingrid's, their fingers tangling.

He set aside the rifle and sank down on a bale of hay.

Ingrid studied him as she stripped off worn leather gloves. "I'll give you this, cowboy. You surprised me. There aren't too many people around here who would stand up to Bull Hammond."

"I'm just glad he couldn't see that I'm almost out on my feet."

Ingrid stepped closer. "Come on. You need to get inside."

She caught his arm, then, seeing the dark look in his eyes, released her hold on him and backed up a step.

"In a minute. Tell me what happened to your wranglers."

"They left after my dad died."

"How long ago was that?"

"Nine months. He died last October."

"So Lily was...?"

"Six."

"And you were...?"

"Twenty-two. I was away at college. Just starting my senior year. I came home to bury my father and never went back."

"That's tough. It had to be hard for all of you. How did he die?"

"Mick said it looked like a heart attack while they were driving the herds down from their summer range."

"You didn't have a medic examine him?"

She shook her head. "He fell from his horse. Mick said he was dead before he hit the ground. We buried him up on the hill."

"I'm sorry." He looked out over the fields, with its fences in need of mending and its outbuildings looking neglected. "Was there no way to keep some of the wranglers?"

"Not when we checked with the bank and found out there was barely enough to pay them their wages. The only one willing to stay was Mick."

"Then why not sell to Hammond?"

Her voice frosted over. "My dad loved this ranch, and he promised it would be mine someday. I'm going to do whatever it takes to hold on to it."

"Isn't that up to Nadine?"

"As Dad's widow, she inherited it, but she wants out. She's always hated the ranch. I've asked her to hold off making a decision until the end of summer, to see if I can get enough from the sale of the cattle to buy her out."

"Aren't the cattle hers, too?"

Ingrid shook her head. "My dad left them to me. Us," she corrected. "Lily and me. But I'm the executor."

"Since you're family, wouldn't Nadine be willing to take a down payment and let you pay it off slowly?"

"You met Nadine. What do you think?"

Luke chose his words carefully, knowing this was deeply personal and none of his business. "I guess, if she holds the title on this place, she gets to call the shots."

"Yeah. And Bull Hammond has offered her cash to walk away." Ingrid glanced at her little sister, who had walked over to feed a carrot to Luke's horse. "Come on." She leaned close. "While Lily's amusing herself, I'll help you get to the house."

He shot her a wicked grin. "Much as I'd like your hands on me, I can get there on my own."

Her eyes flashed fire as she jerked back. "Don't ever confuse me with my mother. You want to play sexy games, call Nadine."

"Sorry." His tone went from teasing to contrite in the

blink of an eye. "I can see that's a sore spot with you." He lifted a palm to her cheek and she flinched and backed away as though burned.

His voice was barely a whisper. "Believe me. I'd never confuse you with Nadine."

At the look in his eyes, she crossed her arms and stared hard at the floor before turning to her sister. "Come on, Lily. It's time for us to saddle up."

Lily hurried over with a nervous look. "Can't Luke come with us?"

"After the work he just did, he wouldn't make it half-way out of the barn on horseback. We'll just check on the herd and get back in a couple of hours."

Over her shoulder she called, "That was my only offer of help. If you don't head up to the house and settle on the sofa, you're apt to pass out in the barn."

"I'll be fine." He watched as she tossed a saddle over her horse and began tightening the cinch.

Beside her, Lily did the same.

As they mounted, Luke called, "You stay close to your sister, Li'l Bit."

That had her smiling nervously.

Minutes later the two were riding across a meadow, heading into high country. After that angry visit from Bull Hammond, Luke wished he could join them, just to calm their nerves, but he knew it would be futile to try.

He turned and made his way slowly to the house, feeling every part of his body protesting the work he'd done.

He knew he was going to pay a dear price for today. But it was the least he could do to repay Ingrid Larsen for saving his hide.

He couldn't help wondering what Bull Hammond

would have done if he hadn't been here. The man looked furious enough to get physical, but it wasn't clear whether his anger was directed at Nadine or Ingrid.

Luke paused and looked out across the hills. He hadn't expected Ingrid's reaction to his touch. He'd bet all his money that Nadine was the reason she chopped all her hair off and hid that lush body beneath layers of bulky clothes. She didn't want to be confused with Nadine. Not that it was even remotely possible. They were as different in looks and temperament as two women could be.

And one of them, working so hard to hold him at arm's length, was doing strange things to his heart.

CHAPTER FOUR

Luke walked into the kitchen to find Mick alone. "I saw a truck hightailing it out of here, spitting gravel."

The old cowboy looked up. "That was Nadine. She likes fast rides and faster cowboys."

"I guessed as much. Ingrid and Lily don't talk about her."

"They live by the rule that if you haven't got anything good to say, don't say anything."

Luke grinned. "As good a rule as any."

"Yeah." Mick ran a wet mop across the floor before rinsing it out in the bucket at his feet.

Luke eased himself weakly onto a wooden chair at the table. "Kitchen duties part of your routine?"

"Not by choice. But I do them better'n the others around here. Ingrid never stops from dawn to dark, and Lily pretty much imitates her."

"What does Nadine do?"

"As little as possible." The old man shook his head. "I've never known her to do a lick of work."

"Even when her husband was alive?"

"Especially then. She liked to call herself a"—he wiggled his fingers to make air quotes—"free spirit."

Luke merely grinned.

The old man moved the mop around. "I think Lars always knew he'd made a bad bargain, so he just looked the other way. And once Ingrid was born, nothing else mattered to him. Father and daughter were like two peas. If he was working in the barn, Ingrid was right there beside him. And when he rode up into the hills, she went along. She rode in his arms until she was old enough to handle a horse on her own. No more'n two or three years old, I'd say." The old man smiled, remembering. "Lars was so proud of that girl. He used to say she was a born rancher. There wasn't anything on this spread she couldn't do better than his wranglers. And that was the truth. She could work circles around all of us."

"What about Nadine?"

"She was happy to leave their daughter to Lars. That freed her to do whatever she pleased."

"I have a grandmother like that. She goes off on camera safaris for weeks at a time, photographing the herds of mustangs up in our hills. She gets amazing amounts of money for her photos. But it isn't the money that drives her. It's the thrill of capturing the beauty of those mustangs." He chuckled. "I swear she works harder than anyone I know when it comes to her photography." He looked over. "So, what pleases Nadine?"

Mick snorted. "You've seen her. Men. Lots of 'em. She craves their attention the way a drunk craves alcohol."

"That's it? That's all she does? Did her husband know?"

"How could he not? Especially when she started staying away for nights at a time. The first time she left Lars for over a month, Ingrid was probably five or six."

"'The first time'?"

"There were too many times to count. Later, when Ingrid was just a teen, Nadine returned to the ranch with a surprise. She was expecting a baby. Lars took her back and loved that baby, even though Lily wasn't his. And because they'd never divorced in the eyes of the law, Lily is his legal heir as much as Ingrid."

"How did Ingrid feel about sharing her father with another child?"

"You've seen them. Ingrid purely loves that girl. And Lily considers Ingrid her mama as well as her big sister."

Luke fell silent, trying to imagine what this family had gone through.

His grandpop often said that everyone had a story. This one was like a fairy tale gone bad.

Mick mopped at a spot in the corner of the room. "Ever since Lars died, Nadine's gone off the deep end. She leaves the two girls for weeks at a time, until she runs out of money. Then she's back, blackmailing Ingrid into giving her whatever she wants, or she threatens to sell the ranch from under her. A couple of weeks ago she brought a cowboy home with her. Said she was going to marry him. His name was Lonny Wardell."

"Wardell?"

Seeing Luke's head come up, Mick peered at him. "You know him?"

Luke nodded. "He worked as a wrangler on our spread for a while, until we caught him stealing."

"It was the same here. He'd done some work for Lars, and Ingrid knew he was a drunk and a thief. When she saw how he was taking over her pa's things, she ordered him off the property at the end of a rifle. It got ugly. He vowed revenge on the 'bigmouthed female who thinks she can order me around.'"

Luke shook his head. "How did Nadine take that?"

"Just like you'd expect. She screamed and hollered at Ingrid, saying Wardell was the first man who'd seriously offered to marry her since Lars, and now her own daughter had spoiled everything. She accused Ingrid of being jealous because she had a life, and all Ingrid had was hard work stretching out in front of her. Then, after she'd said her piece, she headed out to find Wardell in Wayside, the little spit-and-you're-through-it town where she hangs out. When she finally came back, she refused to talk about Wardell. I don't know if that means he walked out on her for good, or if she's seeing him without letting Ingrid know. Either way, as you can imagine, she's been mad as a spitting cat and making everyone dance to her tune."

The old cowboy set aside the bucket and mop and took a chair across from Luke. "What worries me is right after that incident with Wardell, odd things began happening."

"Such as?"

Mick shrugged. "A fire in the hay field left us with no hay for next winter. The authorities said there was no proof it was anything more than a wildfire started by a lightning strike."

Luke nodded. "It would be tough to prove otherwise."

Mick sighed. "Then Ingrid's dog, Tippy, that she'd had since he was a pup, was found dead up in the hills where he'd been guarding the herd. Just a few nights before that, he'd set up a loud yapping out behind the barn, but I figured he'd spotted coyotes. The next morning he was dead. And since there was no blood, I'm inclined to believe he was poisoned. But again, it's just a feeling. I have no proof." He paused before saying, "And now that gunshot that scattered those mustangs. Though Ingrid didn't see anybody but you, who's to say it wasn't directed at her?"

Luke's eyes narrowed. "You think Wardell would go that far?"

The old man shrugged.

"Does Ingrid have any other enemies besides him?"

After a moment Mick nodded his head. "There's Bull Hammond. He's our neighbor to the north."

"I just met him out in the barn."

The old man's eyes widened. "Is that what set off Nadine? I bet she caught sight of him and figured she'd hightail it out of here before she had to deal with him."

"He had fire in his eyes. He threatened Ingrid."

"That bastard." Mick's lips thinned. "I'm glad you were out there, Luke."

"Ingrid said she asked her mother to wait until the cattle sale, to see if she can make enough to buy the ranch."

"That's so. When Hammond heard that Nadine was strapped for cash, he came here and offered to buy her out. She was about to make the deal when Ingrid reminded her their deal had to wait at least until the cattle were sold."

"So that gives Hammond a reason to want revenge, as well. You think Bull Hammond's capable of doing all the things that have been happening around here?"

"I wouldn't put it past him. There was bad blood between Bull and Lars, though I don't know what it was. Lars never confided in me. But if Bull wants to buy this place for a song, all he has to do is wait. With all that's going wrong, Ingrid may be forced to give up and let her mother sell to him. With that field of hay burned, I don't see how the girl has a chance of making it through the winter if she has to buy hay from the grain-and-feed place in town."

"That makes two men with a grudge against Ingrid. Are there more?"

Old Mick took a long look at the sweat pouring down Luke's face. "Son, if you don't lie down right now, I'll be hauling you across the room again, just like I did when you got here, and you'll be swearing a blue streak."

"Yeah. And I'm running out of creative curses." Luke shoved out of the chair and barely made it to the other room, where he flopped down on the sofa, while his mind worked overtime.

Now he understood why Lily was nervous about riding up to the hills with Ingrid. There were too many unexplained accidents.

Not accidents.

Wardell was a drunk and a thief, and Hammond was a known bully.

Leaving two girls and an old man defenseless in the face of danger was no way to repay Ingrid for saving his hide. Not that he wanted to get into Ingrid Larsen's business. But hell, he thought, he was already in her business. And now that he knew, he wasn't certain he could walk away.

He fell asleep cursing this weakness and questioning whether he'd be a help or a hindrance if he joined them in standing up to danger, if these incidents turned out to be the work of someone bent on real harm.

Luke's sleep was disturbed by the sound of a plane flying low enough that it shook the roof and vibrated through the parlor.

He sat up, pressing his hands to his lower back, aching from the springs of the sofa. He'd have been more comfortable if he'd slept on the floor, but the truth was, he'd been so exhausted by his workout in the barn, he could have slept on a bed of nails.

Hearing the rumble of voices on the back porch, he made his way there and stopped short at the sight that greeted him.

His uncle Colin and old Burke were talking to Mick, Nadine, Ingrid, and Lily.

From the way Nadine was invading Colin's space, her hand on his arm, her rough voice laughing at something he'd said, it was obvious that she'd decided to make her move on him.

"Well." Spotting him, Colin eagerly stepped away. Crossing to Luke, he gave him a friendly punch to his shoulder, causing Luke to suck in a breath at the sudden, shocking pain.

"When we got the call that you'd fallen off a cliff, we weren't sure what to expect."

Luke glanced at Ingrid while he rubbed at his shoulder. "You hoping to get rid of me?"

She shrugged. "I figured you'd be ready to get back to your family as soon as possible."

"We're grateful to Miss Larsen. We told her we'd fly up as soon as the weather cleared. So here we are." Colin studied his nephew, noting the red-rimmed eyes and the way he favored his shoulder. "Good thing you were on your horse and not flying across the hills on your Harley. You'd have probably broken your neck."

Ingrid arched a brow. "You ride a motorcycle?"

"When I can."

She frowned. "Why am I not surprised?"

Ignoring her insult, Luke grinned at Burke, who was sporting a black eye. "You look worse than me. Did you fall off a cliff, too?"

The old cowboy chuckled before touching a finger to the tender skin. "I was priming a pump at the range shack up on the north ridge, and the handle hit me in the eye, darned near blinding me."

"See?" Luke turned to Colin. "It's like I always tell Grandpop. There are a lot of things more dangerous than riding a motorcycle. Those pump handles can be deadly. And you ought to see what damage a sneaky shed door can do."

Nadine sidled up beside Luke. "Want to see what I can do behind a shed door?"

Colin shared a look with Luke before turning to Ingrid. "Thanks for taking care of my nephew until we could get here. I'm obliged that we didn't have to listen to his lame jokes for a couple of days." He glanced skyward. "If we're going to get you home in time for Yancy's special supper, we'd better get started."

Without a word, Ingrid crossed her arms over her chest and looked away.

Lily tipped up her head to peer into Luke's eyes. "I guess you need to go back to your brothers and your grandparents."

Luke knelt down and caught her hand. "I see you were paying attention when I told you about them, Li'l Bit."

"Uh-huh." She touched a hand to his cheek. "You're lucky to have all those people."

"Yes, I am." At her touch, he wondered at how light his heart felt. Little girls weren't something he'd had any experience with in his life. Still, those brown eyes were filled with so much sadness, they nearly broke his heart. "But you're lucky, too. You've got your ma and Ingrid and Mick."

She looked away, but not before he saw the knowledge in her eyes. She might be only seven, but in that instant he recognized a depth of wisdom beyond her years.

Luke stood and turned to Colin. "You realize Turnip is out in the barn. I can't leave without him."

Colin held up a hand. "He can keep for a few more days. We debated driving here with a trailer to accommodate Turnip, but we figured your well-being was more important. We decided to use the plane, in case you were so badly injured we needed to get you to a hospital right away. When you're up to it, you can bring a horse trailer over and haul Turnip home."

"That's not going to work. I wish you'd called to tell me you were on your way. I could have saved you a trip."

Burke and Colin were both looking at him with matching expressions of puzzlement.

Colin spoke for both of them. "What's that supposed to mean?"

Luke shrugged, determined to keep things light. "This is the first time I've ever had a chance to use girly soaps and lotions." He winked at Lily. "I don't think I'm ready to give them up yet."

The little girl covered her mouth with her hand and giggled, while Ingrid stared at him with a look of astonishment.

Luke turned to her. "Any objections to having me here a while longer?"

She showed no expression as she gave a curt nod of her head. "No objection from me. It's your life."

"Now I know you fell on your head." Burke looked at him more closely. "What this about, Luke?"

He clamped a hand on his uncle's shoulder and another on Burke's. "Come on. I'll walk with you to the plane."

Colin and Burke said their good-byes to the others before turning toward the plane, parked on a strip of asphalt behind the barn.

Along the way, Luke filled them in on what he'd learned. When he was finished, he added, "I'd like to pay these good people back for saving my hide."

"By putting yourself in the line of fire?" Colin said soberly. "You're talking about taking on a load of trouble."

Luke nodded. "I know. But I'd like to even the odds a bit. Two girls and an old man shouldn't have to stand up to this kind of bullying alone."

Colin hooked a thumb in the direction of the house. "What about the mother?"

Luke shrugged. "As far as I can see, pretty useless."

"But she's got her eye on you, sonny boy."

Luke grinned. "Not going to happen. Besides, from what I could see, she had designs on you, too."

"Honky-tonk angels aren't my type."

As they laughed, Colin glanced back toward the ranch house. "As soon as we're airborne, I'm phoning Sheriff Graystoke."

Luke nodded. "I'm counting on it. Tell him I'd like him to look into this Lonny Wardell. See if anybody's seen him in the town of Wayside. I hear that's where he picked up Nadine. Or where she picked him up," he added. "And see what Eugene can dig up on Bull Hammond. Somebody's going to a lot of trouble to scare this family off their land."

"You always did enjoy a good brawl." Colin gave his nephew a bear hug before climbing into the plane.

Old Burke put a hand on Luke's shoulder. "You take care, son. But keep in mind, this isn't a game. Whoever is going to all this trouble is playing for keeps."

"I agree, Burke."

"You know how you get fired up when trouble comes. You can be more bullheaded than anyone I know. Keep that temper in check and keep a cool head, son."

"Yeah. Sure."

"And pigs'll fly," Colin muttered. The three of them laughed, breaking the tension, as the old cowboy climbed into the copilot's seat.

"One more thing." Colin beckoned Luke close. "I expect you to check in with us on a regular basis. If we don't hear from you for several days, we're flying in to tan your hide. You hear me?"

"Yes, sir. Loud and clear." Luke paused before adding, "I'll remind you it's been years since any of you were able to tan my hide. I'd like to see you try it now."

"Nothing's changed," Colin muttered under his breath. "From the time he was just a pup, he was always trouble. He's still trouble, only older."

"I heard that."

"Figured you would." Colin exchanged a look with Burke.

Minutes later the little Cessna was moving down the rough patch of earth. Luke watched it until it was airborne.

When he turned, Ingrid and Lily were standing to one side of the barn. As he drew close, Lily reached up and put her hand in his. "I'm glad you're staying, Luke."

"Me, too, Li'l Bit."

He looked over her head at her big sister, who said nothing. From the fire in her eyes, he couldn't tell if she was glad or mad.

Not that it mattered, he thought. This wasn't about her, or about the fact that something about this stoic female touched something deep inside him.

He wasn't in this for hot sex. Or even for a quick fling.

She had saved him. He was just trying to return the favor.

He bit back a grin.

Yeah. That was his story and he was sticking to it.

CHAPTER FIVE

Lily bounded up the stairs ahead of Luke. "Come on. Ingrid said I could show you where you'll sleep."

He followed more slowly. He'd suggested the bunkhouse, but apparently they'd allowed it to fall into disrepair. *Like everything else around the ranch*, he thought. Now he would be upstairs, sharing space with three females. As he'd come from a male-dominated family, this was an alien experience to him. But now that he'd made his decision to stay, there was no turning back.

Lily opened a door and stepped inside. "Ingrid said this was Daddy's office."

It was a big room, with a desk and chair and shelves crammed with books and ledgers. The old brick fireplace in the downstairs parlor extended through this room as well, soaring to the ceiling. Judging by the soot on the hearth and the pile of dried logs in a basket, it had been well used.

Leaning against one wall was a wooden bed frame and mattress, apparently hauled down from attic storage by Mick.

Luke set to work putting the frame together before lifting the mattress into place.

Ingrid entered, carrying an armload of bed linens. Without a word she shook out a fitted sheet. Before she could start to fit it onto the mattress, Luke took it from her hands and stretched it into place, before reaching for a top sheet. He shook it out and tucked it around the three sides with an ease of efficiency.

She stood back, arms crossed over her chest. "You look like you've made up a bed or two."

He chuckled. "Yancy does our laundry. But he expects us to haul down the bedding and then make up our own beds. He likes to remind us he isn't our maid."

"I think I'd like Yancy."

"I know you would."

She watched as he smoothed a plaid blanket over the bed and added two pillows.

"Mick's got supper started. You can come down when you're ready."

"Thanks."

As she turned away, he put a hand on her arm. Ingrid reacted as though burned, stepping back just out of reach.

"Sorry." Luke lowered his hand to his side. "I was just going to say I don't want to be any trouble."

She gave him a long, slow look. "I wouldn't bet on that. I think you're nothing but trouble, Luke Malloy." She turned to her sister. "Come on, Lily. Let's give Luke some time to settle in."

The little girl was wriggling like a puppy. It was clear

that she was excited at the prospect of having a visitor staying with them. "I won't be any bother. Can I stay, Luke?"

"Sure, Li'l Bit. Since I don't have anything to unpack, I'm just going to open these windows and air out the room." He forced open the first window, sending the curtains billowing inward. As he started toward the second window, he added, "Then we'll go downstairs and see if we can give Mick a hand."

Ingrid paused in the doorway. "You're handy in the kitchen? Do you cook?"

He gave a nonchalant shrug. "Some. Not like Yancy. But then, nobody can cook like Yancy. I can do plain and simple things like burgers and chili."

Lily sighed. "I love burgers and chili. What else can you cook, Luke?"

"I make a mean grilled cheese sandwich. And one of the wranglers showed me how to grill a whole chicken on a can of beer." He winked. "Best chicken I ever tasted. Of course," he added with a grin, "it might have tasted that good because of all the beer I had to drink before that bird was done."

Lily looked at him with those big eyes. "Are you teasing again?"

"Maybe just a little. But I really do know how to grill a chicken on a beer can. Come on." He steered her toward the hallway. "Let's see if Mick needs a hand with supper."

"That was a great meat loaf, Mick." Luke sat back and sipped strong, hot coffee.

Lily drained her milk. "Do you know how to make meat loaf, Luke?"

He shook his head. "I missed that cooking lesson."

Mick set a platter in the middle of the table. "If anybody wants seconds, help yourself."

Luke didn't need any encouragement. He heaped more meat loaf and mashed potatoes on his plate before digging in.

The old man chuckled. "Looks like you're making up for lost time, son."

"Yeah. I figure I'd better build up these muscles if I'm going to lend a hand with ranch chores in the morning."

"Just don't overdo it. You took one heck of a fall."

"Like Colin said, as long as I landed on my head, no harm done."

While the others laughed, Ingrid sat, quietly watching and listening.

She sat at one end of the table, with Lily beside her. Nadine's chair was empty, and though no one mentioned her, Luke assumed she'd gone to the tiny town of Wayside looking for a little excitement.

"I liked Burke and your uncle Colin." Mick reached for the coffeepot bubbling on the stove. "Though he looked more like your brother than your uncle."

"Yeah." Luke sat back, feeling stronger than he had in days. "He was my dad's younger brother. He was just twenty when my dad and mom died."

"They passed away together?"

Luke nodded. "A car accident on a snowy road. I was ten. My brother Matt was twelve, and Reed was nine."

Mick glanced at Ingrid and Lily, whose eyes were downcast. "It's always tough when there's no time to say good-bye."

"My great-grandfather insists it wasn't an accident. But then, he's always had a flair for the dramatic."

"That so?" Mick held up the pot, and Luke passed over his cup.

When it was filled, Luke took a long, satisfying drink. "The Great One was a director in Hollywood before he came to live with us."

Ingrid's head came up. "The Great One?"

"That's what we've always called him. He loves it, since his ego is as big as his reputation was."

Mick was grinning. "Would I recognize his name?"

"You would if you followed old movies. He's Nelson LaRou."

The old cowboy's eyes widened. "Is that a fact? Nelson LaRou. Huh." He turned to the girls. "I bet I saw every one of the movies he directed. Back in the fifties, his name was as big on the movie screen as all those movie stars' names."

For the first time, Ingrid looked suitably impressed. "And he lives with your family?"

"Yeah." Luke stretched out his legs under the table. "He and Yancy spend their evenings sharing stories about old Hollywood mysteries. There are a lot of unsolved crimes from those days, and both Yancy and the Great One have theories about who did what. As for my parents, the Great One took a handheld movie camera to the scene of the accident, and he swears that before all the cars and trucks arrived, there were two distinct sets of tire tracks in the snow. By the time the sheriff got there, his deputy, a neighboring rancher, and a couple of wranglers passing by were all on the scene, and the sheriff, considering the amount of snow and ice on the road, declared it an accident. Case closed."

Ingrid frowned. "What about your great-grandfather's film?"

"He showed it to the authorities. They studied it, but it's shaky, because he'd gone to the scene in his pajamas and slippers. And the only light was from the moon and stars, so they said they couldn't be certain just what they were looking at." Luke drained his cup. "Water under the bridge. They're gone. And they left an entire family devastated."

Seeing the glitter of moisture in Ingrid's eyes, he added softly, "At first, I figured I'd never get past the pain. But Burke told me something I've never forgotten. He told me to hold on to the happy memories, and one day I'd find something to smile about."

To hide her emotions, Ingrid scraped back her chair and began gathering up the dishes.

When old Mick started to stand, Luke put a hand on his shoulder. "You did the cooking. We'll clean up." He crooked a finger at Lily. "Your sister can wash. You and I will dry."

They carried the dishes to the sink before taking fresh towels from a drawer.

While Mick enjoyed a second cup of coffee, he smiled at the easy banter between Luke and Lily.

"Not there, Luke. The big plates go in this cupboard." It was obvious that Lily was enjoying her new role of teacher.

"Okay, Li'l Bit. What about the knives and forks?"

The little girl opened a drawer. "In here."

"Thanks." Luke scooped up the entire handful of tableware and began drying each one and dropping them one on top of another.

"Not like that, Luke." Lily pointed to the dividers. "The knives in here. The forks here. The spoons"—she picked up the ones he'd already deposited, and rearranged them until they were neatly stored in their proper slots—"like that."

"I can see I'm going to need a lot more practice before I get it right."

"That's okay." The little girl patted his hand. "I'll help you until you learn to do it the way Ingrid likes."

"Thanks, Li'l Bit." He winked at Mick, and the old man bit back the laughter that threatened.

"Now where does this go?" Luke said as he dried the big platter.

"Up there." Lily pointed to the cupboard above her sister's head.

Luke reached up and easily set the dish inside. As he lowered his hand, it brushed Ingrid's hair. He was pleased to note it was as soft as it looked.

He felt her stiffen. He grinned as he met her sharp-eyed look.

"Need anything else put away that's too high for you, Li'l Bit?" If so, he intended to touch that hair again, and this time he'd linger over it.

"No. Everything's done." The little girl took the towel from his hand and placed it on a rack beside hers. "We hang these over here so they can dry."

"Okay. I'll remember." He watched as Ingrid drained the sink before drying her hands. "What do you do when the chores are done for the day?" he asked.

While Ingrid pointedly ignored him, Lily jumped right in. "Do you play cards?"

"Sure. What's your game? Gin rummy? Poker?"

The little girl shrugged. "I don't know those. Ingrid usually plays Fish with me."

"Fish." He thought a minute. "Yeah. I guess my brothers and I played Fish when we were kids."

"Oh boy." She raced to the parlor ahead of him in search of a deck of cards.

As he followed, he turned to Mick. "You in?"

"Not me." Mick got up slowly and turned toward his room off the kitchen. "Tonight's *Perry Mason*. I've seen every episode a dozen times or more, and I still get a kick out of solving the crime."

"Come on." Lily caught Luke's hand and led him to a game table in the corner of the parlor.

He glanced at Ingrid. "How about you?"

She pointed to a pile of papers on a desk across the room. "I need to sort through the bills and see what I can pay."

"Isn't that Nadine's job?"

"It should be. But if I waited for her to take care of it, the heat and lights would be turned off for lack of payment. So I do what I can to stay ahead of it."

He settled himself at the game table and accepted the deck of cards. After shuffling, he separated the cards into two piles and riffled them so quickly, Lily clapped her hands. "How'd you do that?"

"What? This?" He did it again, even faster, until the cards in his hands were a blur of color.

"Ingrid. Watch." Lily was captivated. "Do it again, Luke. Please."

With a twist of the wrist, Luke not only shuffled and riffled, but he also allowed the cards to spill from one hand to the other, then back again.

Ingrid frowned. "I can see that a certain cowboy spends way too much of his time with card sharks. Better watch your hand, Lily, or that shark will bite it off."

"Over a game of Fish?" He grinned at the little girl as he dealt the cards and dropped the rest in the center of the table.

"Give me all your queens." At Lily's singsong voice, he handed over a card.

"Now your kings."

He handed over another.

"Now your jacks."

He gave her a long look. "Are you able to read my cards?"

"No. Do you have any jacks?"

He handed one over.

"Now your tens."

"Finally. Got you. Go fish." Luke watched as she picked up a card. "Now, give me all your aces."

"Aw, Luke. I have two of them."

"Good." He wiggled his brows like a villain. "Now you have none and I have three."

As Ingrid sorted through the bills and wrote out checks for those that were almost overdue, she listened to the voices across the room. It seemed odd to hear that deep, masculine voice teasing her little sister. The more he teased, the more Lily responded. Laughing in delight when he said something outrageous. Giggling each time she requested a card that he had. He would pretend to grumble as he handed over two or even three cards, all the while challenging her to try to beat him. And when she did, her little voice was high with excitement. They would high-five and then begin yet another game of Fish.

By the way Luke handled the cards, it was obvious that he played often. Probably with his wranglers. Or maybe even in town, at one of the saloons. But, though he must find this childish game tedious, he never showed it. Instead, he continued in the same cheerful way, teasing, laughing, and acting as though he'd never had this much fun in his life.

Lily was clearly enchanted by Luke. And for that, Ingrid was willing to overlook whatever faults he would surely reveal as the days passed. After all, it was for Lily's sake that she'd allowed him to stay on, knowing her little sister deserved some peace of mind.

Across the room, the two dissolved into peals of laughter. Ingrid paused in her work and smiled. She couldn't remember the last time Lily had laughed so easily.

She had to admit it. Luke was being really sweet. And as long as she was being honest, she'd admit, too, that Lily wasn't the only reason she'd permitted Luke to stay on.

When Bull Hammond showed up at the barn, she'd felt a momentary flash of fear. Not that she'd have ever admitted it to him. Or to her little sister. But Luke had been calm, cool, steady, and absolutely fearless. With all that was going on around her ranch lately, she would take all the strong backup she could get.

There was an edge of danger about Luke Malloy that frightened her even while it appealed to her.

At another burst of laughter across the room, she turned to watch. At that moment Luke caught her eye and shot her a devilish wink. She felt her face grow hot.

Who was she kidding? It wasn't just his fearlessness that she was drawn to. It was the man himself. That tall, muscled, self-assured cowboy whose simple touch left her breathless.

But her reaction to him frightened her just a little. His mere touch got her feeling all hot and off stride. When his hand had brushed her hair, she'd felt a rush of pure sexual tension down her spine, all the way to her toes. And when she'd glowered at him, he'd merely grinned like he knew a secret.

This cowboy was dangerous. And not just because of the way he handled a rifle.

She had no doubt he knew exactly how to handle women, too. Didn't he already have Nadine and Lily eating out of his hand?

Well, there was one Larsen who wasn't buying what Luke Malloy was selling.

CHAPTER SIX

Oe more game, Luke. Please?"

Luke stifled a yawn. "Sorry, Li'l Bit. I can't keep my eyes open." He glanced at the clock on the mantel. "Besides, shouldn't you be in bed?"

Before she could protest, Ingrid set aside the papers she'd been working on and shoved away from the desk. "Come on, Lily. You're lucky I was too busy to notice the time. You and Luke can always play again tomorrow."

"Okay." The little girl started toward the stairs. On the first step she turned. "Promise me you won't leave after I fall asleep."

"I promise." He winked. "Besides, you beat me six times in a row. I'm looking forward to a rematch. I plan on winning tomorrow night."

Her smile was back as she turned away and climbed the stairs, calling over her shoulder, "Are you going to hear my prayers, Ingrid?"

"I'll be up in a few minutes. I'm going to turn out the lights in the kitchen."

Luke gathered up the cards and set the deck in the center of the table. "What's up with Lily's question? Why did she think I'd leave in the night?"

"I'm not sure, but I think I understand." Ingrid's look was both sad and pensive. "Nadine has a history of leaving. But my dad's sudden death, with no warning, may have her believing that nobody stays for very long. I guess I'll try to get her to open up to me about her feelings." She sighed. "But I intend to wait for the right opening before I do."

She paused in the doorway of the parlor. "Good night, Luke."

"'Night." Luke climbed the stairs and made his way to the office that was now his bedroom.

He was aware of Ingrid moving through the house before coming upstairs and letting herself into Lily's room.

He thought he heard the back door open and close.

Sitting on the edge of the bed, he shoved off his boots and set them aside before unbuttoning his shirt and tossing it over the back of a chair.

Unsnapping his jeans, he turned in surprise when his door was shoved inward.

Nadine's rusty voice was like the scrape of nails on a blackboard. "Hey, cowboy. There was nothing shaking in town, so I figured you might like some company, to keep you from feeling homesick."

He stayed where he was. "Thanks. But I can handle being alone. I'm a big boy now."

She looked him up and down. "Are you ever." She sauntered across the room, swaying slightly, and lifted her hands to his naked chest. Her breath reeked of whiskey and cigarettes. "I've always been partial to good-looking, muscled cowboys."

He caught both her wrists to stop their movement.

His voice was low. "I'm only going to say this once. I know this is your house, but my room is off-limits."

Her eyes went wide before narrowing to angry slits. She yanked her hands free and took a step back. "Just who do you think you are? Accepting my hospitality and treating me like an intruder in my own husband's room?"

"You called it straight. Your husband's room." He glanced around. "I don't see much of you reflected on these shelves. Are you sure you've ever been in here before?"

She frowned. "Lars liked his privacy."

"And you like your freedom."

She put her hands on her hips. "Has old Mick been spilling family secrets? I ought to send that old geezer packing—"

"Yeah. That's just what your daughters need. Get rid of the last man standing. See that they're completely alone, with nobody left to look out for them. How long do you think this ranch could function without the help of old Mick?"

"It doesn't matter. Whether it's now or a month from now, this place is already dead. Ingrid and Lily and Mick are just prolonging the agony." She gave him a hopeful look and stepped closer. "That's why you ought to consider my offer while you still can. I bet I could show you a few moves—"

"You heard me, Nadine. Now get out." He stepped around her and pulled open the door.

"Your loss. Too bad you don't know what you're missing, cowboy."

Seething, she shot him a last look before she stepped through the doorway and started down the hall, head high, hips swiveling.

His glance was drawn to Lily's room at the end of the hallway. Ingrid was standing in the doorway. Her mouth was a tight, grim line of anger. Her eyes were fierce enough to shoot daggers through his heart.

He knew what she was thinking. He'd be damned if he'd say a word in his own defense. Let her think the worst of him.

Without a word she crossed the hall to her bedroom and let herself in before slamming the door.

Luke swore as he retreated inside his room and closed the door.

He couldn't blame Ingrid. It was a natural enough mistake. She'd been too far away to hear the angry words spoken between him and Nadine. And then there was her mother's history. Not to mention his own reputation for hard living. Hadn't Burke and Colin made it clear on their visit? That reference to him riding his Harley over mountain ravines like some crazy drifter. He'd even looked the part of a bearded biker when he first arrived.

He finished undressing and turned out the lights before crawling naked under the blanket. With his hands beneath his head, he stared at the outline of the distant mountain peaks touched by moonlight, framed in the window.

What in the hell was he doing here, in the middle of nowhere, thinking he could do anything to help these people? From what he'd seen so far, they didn't stand a chance of saving this falling-down hulk from sinking under its own debt.

But then he thought about Ingrid Larsen, with that boyish cap of hair and that lush body she kept hidden under layers of bulky clothes, and he knew why he was staying against all odds.

In the beginning it might have been the allure of her rare beauty, which seemed at such odds with her determination to keep it hidden. But now, he had to admit to himself it was much more than Ingrid's good looks.

There was just something about her. The way she fought so hard for an impossible dream. The way she seemed determined to make it on her own. The way she protected her little sister, even from their own mother.

He'd always been a sucker for a hard-luck story.

Ingrid lay in her bed, wallowing in misery. Why was she not surprised? After all, Nadine could no more change her habits than a zebra its stripes. Her mother had a testosterone radar that never failed her. If there was a horny cowboy within miles, it was a certain bet that Nadine would not only find him, but also lure him into bed.

But she'd thought better of Luke.

Not at first, of course. He'd been a wounded stranger, whom she suspected of shooting at a herd of mustangs. And even after he'd convinced her that he wasn't the shooter, she'd been wary of him. There was something bold and dangerous about him. Something...tempting. Like a wild creature that, though badly wounded, would fight anyone who came too close. She admired the stoic way he'd accepted his pain. And he'd caught her completely by surprise when he'd decided to stay and help with the chores, to repay her for taking care of him.

And then tonight, watching him playing a dozen games of Fish with Lily, she'd seen a side to him she never would have expected. Though he must have been bored out of his mind, he'd made it such fun for her little sister.

It had been rare and wonderful to hear Lily's laughter. The giggles behind her hand. The way the little girl got caught up in the game, cheering right out loud whenever she beat Luke. Ingrid had caught that teasing light in his eyes when he'd turned to her and winked. Her heart had actually swelled with pleasure, knowing he was going to such pains to make it fun for her little sister.

For a minute or two, she'd actually thought he was someone rare and special. Now she'd been shot down to earth with a resounding thud. He was just another drifter on his way to someplace else. Someplace more pleasurable. More...adult.

At a knock on her door she sat up.

"Ingrid?" Lily's voice, soft and tentative, had her switching on a bedside light.

"What's wrong, honey?"

Lily hurried over. "Can I sleep with you tonight?"

"Sure." Ingrid pulled back the covers. "Climb in."

The little girl snuggled close while Ingrid pulled the covers over the two of them.

"I heard the back door open and close. I think Nadine's home."

Ingrid sighed, remembering the scene she'd been trying to block out of her mind. "She is."

"Why?" Lily lifted her head to stare at her sister. "She

never comes home this early. Do you think she's sick? Is she going to die like Daddy?"

"Of course not, honey." Ingrid looked away, switching off the light. As she moved lower into the blanket, she sighed. "Maybe she couldn't find anyone interesting to talk to."

"Oh." After a long silence, Lily whispered, "You still awake?"

"Uh-huh."

"I want to talk about Luke. I really like him. He's fun."

"It sounded like the two of you were having a grand time."

"He's so silly. He makes me laugh. Don't you like him, too?"

"I guess. Why do you ask?"

"You frown when you look at him. But I know he likes you."

"How would you know that?"

"I saw him looking at you a lot tonight. Sometimes, when I was dealing the cards, he'd forget to pick them up for a minute 'cause he was too busy staring at you."

Ingrid was grateful for the dark. She knew her cheeks felt hot. "I think you imagined that."

"Uh-uh." Lily snuggled closer. "Luke had a funny look on his face when he was looking at you. Like seeing you made his heart happy."

Her voice grew softer with each word. "I never had a nickname before. Well, Daddy used to call me Lily Lally Lolly sometimes. But only when he thought I needed cheering up. Anyway, I like when Luke calls me Li'l Bit. It makes me feel special, you know?"

"Honey, you shouldn't let yourself get too fond of

Luke. He's...he's a cowboy. They come and go, and they rarely stay in one place long enough for anybody to really get to know them. I don't mean you shouldn't enjoy his silly teasing and jokes, but you don't want to start trusting him to always be around. If you do that, you're bound to be disappointed. It would be better if you could just treat him like a neighbor or one of the wranglers that used to work for us, and not like a real friend. Do you understand?"

She listened to the soft, even breathing that told her Lily hadn't heard a word she'd said. With a sigh she realized the little girl was sound asleep.

She ought to do the same. But all the worrisome thoughts swirling around in her brain had her wide awake and replaying that last glimpse of Luke as he'd held the door for Nadine. Barefoot, shirtless, his jeans unsnapped. And his eyes, those always piercing eyes, looking heavy-lidded and sleepy. And when he'd caught her staring, he'd turned away without a word.

Guilt, no doubt.

She couldn't blame Nadine. The man was sexy as hell.

And at the moment, she hated Luke Malloy with every fiber of her being.

CHAPTER SEVEN

With bright morning sunlight streaming through the upstairs windows, Ingrid stared at the closed door to Luke's room as she made her way to the bathroom.

A short time later she stepped out, wearing a bulky robe. Before turning toward her room, she again stared at the closed door. Was he asleep this late? Or was there another reason there was no sound coming from his room at this time of the morning? Was Nadine in there with him?

She gritted her teeth and dressed quickly, eager to get started on her chores. Maybe then she could dispel all the disquieting thoughts taking over her mind.

As she started down the stairs, Lily trailed behind. "Thanks for letting me sleep with you, Ingrid."

"You're welcome, honey. You know you can always sleep with me when you're feeling worried about something."

As they moved through the parlor toward the kitchen,

she draped an arm around her little sister's shoulders. She realized she was doing it as much for herself as for Lily. She was preparing herself for the pain of having to watch Nadine and Luke coming down the stairs together whenever they managed to rouse themselves. No doubt they'd be laughing and sharing secrets.

In the kitchen, Mick looked up from the stove. "'Morning, ladies."

"'Morning, Mick." Lily glanced around. "Where's Luke?"

Ingrid was quick to intervene. "Honey, that's none of our bus—"

"He's out in the barn." Mick handed Ingrid a mug of coffee, which she immediately bobbled, spilling it across her fingers and onto the table.

She hissed in a breath as she wiped it up, keeping her face averted. "He's in the barn?"

"Been out there for a couple of hours, I'd say. He was heading out the door when I woke up. By now, I'm betting he's worked up a powerful appetite."

"I'll go and tell him breakfast is ready." Lily was already racing toward the back door.

Mick grinned at Ingrid. "We'd better watch out. That little girl's falling hard for our guest."

"She'll have to get in line behind Nadine."

At her flat tone, the old man's look sharpened. "You know something I don't?"

She shrugged. "What they do behind closed doors is none of my business."

"Of course it is. But I'd bet good money you're wrong about this, girl. I can't see Luke Malloy buying what Nadine is selling."

"You mean giving away, don't you?"

At that, the old cowboy chuckled.

Minutes later Luke followed Lily into the mudroom, scraping his boots, then rolled up his sleeves and washed at the sink before ambling into the kitchen.

His shirt, stretched tautly across his muscled chest, was damp from the hard work he'd done. His hair was tied back, but a few wet locks spilled over his forehead. He looked so appealing, Ingrid was forced to clench her hands into fists in her lap to keep from giving in to the temptation to brush it aside.

"'Morning." He accepted a mug of steaming coffee from Mick before taking a seat at the table.

"You're up early." Ingrid hated the accusing tone, but she was determined to steel herself against that devilish light in his eyes.

"I grew up keeping rancher's hours." He sighed when Mick placed an omelet on his plate. "And you, Mick, understand a rancher's appetite."

"That I do." Mick circled the table filling their plates.

"Was there some reason why you wanted to tackle the barn so early?" Ingrid studied him across the table. Even the way he savored his food was annoyingly sexy.

"I figured with that out of the way, we'd get an early start on riding up to the hills to see the herds."

"We only have one herd." Lily drained her milk and wiped her mouth on her sleeve.

"Even better. That'll give us a chance to make sure they're all healthy enough for the end-of-summer roundup. It'll be here before you know it."

"Do you plan on being here for that?" Again, Ingrid thought, there was that note of sarcasm in her tone. But she couldn't quite believe this rolling stone would actually stick around long enough for roundup.

"How would I know? My crystal ball broke." Luke winked.

Lily burst into giggles. "You're funny, Luke."

"It wasn't that funny, Lily." Shoving aside her plate, Ingrid pinned him with a look. "Even without your crystal ball, what do you think? Will you be here, or will you be off on some new adventure, riding your...Harley across some challenging mountain ravines?"

He shot her a lazy smile. "You really ought to try it sometime. It's a feeling like no other."

"Oh, I'm sure you're good at chasing feelings."

"Since I was no bigger than Li'l Bit here."

At her nickname, Lilly's smile lit up the room as she said to Mick, "Did you hear what Luke calls me?"

"Yeah." The old man grinned. "I have to say, it suits you, girl."

Ingrid scraped back her chair. "I'm heading to the barn to saddle up and head to the hills."

Luke picked up his mug. "I'll be along in a few minutes."

Ingrid turned to her little sister, who could be counted on to shadow her. "You coming?"

Lily shrugged. "I'd rather stay here with Luke."

Ingrid stalked to the mudroom to pick up her denim jacket and wide-brimmed hat before slamming out of the house.

"Looks like somebody didn't get enough sleep last night," Mick muttered.

"I slept in her bed," Lily said softly. "Maybe I shouldn't have. Maybe I kept her awake."

"Don't you worry about it, Li'l Bit." Luke winked at her, and her smile returned. "Your sister can catch up on her sleep tonight, while I have my revenge on a certain little card shark."

"You mean we can play more Fish tonight?"

"I'm looking forward to it." He picked up his dishes and Ingrid's and placed them in the sink. "Thanks for that great breakfast, Mick. I'm feeling fortified for the day."

Lily carried her dishes to the sink, and following Luke's example, turned to the old cowboy. "Thanks for breakfast, Mick."

"You're welcome. You're both welcome. Now get out of here and find a way to put a smile on Ingrid's face."

Ingrid's horse was already saddled and nibbling grass outside the corral. Inside the barn Ingrid was busy rubbing oil into an old harness. She looked up briefly when Luke and Lily entered, but held her silence.

Lily opened a stall door and led her mount out into the sunshine, where she proceeded to wrestle a saddle onto the horse's back.

"Need any help with that, Li'l Bit?"

She gave a quick shake of her head. "I can do it, Luke."

He led Turnip outside. "Okay then. But that saddle's bigger than you."

"Ingrid said I have to be able to take care of myself, especially when we're up in the hills. That way, if there's ever an accident, I can go for help."

Luke tightened the cinch. "Your sister's a smart woman." He waited until Lily pulled herself into the saddle before doing the same on his horse.

Ingrid stepped out of the barn and took a pair of worn leather gloves from her back pocket. Drawing her hat low on her head, she mounted and, without a word, took the lead. Lily followed, and Luke took up the rear.

They rode single file until they crossed into a high meadow carpeted with wildflowers. They rode side by side until, at the very top of the hill, Luke reined in his mount.

As he did, Lily opened a zippered pouch hanging around her neck and took out a battered old camera, aiming it at the land below as she snapped off several shots.

"I don't believe there's a prettier picture in all the world than Montana in summer." Luke winked at Lily. "Unless it's Montana wearing a blanket of snow in winter."

"I love winter. Do you like winter, too, Luke?"

He nodded. "And spring and fall. I like all the seasons, as long as I can spend them here in Montana."

"Did you ever go away from here?"

He shook his head. "My grandpop thought I should study veterinary medicine. When I heard how far away I'd have to travel, I decided I'd just learn all I could about doctoring cattle from Burke."

"Did you go to school when you were my age, or did you get homeschooled?"

"Mostly homeschooling. Our ranch was more than an hour away from the nearest town."

"Me too. Miss Sarah, the teacher who checks all my on-line assignments, says I'm really smart." Lily was beaming as she tucked away her camera. "What do you like better, Luke? Riding Turnip or riding your motorcycle?"

"Now that's a tough question, Li'l Bit. You're asking me to compare apples and oranges."

She looked perplexed. "I don't understand. What does that mean?"

"I love oranges. They're sweet and juicy. But I have to peel them before I get to the good stuff. I love apples, too. They crunch when I bite into them. And I can even eat the outer peel. But I couldn't say if I liked one better than the other."

"Oh." She thought about his words. "So you love riding Turnip, 'cause you've had him since he was a foal. And your...Harley?"

"I've been riding bikes since I was thirteen. My first motorcycle was one of Burke's rejects. It was old and rusted and lying in the barn, and I spent months fiddling with it until I got it working. Then I took it out to one of the pastures, where nobody could see me, and taught myself how to ride. Pretty soon I decided it would be fun to try doing some tricks with it. In no time I could jump it clear over a couple of bales of hay. Then over a tractor." He shrugged. "After that, there was no stopping me."

"Didn't your daddy worry?"

"My parents were dead. And poor Grandpop was in a panic over what to do with his ornery grandson."

"Did he punish you?"

Luke shook his head. "He tried. But no matter what, I'd just take my lumps and get right back on my bike. Finally Grandpop gave up. I'm sure he's amazed that I've lived this long."

"What about your brothers? Do they ride motorcycles, too?"

"Matt's too sensible." Luke chuckled. "And now that he has himself a bride, I'm sure he's not going to do anything too dangerous. He's got way too much to live for."

Ingrid's eyes flashed. "Your brother Matt sounds like a smart man."

Luke smiled. He'd caught her listening to their conversation and had known that sooner or later she wouldn't be able to bite her tongue any longer. And though he figured her anger was about what she'd seen the previous night, or thought she'd seen, he had no intention of enlightening her. "Oh, Matt's smart. But so is my brother Reed. We refer to him as our very own technonerd."

Lily's eyes widened. "What's a... what does that mean?"

"Reed's a guy who dearly loves the challenge of learning all kinds of new technology. Give him a complicated gadget with enough directions to fill a book, and he'll sort it out in a matter of hours and have the gadget up and running. He's been that way since we were just kids."

"So." Ingrid's tone was pure ice. "Both your brothers are smart and follow the rules. It seems you're the only misfit in the family."

"That's me." He winked at Lily. "A crazy rebel. I thrive on challenge. Or, as I like to call it, opportunity."

"Do you have any pets, Luke?" Lily guided her horse close to his.

"Just old Turnip here. There's a bunch of barn cats out back of our place, but they're not what I'd call pets. How about you?"

She nodded. "I've got Little."

"Sounds like a hamster or a bunny. Which is it?"

"A chicken. Right after she hatched, I picked her for my very own. And I named her Little 'cause it was the name of a chicken in my favorite story."

"Is she a good pet?"

Lily shrugged. "I used to spend hours dressing her in dolls' clothes and pushing her around in a stroller. But now she just wants to be with the rest of the chickens in the henhouse. But whenever I feed them, she comes right over and sits down so I can pet her."

As they came up over a ridge, the herd of cattle was spread out before them in a rolling meadow of lush grass.

"That's a fine-looking herd." Luke drew back on the reins, allowing Lily to ride ahead, while he remained beside Ingrid. "How many do you figure there are?"

"Nearly six hundred." She dismounted, and Luke did the same. "With the calves born this spring, there should be well over a thousand heading to market this year."

He studied the animals, fat and sleek from the lush grasses in these hills. "You found the perfect place for a summer range. Even without a team of wranglers, they're pretty much fenced in here by the steep hills around them."

Ingrid tossed back her hat to allow the breeze to take her hair. "My dad chose this spot years ago. He divided the herd into three equal parts, leaving some to graze on a higher mountainside, some on a lower plain, and some here. At the end of that season, he realized the herd grazing in this spot brought in the highest profits."

"Your dad was a smart man."

At Luke's praise, she beamed with pleasure and turned to him. "He couldn't hide the love he had for this ranch. All he wanted was to teach me everything he could about ranching, so when the day came for him to slow down, he'd take comfort in the fact that his land was in good hands."

"And it is." Luke lifted a hand to the corn silk strands dancing around her cheeks.

At once her smile fled and she jerked back. "Don't. I told you before. I'm not Nadine."

His eyes narrowed on her. "For the record, there's no way I'd ever confuse you with your mother."

"Then don't try playing those games with me."

"What games are we talking about?"

"You know exactly what I mean. All those sexy moves."

"Really? Sexy?" He was grinning as he reached a hand to her hair. "Like this?"

Her chin came up. "If you want lots of hair, reach for Nadine's."

"Is that why you chopped yours off?" He allowed a silken strand to sift through his fingers. "To prove a point?"

"Well, aren't you the brilliant observer. For the record, there are a lot of things Nadine does that I refuse to do. I don't bother with makeup. And—"

"—and you try to hide your gorgeous body under this bulky shirt." He fingered the rough collar. His smile was quick and charming. "I'll let you in on a secret. It's not working."

She slapped his hand away. "Stop trying to be clever. I know what I am. I'm a rancher who's struggling to stay on the land I love. A big sister working overtime to raise Lily to be the best she can."

"You forgot the most important thing. You're a woman." His voice lowered to a near growl. "Maybe you'd like to forget that, but it's impossible for me to overlook the fact that you're not just a woman, but a gorgeous, amazing, very independent woman."

She actually gasped as he leaned close.

"Just so you know, I'm going to kiss you, Ingrid." His arms came around her and he gathered her close.

He'd known her lips would be soft and inviting. Had known it from the first time he'd looked at them. But he wasn't prepared for the taste of her. Sweet, yet tart. So strong, and yet he could feel the way her breath hitched, alerting him to her unease.

All woman, and yet fighting it. She kept her hands at her sides, refusing to give him any encouragement.

"I won't do anything you don't want me to do. So don't be afraid." He spoke the words inside her mouth.

"I'm not—"

"Just for a moment, Ingrid, let yourself enjoy something."

She responded with a soft purr in the back of her throat. For the space of a heartbeat he could feel her relax in his arms as she gave herself up to the moment.

A burst of heat shot through Luke's veins. His heartbeat was thundering, keeping time with hers. He changed the angle of the kiss and took it deeper, until he could actually feel the fire.

The ground tilted beneath his feet, and he knew he was losing control. He hadn't meant to take it this far. None of this had been planned. He'd merely wanted to kiss her and tease her a little. But now, too late, he realized that one taste of these lips would never be enough.

He lifted his head and held her for another few moments, while he struggled to bring the world around them into focus.

As his breathing settled, he took a step back, keeping his hands at her shoulders to steady himself as well as her.

Before either of them could say a word, Lily's horse trotted over to where they were standing.

The little girl looked down at them, her smile as bright as the sunshine. "Are we heading home now?"

Luke managed to find his voice. "Yeah. I think it's time. Want to race?"

"Oh boy." She turned her mount before calling, "What does the winner get?"

"It's a surprise." Luke would think of something on the ride home. For now, he could barely make his muddled brain work.

He turned to Ingrid, pulling herself into the saddle. "Want to join the game?"

She managed a cool smile. "Sure. I guess I'd be wise to brush up on all my games while you're around."

He shot her a dangerous grin. "Just so you know which ones are games and which are the real thing."

"Are you sure *you* do?" She urged her horse into a run, leaving him in her dust.

CHAPTER EIGHT

Chili." Luke shot a quick grin at Mick as he ladled out their supper.

"I'd better warn you, son. I like it hot."

"Even better." Luke reached for a platter filled with smaller bowls in the middle of the table, holding chopped onion, grated cheese, oyster crackers, and hot sauce. He spooned some of each into his chili before taking a taste. Then he closed his eyes and gave a sigh of pure pleasure. "Now that's what I call ranch chili."

"Around here we call it Mick's fire." Ingrid followed Luke's lead and added the garnishes before digging in.

Lily and Mick were too busy eating to say a word.

As usual, Nadine's chair was empty. Nobody seemed to notice or care. After a day of ranch chores and the long ride into the hills and back, they were ready for the slower pace of evening.

As dusk settled over the land, they enjoyed a leisurely

supper, while the others filled Luke in on some of the family stories from years past.

Luke took a third helping of chili before turning to Ingrid. "So your ranch goes back several generations?"

She nodded. "My grandfather came here from Norway. Dad used to say his father was a happy loner, comfortable with his own company. He didn't marry until he was in his fifties. Then he met a traveling teacher, Winnie, who used to visit ranch families on horseback. He was so taken with her, he asked her to marry him the next day. When she agreed, they rode into Wayside, found a minister, and returned to the ranch that same day. A year later my dad was born. By the time Dad was fifteen, both his parents were dead, and he just continued caring for the ranch like his father before him."

Luke helped himself to coffee, then topped off Mick's cup and Ingrid's. "Where did your father meet your mother?"

"In town. He went in for supplies and came home with a bride. She was a waitress at Barney's. That's the only bar in town. Dad was forty-two. Nadine was just shy of her twentieth birthday. When she realized how isolated this place was, she took off after just two weeks."

"Where did she go?"

Ingrid shrugged. "Back to Wayside. And Barney's. It was all she knew."

"What did your dad do?"

"What he's always done. He tended to the ranch, and when all the chores were finished, he drove his truck to Wayside and found her back at Barney's, slinging drinks."

"How did he persuade her to come back with him?"

Ingrid glanced across the table at her little sister. "If

you'd like, Lily, you can go in the parlor and get the cards ready."

"Okay." The little girl carried her dishes to the sink. Before leaving the room, she said to Luke, "I'll see you when you're ready to play Fish. And remember, you promised me a prize for beating you in our race."

"I haven't forgotten. You'll get your prize, Li'l Bit."

When she was gone, Ingrid sipped her coffee. "In answer to your question...Dad once told me there was only one way to deal with someone like Nadine, and that was to give her time to figure out whether she needed the freedom she craved or the stability he offered."

"Which did she take?"

"Both. Even all these years later."

"How long did she take to come home that first time?"

"A month. Eight months later I was born. And my father said he knew then that he'd never be alone again. He didn't care if Nadine stayed or left, as long as she understood that he was never going to allow her to take me with her."

Mick, listening in silence, let out a chuckle. "I met Lars Larsen when he was running this place all alone. A man who never had time to be a boy. A loner who never felt lonely. And I can tell you that the minute he laid eyes on his baby girl, he lost his heart completely. It was the same with Lily. He just purely doted on his two daughters."

Ingrid smiled. "Dad always lived on the edge. The edge of having the family he'd craved, but never persuading Nadine to stay and make it complete. The edge of making this ranch a success, but never quite attaining it. There were just too many things getting in the way. Nadine's need to party. Debts that never got completely paid. He died still struggling to make it all work."

Seeing the look of sadness coming into her eyes, Luke pushed away from the table. "Okay. We've been lazy long enough. Since Mick made that great chili, it's up to you and me to clean up."

He crossed to the sink and turned on the faucet. While he washed the dishes, Ingrid picked up a towel and dried. As they worked together, Luke kept up a running commentary about his brothers and the silly fights they'd had over the years.

At the table, Mick stretched out his legs and watched the two of them. He could see right through Luke. He was doing his best to keep Ingrid from dwelling on the sad facts of her life. His jokes and funny stories were doing the trick. But if body language could be believed, even though they were both laughing, they were working overtime to keep from touching. Which meant to him that they were probably dealing with some kind of itch to do just the opposite.

His eyes crinkled as a big grin spread across his face. Damned if it didn't look like Luke took his words to heart this morning and found a way to put a smile on Ingrid's face. And wasn't it the warmest smile he'd seen on her in a long time.

It was the way of men and women from the beginning of time. Throw them together long enough, and they were bound to strike sparks off one another. And some of those sparks were just apt to light a fire.

"One more game, Luke. Please."

Luke gathered up the cards and shook his head.

"Thanks for letting me beat you a time or two. It was darned nice of you. But I'm done for tonight. And tomorrow, I think it's time I taught you something new. Gin rummy. Or poker."

She clapped her hands. "Poker?" She turned to Ingrid, seated at the desk across the room, her head bent over the ledgers. "Is it okay if Luke teaches me to play poker?"

Ingrid shot him a look. "Gambling? Why am I not surprised?" To her sister she said sternly, "You'll stick to Fish, young lady."

"We won't play for real money." Luke winked at Lily. "We'll play for something else. Maybe for chores?"

Lily picked up on that instantly. "You mean, if I beat you, you have to do my barn chores?"

"Or, if I beat you, you'll have to do mine."

Her face fell, but only for a moment. She brightened. "Okay. 'Cause I beat you at Fish more than you beat me."

"Yeah. I noticed that. I've been meaning to ask if you've been peeking at the cards."

The little girl put her hands on her hips. "I would never cheat."

Luke laughed at the outraged look on her face. "I know, Li'l Bit."

Her smile returned. "Oh. You were just teasing me again." She dug into the pocket of her jeans and pulled out the dollar bill. "Thanks for my prize, Luke."

"You earned it, Li'l Bit."

"Good night, Luke." Without thinking she threw her arms around his neck and kissed his cheek. "I'll see you in the morning."

"Yeah. See you."

To her big sister she called, "You coming up to hear my prayers?"

"I'll be there in a minute."

Luke sat perfectly still and waited until Lily danced up the stairs. Then he touched a finger to his cheek.

When he saw Ingrid staring, he started toward the kitchen. "I think I'll make a fresh pot of coffee. Want some?"

"Sure. I'll just be a few minutes." She shoved away from the desk and climbed the stairs.

A short time later she returned to the parlor to find Luke on his knees in front of the fireplace, coaxing a thin flame to some kindling. On the coffee table was a tray holding two mugs and a pot of coffee, along with cream and sugar.

Ingrid poured the coffee and crossed the room to hand Luke a steaming mug.

"Thanks."

She nodded toward the fire. "That feels good."

"Yeah. Getting chilly in here. The temperature must be dropping."

"Mick said rain's coming in."

"He watched the news?"

She shook her head and picked up a mug of coffee for herself. "He claims his bones let him know when rain's coming."

They shared a laugh as they settled into two over-stuffed rockers in front of the fire.

Luke stretched out his long legs to the heat. "This is nice."

"Yeah." Ingrid fell silent while she sipped her coffee.

"I saw you going over the bills." He indicated the desk across the room. "Everything okay?"

She shrugged. "I do the best I can. I pay the most important bills first. Taxes. Insurance. But I lost a field of hay, and that's going to cost me this winter."

"You could sell off the entire herd after roundup, and then you wouldn't need the feed."

"What's a cattle ranch without cattle?"

"You could keep a bare-bones herd. A bull. A couple of broodmares."

"And start over?"

"It's what ranchers do when they're up against hard times. You'd not only save the cost of feed all winter, but you could also start saving to pay the salaries of a couple of wranglers next spring."

"There's not much need of wranglers without a herd."

"There are fences to mend. Buildings to repair. By the time you've built up a new herd, your ranch would be in good shape and you could concentrate on being a cattle rancher."

She gave a long, deep sigh. "Oh, Luke, you make it sound so easy."

He set aside his coffee. "It's never easy. If people like us wanted easy, we'd sell everything and take up a trade. Nobody around here is ranching because we're looking for a slick life. But this is our heritage. It's what our fathers did. Our grandfathers. It's in our blood."

He saw a tear slide down her cheek. Alarmed, he dropped to his knees in front of her and caught her hands in his. "Hey. I'm sorry, Ingrid. I didn't mean to make you cry. I always say more than I—"

"Shhh." She touched a finger to his lips to stop his words. "I never knew anyone else felt this way. I've never been able to put it into words. But you said exactly what's in my heart. I love this ranch, Luke. I want, more than anything, to make it work so Lily and I can stay here. And I'm so afraid I'll fail."

When she started to withdraw her hand, he caught it between both of his and lifted it to his lips, pressing a kiss to the palm and closing her fingers around it.

Stunned, she merely stared at him, her eyes swimming with tears.

Maybe it was the tears. Maybe it was the moment. Whatever the reason, he leaned into her and framed her face with his big hands.

And then his mouth was on hers, and his fingers were in her hair, and they strained toward each other with a hunger that caught them both by surprise.

The old rocker creaked as Luke stood, his arms going around her, dragging her to her feet.

She clung to his waist, offering her mouth for another drugging kiss. He took what she offered with a fierceness that had her gasping before she allowed herself to sink into the pure pleasure.

There was such strength in him. In the arms that gathered her close. In the control she could feel in him as he kept his kiss gentle, even though his breathing was ragged.

When at last she pushed slightly away and dragged in a rough breath, she saw the fierce look in his eyes and knew he could easily take this further. But to his credit, he respected her enough to allow her to set the pace.

"Fear is always biting at a rancher's heels. Fear of bad weather. Fear of a failed herd or crop. But we fight back the fear and keep going. It's what we do."

"Thank you, Luke."

He shot her a rogue's grin. "For the kiss?"

She flushed. "For the words. I needed to hear them."

Seeing him watching her closely, her flush deepened. "Well, for the kiss, too. I guess I needed it more than I realized."

"Always happy to oblige, ma'am. You just let me know whenever I can be of help again."

"So noble." She couldn't help laughing. "Don't let it go to your head, cowboy."

She walked to the stairway and turned to him. "You'll bank the fire before coming up?"

"Looks like I have no choice."

At his double meaning she laughed again.

And continued laughing as she climbed the stairs to her room.

CHAPTER NINE

Luke's sleep was disturbed by the sound of a door slamming and voices raised in anger. One he identified as Nadine's. The other was a male voice he hadn't heard before. He pulled on his jeans before reaching for his rifle beside the bed. Shirtless and barefoot, he started down the hall.

Ingrid's door opened. Her hair was tousled, her eyes heavy lidded from sleep. She was barefoot and wearing a faded football jersey that fell below her knees.

They stared at each other in silence, before Ingrid led the way down the stairs.

She paused in the doorway of the kitchen, and Luke stepped up behind her to stare at Nadine, hands on hips, facing a heavyset, grizzled cowboy who was shaking a fist in her face.

Neither Nadine nor her cowboy took any notice of Ingrid and Luke as they lobbed a fierce volley of curses at each other.

"I told you." His voice was fierce. "The money first. Then we'll go to your bedroom."

"And I told you. You'll get your money in the morning." A rough, scratchy chuckle. "If I think you earned it."

"Why you—" The stranger caught a handful of Nadine's hair and tugged her head back so hard she cried out. At the same instant, his hand was around her throat.

Luke stepped in front of Ingrid and took aim with his rifle. "Step away from the woman."

Two heads came up sharply as Nadine and the stranger turned to the doorway.

Luke's voice was pure ice. "I said step away from her. Now."

At once the man released his hold on Nadine, before turning on her with a look of absolute fury. "Who the hell is this guy?"

"Some cowboy who thinks he has the right to butt in where he isn't wanted." Nadine glowered at Luke, and then at her daughter. "You've got no right to interfere in my business."

"Some business." Ingrid's tone revealed a depth of sadness. "Are you reduced to paying for his service now?"

"Since you drove him off the property at the end of your rifle, he said he wouldn't come back unless he was paid."

Luke realized this was Lon Wardell. He wouldn't have recognized this bloated, worn-out cowboy as the cocky, muscled wrangler who had once worked on his family's ranch over twenty years ago. That Lon Wardell had walked with a swagger and had bragged about owning his own ranch one day. A sprawling ranch that would rival the Malloy spread.

Ingrid turned to the cowboy. "What's the matter, Lon? Can't afford a room in Wayside?"

His voice was old. Weary. "She wanted to come here."

"Well, she's here." Ingrid pointed to the door. "And you're still not welcome. So get. Now."

He opened his mouth, then shut it quickly when Luke took careful aim, backing up Ingrid's order.

He directed his fury at Nadine. "I'm done, you hear? I'm sick and tired of your empty promises."

"They weren't empty." Nadine shot a hateful look at Ingrid. "This ranch is still mine. And I can give it to whoever I please. You make the right choice, Lonny honey, you could still have that dream of owning your own place."

"Over my dead body."

At Ingrid's words, he shot her a chilling smile. "Careful what you say. It can be arranged"—he snapped his fingers—"like that."

Luke took a step toward him. "You've got to the count of five to be out of here and off the lady's property."

It was obvious the cowboy was giving some thought to testing him. Then, seeing the look in Luke's eyes, he turned and beat a retreat.

As the sound of his truck faded in the night, Nadine vented all her fury on Ingrid. "How dare you interfere in my life?"

"Interfere?" Ingrid hissed out a breath. "He was about to use you for a punching bag."

"He didn't mean it. It was just love play."

"Of course it was." Ingrid faced her mother, her voice trembling with emotion. "If you believe that, you've got a twisted sense of love."

"You'd better be very careful how you treat me, missy. I'm still legal owner of this place. And if I feel like it, I can give it to anybody I please. Even Lonny."

"Then you'd have to live here. And being a rancher's wife has never been your style."

Nadine brushed past Ingrid and Luke and headed for the stairs, swearing a blue streak as she did.

When Nadine was gone, Ingrid sank down on a kitchen chair. Her hands, Luke noted, were shaking.

He set the rifle in a corner of the room. "I'll make some coffee."

Within a few minutes the air was filled with the fragrance of coffee bubbling on the stove. Luke filled two cups and handed one to Ingrid.

"Thanks." She sipped, and some of the color began returning to her cheeks. "And thanks for backing me up. Judging by Lon's temper, and the fact that he was very drunk, I doubt he'd have given up if I'd faced him alone."

"You should never be alone with that guy." Luke sat across from her. "Neither should Nadine. I didn't like what I saw in his eyes." When she raised a brow, he added, "A look of desperation. That can make a man do dangerous things."

He took his time, giving her the chance to steady herself before asking, "Is this a pattern with Nadine? Violent men?"

She shook her head. "Except for Lon Wardell, I've never met any of the men in her life. And Lon's temperament is as far from my father's as possible. My dad was soft-spoken, hardworking, and, with all of us, as gentle and accepting as a lamb. Whenever she came home after one of her absences, he always welcomed her back as though it was the most normal thing in the world for his wife to be gone for long stretches of time."

Luke fiddled with his spoon. "She seems a bit... desperate."

Ingrid nodded. "I agree. But I don't know what to do about it. Dad used to call it her crazy side. He said there was a crazy lady hidden inside her that fought to get out. And whenever it succeeded, all he could do was stand back and watch her go. Sometimes it took weeks, sometimes months." She shook her head. "Or years. Then she'd come back, all happy and normal until the next time."

Ingrid ran a hand through her cap of hair. "I'm so tired of it all. The threats of giving away all that Dad worked so hard to own. The drunken trips to Wayside. The strangers she hangs with."

"It's a lot of drama."

"And I'm sick and tired of it."

Hearing the weariness in her tone, Luke topped off their cups.

"Thanks." Ingrid eyed him over the rim of her cup. "Why are you staying here, Luke?"

He gave a nonchalant shrug. "Why not? You saved my life. I'd like to do something in return to help you."

She eyed him squarely. "Most people would say thank you and move on. If that wasn't enough, maybe a note, or flowers, or..." She sighed. "Most people would be so eager to get away from all this, they'd run screaming into the night."

He gave her an unexpected wink. "I guess I'm not most people."

"You're not like anybody I've ever known."

"Good. That's part of my charm."

She laughed out loud. "You always have the perfect answer to everything."

"Just part of the package, ma'am." He gave an exaggerated drawl. "Not only charming, but smart as a whip, too."

Before she could think, she closed a hand over his. "Oh, I needed to have something to laugh about." Realizing what she'd done, she lifted her hand away.

Luke caged her hand between both of his. "It's nice to have someone to share the laughter with."

She looked at their joined hands. "Yeah. It is nice." She paused a beat, letting her gaze trail that muscled chest and torso before adding, "Just don't fool yourself into believing that I'm falling for all that muscle and charm."

He bit back a grin. "Not for a minute, ma'am."

Seeing that their cups were empty, Luke picked up his rifle and caught her hand. "Come on. You can still manage a couple of hours of sleep before you have to start your chores."

Upstairs, Ingrid paused outside her bedroom. "I know I already thanked you, but let me say it again. I'm really grateful you're here, Luke."

"So am I. Good night."

He waited until she stepped inside and closed her door before moving on to his own room. Once inside, he walked to the window and stared out at the midnight blackness.

He admired Ingrid for fighting to salvage her father's heritage. He knew, in her place, he'd do the same. But a clear-eyed look at the odds against her had him wondering how much longer one determined woman could hold out for the proverbial happy ending. Maybe he should encourage her to cut her losses and go to a place where she and Lily could be safe. At least then they could live to fight another day.

He thought about the very different lifestyle he was accustomed to at the family ranch. Teasing. A lot of trash talk between brothers. The occasional fight that ended in raised fists. But more, there was concern and love and laughter. So much laughter.

It had been good to hear Ingrid laugh. She deserved to do it more often.

While he peered out the window, he saw a flash of light as the rusted pickup chugged to life. He could see Nadine clearly outlined in the interior light of the truck as she put it in gear and took off with tires spinning.

Apparently she hadn't had her fill of Wayside or its cowboys yet.

The crazy woman inside her had won another round over common sense.

After breakfast, Mick joined Luke, Ingrid, and her little sister in the barn, mucking stalls after turning out a string of horses into a fenced corral. With four sets of hands, the chores were quickly completed.

Mick looked over at Luke, hanging his pitchfork on a hook along the wall. "How's the shoulder holding up, son?"

"Good." Luke massaged the muscle. "Hardly a twinge now."

"You up to lending a hand with the shed?"

"Sure thing." Luke turned. "Lead the way."

The two crossed a pasture and headed toward a small shed in the distance. Once there, they took down a sagging door. While Mick replaced the rusty hinges, Luke removed his shirt in the hot sun before laying the door across a couple of sawhorses, and he began working a plane across the surface in smooth, even strokes.

While they worked, Luke brought the old man up to speed on what had happened the night before.

Ingrid and Lily came riding across the pasture and reined in their mounts.

Ingrid had to call on all her discipline to tear her gaze from Luke's muscled, sweaty body. He was, quite simply, beautiful.

"You two need our help?"

Mick shook his head. "We've got this, girl. You heading up to the herd?"

"Yeah." She decided to say no more, afraid to trust her voice over the knot of lust she couldn't seem to swallow.

Lily's voice was almost pleading. "I was hoping you'd be able to come with us, Luke."

He winked at her. "If you'll give me a few minutes, I'll go along." He lifted the door and held it in place while Mick tightened the hinges.

Luke opened and closed the door several times to be certain it was level. Then, snatching up his shirt, he grabbed Turnip's reins.

"If you have any more chores, Mick, I can get to them in a couple of hours."

"There's always tomorrow, son." The old cowboy lifted his Stetson and wiped a sleeve across his brow. "The chores will still be waiting."

"Can we race again, Luke?" Lily was already crouching in the saddle, determined to win.

"Sorry, Li'l Bit. I think this hot sun calls for a slow, easy ride so our horses don't get overheated." He pulled Turnip beside Ingrid's mount, and the two exchanged a look.

As the three horses started across the meadow toward the distant hills, Mick stood watching. Luke hadn't fooled him. That young man wasn't so much interested in the herd as he was in keeping Ingrid and Lily safe.

After hearing about their midnight encounter with Lon Wardell, he was grateful for Luke Malloy's presence on their ranch.

The old man squirted oil on the hinges and tested the door one more time before turning toward the house. He'd seen a hunk of beef in the freezer and figured it was time for some good old-fashioned pot roast. Comfort food. After the scene Ingrid had been forced to witness last night, it was just what the doctor ordered.

Of course, so was Luke Malloy. He was more than the doctor ordered.

His presence on the ranch gave the old cowboy a feeling of security he hadn't felt since Lars had passed away so suddenly.

CHAPTER TEN

Luke, Lily, and Ingrid enjoyed a leisurely ride across the meadows before pausing at the top of the ridge to study the herd below. As before, Lily urged her mount into a fast run down the hill, where horse and rider moved slowly among the grazing animals. These hills, and this herd, were part of the child's comfort zone. She was as easy with these cows as a city kid would be with a skateboard.

While Luke watched, something in the scene below looked out of place, but it took a minute for it to register in his mind. "That can't be right."

Ingrid saw the grim set of his jaw. "What?"

He shook his head slowly. "I hope I'm wrong. But from what I can see, there can't be more than a couple of hundred head of cattle down there."

After scanning the scene, she tried to cover the little cry that escaped her lips before she bit down hard. "That's impossible."

He drew his mount closer to hers. "With no wranglers, it wouldn't be hard for anyone to help themselves to your cattle."

"Rustlers?"

"With enough cattle haulers, they could truck away an entire herd in a couple of nights."

"But who...?"

His eyes narrowed. "I can think of two men who would benefit from stealing your herd."

He saw her eyes fill before she turned away.

He left her alone while he slowly circled the herd, mentally tallying as he did. By his calculations, there were less than four hundred cattle in this meadow, when there had been more than six hundred earlier.

And for every cow missing, Ingrid's chances of buying the ranch from her mother narrowed considerably.

When he returned, she and Lily were standing together, talking quietly, while holding to their horses' reins.

"Maybe they wandered off." The little girl put her hand on her big sister's arm.

"A couple of hundred?" Ingrid wrapped her arms around the little girl and hugged her hard. Against the top of her head she muttered, "I don't want you to worry. It's only cows. At least we're safe, honey."

Luke managed a smile for Lily's benefit. "I checked my phone and there's no service up here. Why don't we head back down to the house and see if we can make a call?"

While Lily mounted and started ahead, Luke waited for Ingrid. As they rode slowly behind the little girl, he said quietly, "As soon as you get phone service, you need to phone the sheriff and report what you suspect. There may be other ranchers around here who've lost cattle, too. If so, he'll be aware of a pattern. But even if yours is the only ranch hit, someone may have spotted a convoy of cattle haulers in the area."

"If they came in the night, they could be across the border into Canada by now."

He heard the note of grim resignation in her voice and wished he could think of something to lift her spirits. But they both knew this was serious business.

Neither of them could pretend any longer. This was one more in a string of unexplained incidents. And they were all directed against Ingrid.

Several hours later, Sheriff Eugene Graystoke pulled up to the Larsen house. A beefy man with a booming gravel voice, he commanded respect from the ranchers in the area.

He climbed the back steps, but before he could knock on the door, Ingrid opened it.

"Miss Larsen?" He removed his hat and held it at his side while extending his other hand. "Sheriff Eugene Graystoke."

"Hello, Sheriff." She returned the handshake before indicating the girl behind her. "This is my sister, Lily."

The sheriff smiled at the little girl. "Hello, Lily."

"Hello. You look like those men on TV." Lily couldn't hide her fascination with his badge and uniform.

He chuckled. "Now if only I could be paid what they're paid, life would be good."

Ingrid stood aside. "Thank you for coming so quickly, Sheriff."

He walked into the mudroom and hung his hat on a peg by the door before scraping his boots.

She led the way into the kitchen, where Mick had a pot of coffee perking. "Sheriff Graystoke, I believe you met my foreman, Mick Hinkley."

"Yes. When your field caught fire. Hello again, Mick." The two shook hands. "Sorry I couldn't determine the cause of the fire, but with so many lightning strikes during summer storms, it was a good bet that it was purely nature and not anything sinister."

"I understand. Coffee, Sheriff?"

"I've never been known to refuse." He looked over when Luke walked into the room from the direction of the parlor.

"Luke Malloy. Didn't expect to see you. What are you doing way over here?"

"I took a nasty fall up in the hills and Ingrid brought me to her place and tended my wounds."

"You doing crazy tricks on that Harley again, Luke?"

Luke grinned and shook his head. "I was riding Turnip this time. Anyway, considering all the trouble it took getting me here, I figured I'd repay the favor by hanging around awhile and giving a hand with the ranch chores."

"That's nice of you. I'm sure your help is appreciated." The sheriff turned to Ingrid. "I knew your daddy. Lars was a good man. And an honest one. I never had a single complaint about him, and that's more than I can say about a lot of folks in this county."

He accepted a cup of coffee from Mick and then indicated the table. "Why don't we sit and you can tell me about this suspected rustling."

As quickly as she could, Ingrid explained about their late-morning ride and the number of cattle that were now missing from the herd. The sheriff listened intently and waited until she'd given him as many details as possible before he began asking a few questions.

"How many wranglers do you employ, Miss Larsen?"

"Just Mick. He can do just about anything around the ranch. He cooks, he does barn chores, and he often rides up to check on the herd."

"How about this spring? You say you had a record number of calves born this year. How many wranglers were here to lend a hand?"

"Just Mick and me. And my sister, Lily."

"Most calves need a lot of help being born. You and your little sister don't look strong enough to pull a calf from its ma."

"We were born on this ranch. We know how to do whatever's needed to survive."

The sheriff gave her an admiring look before flipping a page and making notations. "You say the herd numbered close to six hundred?"

She bit her lip and nodded.

"Did you comb the hills for your missing cattle?"

"No. There wasn't time."

"I see. Have you fired anybody lately?"

"Not since last year. After my father died, I had to let all the wranglers go. But I paid them their fair wages."

"I heard. I was sorry about your daddy. As I said, he was a good man." He looked up, meeting her direct gaze. "You have any known enemies, ma'am?"

She flushed. "There is a cowboy I ordered off my ranch at the end of my rifle."

"You threatened to shoot him?"

She nodded.

"Can you tell me why?"

She stared hard at the table. "I didn't like him. And I didn't trust him."

The sheriff set aside his empty cup. "Would you care to elaborate? What did he do to make you distrust him?"

"He..." She ran a finger around and around the rim of her cup before clenching her hands together in her lap. "My mother brought him home and said she was going to marry him. I couldn't stand to see him sleeping in my father's bed, sitting at my father's place at the table. He even started driving my father's truck."

Sheriff Graystoke's voice softened. "That's not a crime, ma'am."

"I know. But he was...I had a very bad feeling about him."

"You were about to say something more. He was what?"

She sighed. "Creepy."

"So you aimed your rifle at your mother's...friend and ordered him off the ranch. Could he be angry enough to want to retaliate?"

She nodded. "He said as much."

"Can you give me his name?"

"Lon Wardell."

He scribbled in his notes before looking up with a distinct frown. "Are there any more people you can think of who might want to do damage to you or your ranch?"

"My neighbor, Bull Hammond."

"He has a reason?"

"He offered to buy the ranch from my mother. I asked

her to wait until roundup, to see if there was enough profit from the herd to buy it myself."

The sheriff looked puzzled. "If your mother owns this ranch, doesn't the herd belong to her?"

Ingrid shook her head. "My father's will stated that my mother owns the ranch, with all its property and buildings, but the herd belongs to me."

"So the only one harmed by this theft is you. It doesn't affect your mother's interest in the ranch?"

"That's right."

"Would that be common knowledge to Wardell or Hammond?"

She shrugged. "Only if Nadine told them."

Within half an hour he had as many facts as she was able to give. When the sheriff got ready to leave, Luke offered to walk with him to his vehicle.

They paused outside the police car. Luke leaned close. "You heard what Ingrid had to say. What do you know about Wardell and Hammond?"

"Wardell's bad company. A loose cannon. I have a file of paperwork on him as long as my arm. Wardell has been drifting from ranch to ranch in these parts for as long as I've been sheriff here. He's never been able to hold a job for long."

"He worked our place when I was just a kid. I know he was fired for stealing. Is there more?"

Eugene Graystoke shrugged. "Larceny, mostly. If it isn't nailed down, Wardell will find a fence willing to buy just about anything. Then he spends the money on booze. Most bartenders know whether he stole something big or small by the amount of time he stays drunk."

"Bull Hammond? What do you know about him?"

"A bully. Likes to throw his weight around. I heard years ago there was bad blood between him and Lars Larsen. Never heard what the beef was about, but I wouldn't be surprised if he still carries a grudge, even though Lars is in the ground. But there's no official complaints on file. I'd say Larsen's daughter better watch her back with those two out to cause trouble."

"There's more." Luke proceeded to tell the sheriff about the shot fired at the mustangs, the suspicious fire in the hayfield, the mysterious death of Ingrid's dog, and the ugly incident between Nadine, Lon Wardell, Ingrid, and himself the night before.

With a muttered oath, Sheriff Graystoke tossed his notebook into the car before settling himself in the driver's seat. "I think I'll take a ride to Wayside and have a chat with the bartender at Barney's. See if he knows anything. Most bar owners are able to hear more in a single drunken night than a lawman can learn in weeks of investigating."

He gave Luke a long, level look. "It may be nothing more than cattle straying from their usual pasture. Or we may be dealing with cattle rustling. But if what you've told me turns out to be deliberate, and not accidental, we may have something much more serious going on here. That young woman's life could be in danger."

"Then I guess that means I'm staying on."

The sheriff raised a brow. "You in this for the excitement? Or is that pretty lady the reason you're staying?"

Luke gave the sheriff the famous Malloy smile. "I'm not sure myself. I guess a little of both."

CHAPTER ELEVEN

R oast beef and mashed potatoes?" Ingrid stepped into the kitchen and breathed deeply. "What's the occasion, Mick?"

Luke stepped in behind her, trailed by Lily, who'd worked alongside Ingrid and Luke in the barn, finishing up the last of the evening's chores.

Mick looked up from the oven, where a cloud of fragrant steam was drifting. "Are you saying there has to be something special to enjoy a good meal?"

"All your meals are great, Mick." Ingrid paused beside her place at the table and held up a tall glass filled with ice water. "But this is the first time I've ever seen you do this." She drained it in one long, parched swallow.

"I figured you'd be thirsty after all that work." Mick reached into the refrigerator and removed two frosty longnecks, handing one to Luke. When Ingrid shook her head in refusal, he twisted the top off the other and took a drink. "Figured you've earned a thirst quencher, too, son."

After a long pull, Luke shot the old man a wide smile. "Now that was worth working up a sweat. Thanks, Mick."

Lily spotted the glass of milk beside her plate and needed no coaxing to enjoy the surprise.

"You can all sit." Mick began setting out a platter of roast beef swimming in gravy. The meat was so tender it fell off the bone. There was also a big bowl of steaming mashed potatoes, dotted with butter. The green beans were from the little patch of garden Mick tended all summer on the far side of the house. There was even a plate of store-bought rolls from the freezer, thawed in the oven until they were all soft and doughy, to mop up the gravy.

For nearly ten minutes nobody said a word. The kitchen was peppered with sighs and murmurs of approval as they dug in.

Finally, after her plate was empty and she'd finished her second glass of milk, Lily looked across the table at Luke. "Does your cook make roast beef like Mick?"

"He makes a lot of beef dishes. We are, after all, a cattle ranch." Luke shot the old man a smile. "But right this minute, I doubt anybody could match what your cook just did."

Mick gave a loud laugh. "Looks like all that flattery means somebody's hoping for thirds."

Luke shook his head. "I've already had seconds, and I'm as stuffed as a sausage."

That had Lily giggling.

Luke was careful not to look at Ingrid, but instead kept his eyes downcast. "I've been thinking that you all deserve a break from ranch chores. What would you think about driving over to my family ranch?"

Lily clapped her hands and turned to her sister. "Oh boy. Can we, Ingrid? Can we? Please?"

"A break would be nice if we had wranglers." Ingrid looked away from the pleading look in her sister's eyes. "But I don't see how it's possible. The ranch depends on all of us working together. Who would muck the stalls? What if the rest of the herd should disappear?"

Luke drained his beer. "The horses could be put to pasture. As for the rustling, it happened when we were all here. If thieves have targeted your herd, nothing will stop them except the presence of wranglers keeping watch."

"Fine." Ingrid crossed her arms over her chest. "Then I'll keep watch tonight."

"You think men bent on stealing are going to be stopped by one woman?"

She narrowed her gaze on him. "A woman with a rifle holds the same firepower as a man."

"I'll grant you that. But if there are enough rustlers, their sheer numbers will overwhelm you before you can stop all of them."

"If my dog Tippy were still here"—she looked on the verge of sudden, unexpected tears—"this never could have happened. That herd was as much his as ours, and he'd have fought to the last breath to save them from strangers."

Luke arched a brow. "Did anyone else know he was attached to the herd?"

She shrugged. "I guess just about everyone around here knew. Tippy could do the work of half a dozen wranglers. And he didn't need a rifle. He had his teeth. He used them to nip at the stray cows, and he'd have used them on anyone trying to encroach on his territory."

"So his death was more than a personal loss. He was the herd's guardian." Luke considered before adding, "All right. If you insist on staying with the herd tonight, I'm going along."

"I don't need a babysitter."

He merely smiled. "I'm well aware of that. But you have to admit that a second gun would be comfort during a raid."

Lily spoke up in a sad voice. "What about me? If you both go, I'll be all alone upstairs."

"It's only for a night, honey." Ingrid glanced at Mick, hoping he might calm the girl's fears.

Instead, the old man sided with Lily. "I don't like the idea of us splitting up. Too much going on around here. There's safety in numbers. If you want my vote, I say we either all stay in the hills with the herd, or we all stay here and trust that the cattle rustling was a onetime incident."

Ingrid fell silent as she mulled their options. On the one hand, she needed to hold on to what was left of her herd. On the other hand, she had no right to deny the rest of them, who worked so hard all day, the chance for a little rest from the grind.

Tapping her finger against the table edge, she gave voice to her thoughts. "I'm trying to think like someone with a grudge to settle. I guess it doesn't much matter whether we stay here or spend a night up in the hills. If we're here, the rest of the cattle could be gone by morning. If we go, we're draining our energy for the day ahead."

Mick watched her for a minute longer. "So. What'll it be?"

Ingrid gave a curt shrug of her shoulders. "We'll stay here."

Luke shoved away from the table. "Well, now that that's settled, it's time to thank Mick by cleaning up this kitchen."

As Ingrid started to rise, he turned to Lily. "I'm thinking we'll give your big sister a break, and you and I will do the dishes."

"Okay." The little girl was up and reaching for a dish towel before Luke had time to fill the sink.

Grateful for the break, Ingrid headed to the parlor to work on her ledgers.

Mick, free for the evening, drifted off to his room to watch television.

"Tell me more about your grandparents, Luke." Lily picked up a plate and dried it carefully before setting it on a shelf.

Luke realized the little girl was fixated on the things she'd never had. "My grandfather is Francis Xavier Malloy."

"That's a funny name."

"You think so?" He considered. "I guess it is to some people, but it doesn't matter. I never call him that anyway. I call him Grandpop, but my grandmother calls him Frankie."

"What's your grandmother's name?"

"We all call her Gram Gracie. And Grandpop calls her his Gracie Girl."

"Is she real old?"

"She would probably seem that way to you. But she's not as old as her father, the Great One."

"Why do you call him that?"

"Because when I was a kid, it was easier to say that than to call him Great-Grandpop. Besides, when he first came to live with us, he was a stuffed shirt, and not at all like the grandfatherly type. So he became the Great One. He loves the name."

"What's a stuffed shirt?"

"A person who's so stiff and formal, he'd probably break in half if he ever tried to bend the rules a little."

"Is he still like that?"

Luke thought a minute. "He's about as far removed from being a stuffed shirt as he'll ever be. He still misses the good life he left behind in Hollywood, but he's learned to love the ranch, too."

"Do your grandpop Frank and gram Gracie sit by the fire with a blanket over their laps, like the grandparents in my books?"

That had Luke chuckling. "Don't ever suggest that if you're around them. Grandpop can still work as hard as any wrangler on our ranch. And my gram Gracie often rides up in the hills for weeks at a time on her safaris."

"What are safaris?"

"That's what people call travels in Africa to study wild animals. But here it just means a trip to the hills for a few days."

"Oh. I read about Africa in my geography book. Next time, I hope I read about safaris. How about your...Great One? Does he sit around with a blanket on his lap?"

"Never. He keeps everyone in the family on their toes with his outrageous demands."

"Like what?"

"Well, for one thing, he loves exotic food and drinks."

"What's exotic?"

"Fancy-schmancy meals you'd find in the most expensive restaurants in the world."

That had Lily giggling behind her hand. "Does he ever get any?"

"Does he ever. Yancy is constantly surprising him by making them exactly as the Great One remembers from his younger Hollywood days."

"You keep saying that. What are Hollywood days?"

"That's where the Great One lived and worked."

"Oh." The little girl looked suitably impressed. "Does the Great One drink"—she had to think a moment before continuing—"fancy-schmancy drinks, too? Or does he drink longnecks like you and Mick?"

Luke gave a snort of laughter. "Li'l Bit, he considers beer lower than soda pop. He prefers martinis. He calls that a gentleman's drink."

"And does Yancy make what the Great One likes?"

"You bet." He bent down, as though telling her a grand secret. "You know what?"

"What?" The single word was a whisper while her eyes went wide.

"I'd rather have an ice-cold longneck and Mick's roast beef anytime, but I'd never admit that to Yancy or the Great One."

She giggled.

After finishing the dishes, they strolled into the parlor, where Ingrid was busy at the desk.

She looked up at the clock on the mantel. "You two took your time."

Lily's smile was radiant. "Luke was telling me all about his grandparents, Frankie and Grace, and his great-grandfather the Great One. His grandma goes on ..." Forgetting the rest of it, she looked over at Luke.

"Safaris."

"That's right. Safaris. That's what they call adventures in Africa to see wild animals."

Ingrid arched a brow. "That's pretty impressive." She turned to Luke. "You sure you aren't a teacher posing as a rancher?"

He gave a mock bow. "Just one of my many talents, ma'am."

They shared a laugh.

Seeing Lily yawning behind her hand, Ingrid said, "You may want to skip playing Fish tonight and save it for another night when you're awake enough to beat Luke."

"Okay." Lily smiled up at him. "Can we play tomorrow instead?"

"Sure thing." He winked. "Since I intend to win, I'd rather beat you when you're in fighting form."

Laughing, she called, "'Night, Luke. I loved hearing about your family."

"'Night, Li'l Bit. I loved talking about them."

Ingrid sealed an envelope and returned a pile of bills to a file folder. "I'll be upstairs in a few minutes, honey."

A short time later, as she got to her feet and started up the stairs, she hugged her arms to her chest at the sound of thunder in the distance. "Getting colder outside. Storm's coming."

Ingrid descended the stairs to find Luke in the parlor, seated in front of a roaring fire.

Some of the sadness disappeared from her eyes. "Oh, that feels good."

Seeing the way she eyed the paperwork piled on her desk, he held up a longneck and indicated the rocker beside his. "Let it go. You've done enough for one day."

She settled herself in the rocker and gave a soft sigh. "No matter what I do, it's never enough." She glanced at the bottle in his hand. "Where did you find that?"

"Hidden behind the milk. I hope it's not part of Mick's stash." He took a long pull before passing it to her.

She took a grateful sip. Suddenly, her eyes danced with laughter. "That old sweetie. Do you think he was hiding this?"

"Could be. But at least he shared some over supper. If I find out this one is his last, I'll have to make a trip to town tomorrow and restock the larder."

Ingrid laughed and leaned her head back, letting the heat of the fire seep into her bones. "Do you want to know what Lily prayed for tonight?"

He looked over.

"You and your family." She turned her head slightly, meeting his gaze. "She's falling under your spell, you know."

"That's awesome."

"You mean an awesome responsibility."

"What's that supposed to mean?"

She took another drink of beer before passing the bottle back to him. "It means you're becoming important in her young life. She looks up to you, Luke. I hope you realize how serious that can be to a little girl."

He nodded. "She's become special to me, too. She's a really sweet kid. And that's a tribute to you. Mick told me you're more a mother to her than Nadine is. Seeing the two of you together, I agree. You're setting a fine example for Lily. She's smart and independent. She's got the whole world ahead of her."

"I hope you're right."

When he offered her another drink, she shook her head. "Thanks. I've had enough. You finish it."

He emptied the bottle and set it aside.

They sat in companionable silence for long minutes, enjoying the sizzle of flames, the soft patter of rain on the roof.

Ingrid roused herself enough to push out of the rocker and get to her feet. "If I stay here any longer, I'll be asleep. This was nice. Thanks for sharing. Good night, Luke."

"'Night."

At the stairway she paused. "Do you want the light on or off?"

"You can turn it off. I'll just wait until the fire burns low before I head up."

When she was gone, he sat staring into the flames. He couldn't remember the last time he'd spent an evening just sitting with a woman in front of the fire, without making a move. But with Ingrid, it seemed the most natural thing in the world.

Had it been his imagination, or was she beginning to soften toward him?

Not that it mattered, he thought. Neither of them had time to develop a relationship. He was just putting off the inevitable. Though he was reluctant to leave until the sheriff resolved this situation, he knew it was only a matter of time. Sooner or later they would be able to get on with their lives, and he would return to his own ranch. He knew his family was able to function without him, but there was a certain amount of guilt knowing he was neglecting his own herds to help Ingrid with hers.

He checked the grate and closed the fire screen before heading up the stairs.

In his room he didn't bother with the light as he nudged off his boots and tossed his shirt on a chair.

He'd just unsnapped his jeans when he heard a sound like a gunshot, and for a moment his hands paused in midair.

Thunder? It sounded close, too.

At the same instant, he heard the distinct splinter of glass.

In one quick motion he snatched up his rifle and made a frantic dash down the hall, kicking in the door to Ingrid's room.

She was standing in a pool of lamplight, staring at the shattered glass that littered her bedroom floor.

Luke snapped off the light and threw himself against her, using the weight of his body to press her into the shadows before rushing to the broken window.

Instead of gunshots, all he could hear was the sound of an engine. Instead of a shooter, all he could see was the glare of red taillights as a truck disappeared into the night.

CHAPTER TWELVE

Luke turned to Ingrid. She hadn't moved. Her eyes, wide and unblinking, mirrored the shock she was feeling. She looked absolutely thunderstruck.

He crossed the room and cupped his palm to her cheek. "You okay?"

"I...yes. I guess so. I didn't even know what I'd heard at first. Then the window shattered, and I..." A shudder passed through her.

Seeing her delayed reaction, he gathered her close and simply held her as tremor after tremor rocked her.

She stood still, absorbing his quiet strength and breathing deeply before pushing a little away. "I know I should have dropped to the floor, but I couldn't seem to move. I felt nailed to the spot. I know it was wrong. I was making myself even more of a target, but I..." She let the words trail off.

"It's a natural reaction when your life is threatened. You freeze."

"I've never..." She tried again. "I've never been in the line of fire before." Her hand went to her mouth. "Oh, Luke, what if that had been Lily?"

"Hey now. Don't go there." He closed his hands over her shoulders and simply held her.

Mick raced into the room, red-eyed and bewhiskered, wearing a ratty robe hastily tossed over his long johns. "I heard a gunshot."

He looked down at the glass littering the floor, before his eyes narrowed on Ingrid. "You hurt, girl?"

"No. But whoever fired that shot had time to fire again. If Luke hadn't come racing in to drag me out of the light, I could be dead by now."

The old man had to clear his throat several times before he managed to say, "I'm glad you were here, son."

"Me too." Luke kept his hand on Ingrid's shoulder, propelling her toward the doorway. "Let's go downstairs and call the sheriff."

Seeing the door to Lily's room still closed, Ingrid stepped inside quietly to assure herself that the little girl was safe and sleeping.

Luke took those few moments to return to his room for his shirt and boots.

When Ingrid emerged, she said softly, "I guess she slept right through it."

"Good." Luke took her hand as they descended the stairs, as much for himself as for her. He felt the need to hold on to her, to be assured that she was truly safe.

Once in the kitchen, Luke phoned Eugene Graystoke, while Mick started a fresh pot of coffee.

The three of them sat around the table, talking in low tones.

"Did you recognize the vehicle?" Mick eyed Luke over the rim of his cup.

"It was too dark. All I could see were the taillights."

"I wonder how long the shooter was standing out there in the night, waiting for a light to go on upstairs."

Luke nodded. "I was just wondering the same thing." He turned to Ingrid. "If you had a dog, a big, barking dog, this couldn't have happened. You would have had plenty of warning."

"Tippy was big. And loyal. And fierce." She pressed a fist to her mouth to stop her lips from trembling. "A lot of good it did."

He reached over to close a hand on hers.

By the time they heard the crunch of tires on the gravel driveway an hour later, the three of them had gone over every detail of those few moments, speculating on the shooter, without once mentioning the names of the two men they suspected of having done the deed.

Sheriff Graystoke's face was grim as he greeted them and sat at the table to hear the details.

Mick handed him a steaming cup of coffee, which he barely tasted. "I want to see your room, Miss Larsen."

When Ingrid started to stand, Luke saw the weariness in her eyes and gave a quick shake of his head. "I'll go up. You stay here with Mick." To the sheriff he explained, "Lily is still asleep up there. We'll need to keep things quiet."

Eugene nodded in understanding. "No need for words. I just need to see the crime scene."

Luke led the way up the stairs. Once in Ingrid's bedroom, Luke snapped on the light to allow the sheriff to study the shattered window and the shards of glass littering the floor.

After several minutes staring out the window, Eugene Graystoke turned toward the doorway. "Leave the light on while I head downstairs. I want to see what it looks like from outside."

In the kitchen, the sheriff asked Ingrid to go to her room and stand in the spot where she'd been standing when the gunshot occurred.

Seeing the look in her eyes, Mick got slowly to his feet. "I'm going with you, girl."

While Ingrid and Mick made their way to her room, Luke and Graystoke walked outside to stand in the yard below Ingrid's window.

As she came into view above them, the sheriff's eyes narrowed in concentration. "Look at her. As clear as if she's onstage in a spotlight." He hissed out an oath of frustration. "Nobody in these parts ever feels the need to draw down a shade or close a drape. We don't expect something like this in the middle of nowhere. At least"—he spat a curse—"not on my watch."

Luke's voice was rough with anger. "I know you take it personally, Eugene. So do I."

The sheriff turned to look at him. "What's eating at me is the fact that I don't have the manpower to keep Ingrid and her sister safe, Luke."

"I do." Luke's eyes were hard as flint. "Now I just have to find a way to persuade them to come home with me."

"That would solve the problem, at least in the short term." Eugene started toward the back porch. "Maybe I can help."

* * *

The sheriff sat at the kitchen table, completing his report. While he worked, he accepted a plate of scrambled eggs and bacon from Mick's hand. He watched as the old man worked off his frustration at the stove. But when Mick tried to get Ingrid to eat, she refused, choosing instead to drink coffee and pace the length of the kitchen and back.

Across the room, Luke watched in silence, knowing each of them had to deal with their fears in their own way.

Finally Eugene Graystoke tucked away his papers and drained his fourth cup of coffee.

Ingrid stopped her pacing and took a seat across from him at the table. "Well?"

He steepled his hands. "I'll send my deputy Archer Stone out here at first light to scour the area and see if he can find any shell casings. The rain will probably wash away the tire tracks. If there's even a trace, I'll have Archer make a mold for the state police to trace. I also intend to interview both Lon Wardell and Bull Hammond. But I have to confess, without hard evidence, this isn't something easily resolved. And while I'm in the mood for some honesty, I might as well tell you that this was no random act. You were clearly the intended victim of this shooting. From where I was standing outside, there was no mistaking you in the window."

He watched Ingrid's face grow pale and lowered his voice. "Miss Larsen, it's my duty as a lawman to advise you to seek a safe haven."

Her chin lifted in a gesture of defiance. "Are you saying I should leave my own home?"

"I'm not talking about forever. But I do believe you

should leave here for a while. At least until this shooter is identified."

She got to her feet. "I have a ranch to run. A ranch I could lose if I don't keep a tight rein on things."

"The ranch isn't nearly as important as the life you could lose." Before she could protest, he added, "If you're not worried about yourself, I urge you to think about that little girl asleep upstairs."

"Lily?" Visibly shaken, she sank back down to her chair. "You think someone would harm her?"

"What better way to hurt you than to hurt the ones you love?"

His words brought a stunned silence to the room. Ingrid turned to look at Mick, whose hand had paused in midair. His brow was creased in a frown.

"My family ranch can offer a safe haven, Sheriff." Luke's voice, calm and assured, had Ingrid looking up. "Our house is big enough to accommodate a dozen houseguests without even feeling crowded. And there are enough wranglers around that anyone foolish enough to try to invade our space and cause any trouble to a guest would be outnumbered ten to one."

The sheriff sat back with a look of satisfaction. "There you go, Miss Larsen."

She was already shaking her head. "We're strangers. We couldn't possibly just barge in and—"

"But you're not strangers. You're my friends." Luke's tone was calm and reasonable. "You've already met my uncle Colin and our foreman, Burke. The rest of my family will make you feel so welcome, you'll think you're part of the family in no time."

"Luke isn't exaggerating. The Malloy family is just

about the most accommodating in Montana." Eugene Graystoke got to his feet. "At least think about it, Miss Larsen. For the sake of your little sister."

He reached across the table to shake Ingrid's hand and then Mick's, before heading for the mudroom and motioning for Luke to follow. At the back door he took his hat from a hook on the wall before stepping outside.

Luke offered his hand. "Thanks, Eugene. I think using her fear for Lily's safety will be the deciding factor."

The sheriff gave a grim smile. "That may take care of the immediate danger. But think about this, Luke. This thing could go on for months. And I'm worried that our shooter will try again, whenever he gets an opportunity. Next time, he may not miss."

"You think I haven't already thought of that?" Luke was equally grim. "But for now, I just want them all safe and out of harm's way. After that, I'll have to take it day by day."

The sheriff started down the porch steps. "I intend to ask the state boys for help in this. In the beginning, it sounded more like an insult against the mother's boyfriend, or a feud between neighbors. Now it's become attempted murder. This is getting too complicated, and too dangerous, to stand by and wait for the next shoe to drop."

"I agree. Tonight has changed everything." Luke took in a breath. "Thanks for all your help, Eugene."

He turned and made his way back to the kitchen, where Ingrid and Mick were having a spirited conversation.

"What do I do about the herd up in the hills?" Ingrid was pacing, arms crossed over her chest. "Or what's left of them?"

"They're up there right now without any wranglers.

They can certainly make it a few more days without you, girl." Mick scrubbed the skillet until it gleamed, then continued scrubbing it viciously, taking out his frustration in any way he could.

"And this house?" Ingrid stabbed a finger in the old cowboy's chest. "What if Nadine comes home and finds it empty?"

"So what?" Mick caught her wrist and lowered her hand to her side.

"So, she could decide to move Lon in while we're away. What's to stop her?"

"Let him move in." The old man looked around. "What can he do to this old place to make things worse than they already are?"

Ingrid flinched. "I'm not worried about him trashing it. But he'll be free to go through my private things. The mail. The bills and receipts. The ledgers. I don't want him knowing my business."

"Neither do I, girl. But if it's a choice between staying here and being shot at like fish in a barrel or leaving the house open to prying eyes, I vote for hightailing it out of here and taking Luke up on his generous offer."

Ingrid's eyes flashed fire as she turned away and began more pacing.

Luke poured himself yet another cup of coffee and sat quietly, letting the two of them go at it.

It looked as though it would be a very long night, with no one but Lily getting any sleep at all. But at least, he thought with a clenched jaw, they'd make it through the night alive.

Things could have taken a very different, and very violent turn, if the shooter had been successful.

The thought of someone standing in the dark, taking aim at an unsuspecting woman, had Luke itching for a good knock-down, drag-out fight. It would be so much more satisfying than sitting around and watching Ingrid and Mick verbally sparring. But for now, since the coward had slunk away under cover of darkness, he was forced to make do with this.

And to hope that in the light of morning, Ingrid would relent.

CHAPTER THIRTEEN

Oh boy. Are we really going to stay at your ranch overnight?" Lily was too excited to sit still. She and Mick were in the backseat, where Lily continued to bounce as much as her seat belt would allow.

Ingrid drove her battered truck, with Luke in the passenger seat. Towed behind them was a horse trailer holding Turnip.

Before Lily woke, the three of them had agreed to say nothing to her about the shooting. The little girl was told only that Luke needed to see his family and had invited them along. After morning chores, the horses had been turned out into a fenced meadow.

"Yes, we are, Li'l Bit. Or maybe more than a night, if we can persuade your sister."

Ingrid shot Luke a dark look before returning her attention to the highway. She had agreed to one night. Beyond that, she'd refused to speculate.

Lily missed the look. She was too busy playing tutor to poor, patient Mick.

"Now remember their names, Mick." Lily held up her hand, counting off each name on a finger. "There's the Great One. He's Luke's great-grandfather. He likes to eat and drink fancy-schmancy stuff like he did in Hollywood. Isn't that right, Luke?"

Luke couldn't help chuckling at her dead-on repeating of his own words. "Right you are."

"And then there's Gram Gracie and Grandpop. That's Luke's grandpa, Frankie," she added in an aside. "Then there's Luke's uncle Colin and Burke, the ranch foreman. We already met them when they flew in to take Luke home. But you didn't go home with them, did you, Luke?"

"That's right."

"Next are Matt and Reed, Luke's brothers, and Matt's new bride, Vanessa. Luke says she's really pretty, and down-to-earth for a big-city lawyer. And there's Yancy, the cook and housekeeper."

"You might not want to call him our housekeeper," Luke said with a wink. "He prefers to think of himself as simply a cook."

"Okay." The little girl was beaming. "When will we be there?"

"Not long now. We've been on our land for the last half an hour."

Ingrid's eyes went wide. "This is all your land?"

Luke leaned an elbow out the window, enjoying the view. "Yeah. I didn't realize how much I've missed it."

"But"—she allowed her gaze to sweep the rolling hills, folding one into the other, and all of them dotted with cattle as far as the eye could see—"it goes on for miles."

"That's Montana for you. More cattle than people."

Her voice lowered. "Looks like half the state belongs to you."

"To my family," he corrected with a grin. "Just around this bend you'll see the house."

They came up over a rise, and as they followed the curving gravel road, they caught sight of the sprawling ranch house in the distance and, beyond it, several barns and outbuildings, and not a one of them in need of paint.

The house was an ageless structure, three stories of stone and wood, looking as though it had sprung fully built from the towering hills and mountains looming up behind it. The barns and outbuildings were the same dark wood, gleaming in the sunlight.

For the longest time everyone fell silent. Then, as they drew near, Ingrid couldn't contain herself. "Oh my." She pulled up behind several ranch trucks parked in a row, and all bearing the logo of the Malloy Ranch.

Luke's smile grew. "Looks like everyone's here." He held up his cell phone. "I called ahead."

"It's nice to know we're not just crashing." Ingrid turned off the ignition and sat very still, fighting nerves.

Seeing it, Luke stepped down and circled around to open the driver's-side door and take her hand. "Come on. They don't bite."

Lily and Mick were already out of the truck and stood waiting for Luke and Ingrid to lead the way. Before they could climb the steps, the back door was thrust open and the family spilled out onto the wide porch.

"About time you came home, sonny boy." Frank

slapped Luke on the shoulder hard enough to jar his teeth.

Gracie hurried forward to hug her grandson before turning to the others. "Welcome to our home. We're so happy to see all of you."

"Gram Gracie, this is Ingrid Larsen and her sister, Lily."

Instead of the expected handshake, Gracie surprised Ingrid with a warm embrace, before turning to Lily and gathering her close with a murmured, "Oh. Finally. Some girls to even the score against all these Malloy men."

The smile on the little girl's face put the sunshine to shame.

Grace indicated the immaculately groomed man standing in the doorway, his white hair flowing like an aged lion's mane; a blue silk ascot was tied rakishly at his throat. "This is my father, Nelson."

"I know you," Lily said with excitement.

The old man's eyes lit with pleasure. "A bit young to know about my reputation, don't you think?"

"You're the Great One. Luke's great-grandfather."

"Oh, that." He gave a shrug of his shoulders. "Yes, indeed, I am. And you may call me Great One."

Luke indicated the old man in faded denims and scuffed boots. "This is Mick Hinkley, Ingrid's foreman."

Frank and Grace shook the old cowboy's hand before turning to handle the rest of the introductions.

"You've already met Colin. And this is our oldest grandson, Matt, and his wife, Vanessa."

While the others shook hands, Lily couldn't hold back. "You're as pretty as Luke said."

Vanessa dimpled. "Thank you, Lily." She turned to Luke. "And thank you, brother-in-law. You think I'm pretty? I don't believe you've ever said that before."

Luke shot her a wicked grin. "Just a slip of the tongue. Don't let it go to your head."

Frank turned to the others. "This is my youngest grandson, Reed."

Lily stared up at the tall, handsome cowboy to say loudly, "Youngest? But you're as old as Luke."

"Wrong, Li'l Bit," Luke said above the laughter. "He may be taller, but he's a year younger. That makes him the baby of the family."

Reed knelt solemnly in front of the little girl and held out his hand. "Hi, Lily. I'm sorry you had to put up with my brother, but now that you're here, I'll show you how to avoid being stuck with him."

"Oh, I don't mind." She missed the joke entirely as she looked at Luke adoringly. "Luke said he likes tomboys. Luke's my friend."

Reed got to his feet. "Just so he's not your boyfriend."

She put her hands on her hips. "He's too old for that. Besides, I think he'd rather be Ingrid's boyfriend."

That had everyone laughing and punching Luke's shoulder, while Ingrid's face flamed.

Gracie turned to the man with the bowl haircut standing in the doorway. "This is Yancy Martin."

As the others shook Yancy's hand, Lily dashed forward, then stopped in her tracks, her eyes growing round. "You're not much bigger than me."

Grinning, Yancy held out an arm, as though measuring her against himself. "Oh, I know I'm short, but I think you need a couple of years to catch up to me."

"I like having someone almost my size. Luke said you're the best cook in Montana."

Yancy's smile went up several notches. "He did?"

Luke shrugged. "I must have said it in a moment of weakness."

"Or hunger," Reed said to the others' laughter.

Burke ambled up from one of the barns after turning Turnip into a stall and joined in the handshakes.

"Let's go inside." Gracie led the way through the mudroom and into the large kitchen, with everyone following.

While the others laughed and chatted, Ingrid paused in the doorway and simply stared around the big, sunny room, where an oversized harvest table was set for supper, with colorful, matching plates and napkins. Across the room in an alcove of tall windows stood several overstuffed chairs and a sofa, where the family now gravitated while Yancy set out several plates of fruit and cheese, assorted crackers and small, round slices of bread, and a bowl of cheese dip on the low coffee table. A tray on the kitchen counter held frosty longnecks and several glasses of different beverages.

Luke offered Lily a glass of lemonade before handing a longneck to Mick. The old man shot him a grateful smile.

Gracie crossed the room to loop her arm through Ingrid's. "Feeling a little overwhelmed?"

Ingrid nodded. "Yes. Does it show?"

"Not at all. Come on." The older woman handed her a glass of white wine and walked beside her, drawing her toward the others, who were all enchanted by Lily, who was chattering like a magpie.

"Luke and I play Fish every night before I go to bed, and he hardly ever beats me."

"Fish?" Reed shot his brother a look. "Just don't let him offer to teach you poker, Lily."

"He's trying to. Ingrid said she wants us to stick to Fish."

"Smart woman." Reed turned to include Ingrid in the conversation. "Luke may be a lousy Fish player, but nobody can beat him at poker. So if you play him, don't play for money."

Lily said proudly, "We play for chores. And Luke has to do my share of mucking stalls whenever I win."

Nelson looked up from his favorite overstuffed chair, where he was enjoying a martini. "You play for chores?" He looked from Lily to his great-grandson. "I guess that makes sense."

He turned to his daughter. "Grace Anne, watching and listening to this lovely child has made me realize she would have been perfect in the role of Megan in my movie *Divine*."

Grace studied Lily before nodding. "I believe you're right, Dad. It wouldn't have been a stretch for her to play a girl who talks to animals. And she'd have been so much better than that awful child star you hired."

"A horrid little diva. And her mother was even worse." He gave a mock shudder.

Ingrid went very still as the truth dawned. "Oh my goodness. You're that Nelson LaRou. The famous Hollywood director."

Nelson couldn't have been more pleased. He puffed up his chest. "Right you are, Ingrid. I thought perhaps Luke would have mentioned me."

"He did. But I must have missed the part where he said how famous you are."

"Yes, he did." Lily looked confused. "He said you're his great-grandpa. Aren't you?"

"Indeed I am. But long before Luke was born, I was a Hollywood director, handling all the rich and famous movie stars."

Lily's eyes went wide. "Do you know Justin Bieber?"

It was Nelson's turn to look confused. "I haven't a clue whom that might be. And I pride myself on knowing the name of every famous actor from the thirties to the sixties."

Ingrid sighed. "He sings. And happens to be Lily's current crush."

The little girl shot her sister an indignant look. "He is not. You take that back. You know I don't like boys."

Ingrid gave her a gentle smile. "Sorry. You're right. That's too personal. Justin isn't your current crush."

"I think Luke is," Reed said with a wink.

Instead of a denial, Lily's face colored.

Grace quickly changed the subject to spare the poor child's feelings. "Tell us about your ranch, Ingrid."

Ingrid took a sip of wine to cover her embarrassment at being singled out. "I'm afraid it's small and insignificant next to all this."

"Nonsense," Frank Malloy was quick to add. "Every rancher knows it isn't the size of the ranch that matters; it's the heart and soul the rancher pours into it that counts."

"If that's all it takes," old Mick said with a grin, "then Ingrid's spread is as big as the state of Montana. She pours everything she has into that place."

"Good for you, Ingrid." Frank glanced out the window at a clap of thunder. "It was sunny just a few minutes ago."

Old Mick rubbed his shoulder. "I could've told you

it was going to rain. These old bones know long before those TV weatherpeople do."

Burke nodded. "I know what you mean. I'm getting better at predicting the weather every year."

Lily looked from one to the other. "Can my bones tell me when it's going to rain?"

"I'm afraid you're just going to have to wait until you're as old as us," Mick said with a laugh.

Lily turned to Nelson. "Your bones are even older than theirs. Can you tell when it's going to rain, Great One?"

His laughter rang through the room. "When you get to be my age, every little ache and pain can predict rain, snow, and even a cloud in the sky."

"See." She looked around at the others. "And that's why he's the Great One."

Luke winked at Ingrid before turning to her sister. "You got that right. And don't you forget it, Li'l Bit."

Just then Lily caught sight of a framed photograph hanging across the room. She pointed. "Look, Ingrid. They have the same picture I have hanging in my bedroom. Only mine is smaller."

"You have this one?" Grace started across the room.

Lily trailed behind her. "Uh-huh." She pointed to the stallion watching over his herd of mustang mares. "I've seen him. I've seen all of them. They're my herd."

Grace's brows shot up. "Yours?"

"Well, not mine exactly. But I see them sometimes up in the hills. I even took some pictures of them, didn't I, Ingrid?"

Her big sister nodded. "Quite a few, as a matter of fact. I don't know which she loves more: her herd or her camera."

"You love taking pictures?" Grace looked excitedly at the little girl.

"Uh-huh. Ingrid gave me our daddy's camera. I take it with me everywhere."

"Remind me to show you some more pictures I've taken of . . . your herd as well as several other herds."

"This is yours?" Lily moved closer, and as she read the name in the lower right hand corner, her eyes went wide. "This says Grace Anne LaRou Malloy." She turned to Grace. "I've got your picture hanging in my bedroom. Are you famous?"

"Maybe. To some who love photographs of mustangs."

Frank ambled over to drop an arm around his wife's shoulders. "My Gracie Girl is being modest. She's spent a lifetime photographing mustangs here in Montana and has earned quite a fine reputation around the world for her work."

"Oh boy." Lily's eyes were shining with excitement.

Yancy announced that supper was ready. As they gravitated toward the table, Lily saw Nelson struggling to ease himself out of his overstuffed chair.

She raced over and caught his hand. "Come on, Great One."

As the rest of the family stared in surprise, Nelson kept the little girl's hand in his as he allowed himself to be led to the table. When he was seated, he patted the chair beside his. "You can sit here, Lily."

"Thank you." As she settled in, looks were exchanged.

The stern Hollywood director they all knew and loved had made no secret of his disdain for the children he'd been forced to work with through the years. He'd once remarked that he'd rather work with the devil himself than deal with a single heavenly cherub who always proved to be sugar and spice only on the outside, with vinegar and acid in his or her tiny, shriveled little heart.

Apparently the little tomboy with the wild tangle of hair and the wide, trusting eyes had just become the exception to Nelson's self-proclaimed rule. The family wasn't quite certain how this had happened.

Was it her admiration for his daughter, Grace Anne, that endeared her to him? Or was it her sweet, sunny nature and her concern for an old man's welfare?

Whatever the reason, he seemed genuinely charmed by her.

CHAPTER FOURTEEN

I knew your daddy." Frank held a big bowl of mashed potatoes so Ingrid could help herself.

She paused with the spoon hovering over her plate. "You did?"

Frank nodded. "A good man. And from what I heard from the wranglers who worked for him, a fair one."

Ingrid's tension eased and she let out a long, slow breath before passing the bowl Luke's way.

He winked. "I figured you probably knew Lars Larsen, Grandpop. I guess you've met just about every rancher in these parts."

"That I have." Frank took a bite of beef burgundy and paused a moment to savor the taste before turning to Yancy. "This may be your best recipe yet."

"I was just about to say the same." At the other end of the table, Nelson cut off a second piece before giving a nod to the cook. "Even Pierre, head chef at the Bistro, couldn't have done it better."

Lily looked up at the old man beside her with eyes wide. "Is this one of those fancy-schmancy foods you love, Great One?"

Luke nearly choked on his beef.

Nelson glared down at the little girl. "Where did you hear that?"

"Luke said you only drink fancy-schmancy drinks and eat fancy-schmancy food. Isn't that right, Luke?"

Nelson speared a glance at his grandson. "I figured an innocent like this couldn't have come up with such a phrase on her own."

"You have to admit it defines you, Great One."

Silence descended over the room.

Nelson slapped a hand on the table. "That it does, Luke. That it does."

He looked at Lily. "Fancy-schmancy, am I?" Then, without waiting for her response, he threw back his head and roared with laughter, and the others joined in.

With everyone relaxed, the conversation around the table turned, as always, to the weather, the herds, and the expectations of market prices for roundup at the end of summer.

During a lull in the conversation, Grace turned to Ingrid. "You haven't said anything about your mother, dear. Did she pass away, too?"

"She's...alive."

"You left her alone at the ranch?"

Ingrid turned to Luke, feeling her face flame.

"She isn't at the ranch." Without thinking, Luke placed a protective hand over Ingrid's. "She's spending some time in Wayside."

Grace shook her head. "I'm not familiar with Wayside. Is it far from Glacier Ridge?"

"About an hour or so. It's much smaller than Glacier Ridge, just a few shops and such. But it's closer to Ingrid's ranch than our town."

"I see. Well, as long as she's safe there. But if she'd care to join you and Lily here, please let her know she's welcome, Ingrid."

"Thank you. I will, Mrs.—"

"Gracie." Grace reached over and, like Luke, squeezed her hand. "We don't stand on formality here. Just call me Gracie, or if you'd rather, call me what the boys call me. Gram Gracie."

"Oh boy." Lily couldn't contain her excitement. "I never had a grandma." She turned to Frank. "Or a grandpa. But I've got Mick, and Ingrid says he's like a grandpa, aren't you, Mick?"

The old cowboy chuckled. "As long as I'm everything else around the ranch, I may as well be your grandpa, too, girl."

Grace smiled at the little girl. "And I feel lucky to have a little girl call me Grandma, since all I've ever had around here is boys."

"Oh boy. Gram Gracie." Lily was beaming as she finished her meal.

The family left the kitchen to take dessert and coffee in the great room. They were treated to Yancy's chocolate layer cake and chocolate-marshmallow ice cream as they sat around a roaring fire that managed to drown out the sound of a summer storm that had begun raging outside.

Afterward, as Nelson enjoyed a glass of bourbon,

and the others sipped coffee or longnecks, Luke found a deck of cards and challenged Lily to a game of Fish, with the loser having to tend to Turnip's stall in the morning. It was all Lily needed to forget the storm and her weariness, and she threw herself into the game with renewed energy.

Reed took a seat beside her, cheering her on each time she beat his brother, and commiserating with her each time she lost, until Luke insisted Reed join the game. Then it became a fever-pitched contest that had the winner boasting, and the losers loudly grumbling and calling for a rematch.

Late into the night, when Lily could barely keep her eyes open, Luke took pity on her and suggested they continue the game another night.

"But I need to beat you two more times, or I have to clean Turnip's stall in the morning."

Like shook his head. "I'll clean it. Just this one time. And then we'll play again to see who wins the match. But right now, you need to get to bed."

Grace looked up. "Would you like me to show you to your rooms?"

Luke was already on his feet. "I'll take them up, Gram."

"All right." Grace turned to Yancy. "Will you show Mick his room?"

Yancy nodded. "You've got the room beside mine off the kitchen. Best spot in the house, if you like late-night snacks."

Mick said his good nights and followed Yancy from the great room.

Grace walked over to hug the little girl and her sister.

"Good night. If you need anything at all, be sure to let Luke know."

Ingrid closed her eyes for a moment, inhaling the lavender scent of the older woman as they embraced. "Thank you. I'm sure we'll be fine."

"I know you will."

Grace indicated Lily, who was almost asleep on her feet. "I think Lily might enjoy a horseback ride up to her room, Luke."

"Good idea." He knelt down and caught Lily's hands. "Climb on my back, Li'l Bit."

Lily giggled and called good night to the others before wrapping her arms around Luke's neck as he started up the stairs.

Ingrid trailed behind them, and she couldn't help laughing until she felt her heart suddenly hitch at the sight of Lily snuggling against Luke's broad back.

Once upstairs, Luke galloped down a hallway before stopping at a closed door. He opened it and stepped inside, turning on a light before pausing beside a big bed. "Here's your stall, Li'l Bit."

He knelt down, allowing her to climb down from his back.

She looked around with eyes gone wide, studying the desk and chair, a long, low dresser on which rested a flat-screen TV, and floor-to-ceiling windows overlooking the hills in the distance. "You mean this is just for me?"

"It's all yours." He crossed the room and opened a door, revealing a gleaming bathroom with both tub and shower and a wide expanse of marble counters.

"Ingrid's room is next door, and it's exactly the same."

"So," Ingrid said softly, "if you feel a little lost or uncomfortable, you can come to my room and climb into bed with me."

Lily rubbed her eyes. "I think I'm too tired."

"Okay." Ingrid indicated the bathroom. "Why don't you wash up and settle into bed, and I'll come back in a few minutes to hear your prayers."

"Okay."

Ingrid followed Luke out of Lily's room and paused as he opened the door to the next room.

As she stepped inside, he followed and turned on the light.

She looked around with a shake of her head. "This is...all too much."

He winked. "Yeah. I know it's pretty humble, but hey, it's home."

She couldn't help laughing with him. "It's so beautiful. So big and cozy and..." She shrugged. "I'm rambling. This is all wonderful. Like your family."

"Yeah. They're great. And they like you and Lily."

"I like them, too." She looked up at him. "Thank you."

"You're welcome. You heard Gram Gracie. If you need anything, just let me know."

As he turned away, she lay a hand on his back. He froze, before turning slowly toward her.

"I know I've been...difficult, Luke."

"It doesn't—"

She touched a hand to his mouth to still his words. "You knew I didn't want to leave, even though we weren't safe at the ranch anymore. And you pushed as hard as I resisted."

Unable to stand the heat of her hand on his mouth, he caught it between both of his. "I'm sorry about that."

"Don't be. This isn't easy for me to say, but I need to thank you for insisting. Now that we're here, I feel such relief at being somewhere safe. Not just for my sake, but even more for Lily's. It's plain to see that in a matter of hours she's fallen in love with your entire family."

"And they love her, too. How could they help it?" He looked down at their joined hands, before meeting her steady gaze. "Ingrid..." Something flickered in his eyes. Even the tone of his voice changed slightly. Gentler. More intimate.

She started to pull away, but he cupped the back of her head before lowering his face to hers.

The kiss was soft. Tentative. Testing. Tasting.

When she didn't resist, he leaned into her, taking her fully into the heat that flared up between them. He gathered her close, sinking into the pleasure as she made a soft sound in her throat. Surprise? Delight?

There was no time to wonder as a wave of desire, hot and swift, nearly swamped him. One minute he was simply acting on a whim. The next he felt the pull of raw, sexual need taking over his mind, his will, his senses.

Without a thought to what he was doing, he drove her back against the wall, touching her at will. His hands roamed her back, then skimmed her sides until they encountered the swell of her breasts. His thumbs moved over them, feeling her body's reaction, and all the while he spun out the kiss until they were both struggling for breath.

"Luke."

The sound of his name torn from her lips had him lifting his head. His eyes narrowed on her, and he became aware of just how far he'd taken her. Had taken them both.

He lifted his hands from her, forcing them to his sides. "Sorry. I didn't mean...I was rough."

"I should..." She swallowed and tried again. "I need to hear Lily's prayers."

"Yeah." But he didn't step away.

Instead, he pressed both hands against the wall on either side of her and leaned in to brush his mouth ever so softly over hers. Hot desire sparked between them before she put a hand to his chest.

He shot her a knowing smile. There was no denying that she was as aroused as he. "If you need anything through the night, I'm one room away."

"How...convenient." Her words were a little too breathless. She couldn't quite meet his eyes. "Good night, Luke."

"'Night, Ingrid."

He watched as she stepped around him and into the hall before returning to Lily's room. As he made his way along the hallway to his own room, he was still vibrating with need. A need that was slowly driving him mad.

He stepped into his room and closed the door, leaning against it as he drank in the sight of the darkened hills outside his window. He'd always loved the sight of those hills. Right now, he couldn't focus on them. All he could think about was Ingrid and that kiss.

He fully understood her intention to prove herself stronger than Nadine. Her reaction to his kisses was natural enough, under the circumstances. But for every time she retreated, he wanted her more.

He'd hoped that having her here at his family ranch,

surrounded by so many people, would prove a distraction for him. Now he realized that it had only made things worse.

Seeing her being charmed by the people he loved made him more aware than ever just how special a woman she was.

He undressed, giving vent to his frustration by kicking his boots against the wall. Naked, he climbed under the covers and lay with his hands beneath his head, deep in thought.

Until Ingrid Larsen, he'd never met a woman who cost him sleep. Until Ingrid, he'd never wasted a minute of his time worrying about the next step in his life. He'd been wild and carefree and loving every minute of his freedom to ride his Harley, wrangle his herds, and live the life of a cowboy.

Now the only thing that mattered was Ingrid. Her safety. Her ranch.

Who was he kidding?

He lusted after her like a teenager with raging testosterone. But he did care about her ranch, her safety, her sister, and old Mick.

More than anything, though, he just wanted her. Wanted to do all the things he'd been thinking since that first time he'd seen her, with that cap of fine blond hair and those big, haunted eyes that touched something deep inside his soul.

He turned and punched his pillow before giving voice to a string of curses. Yeah. He wanted her right now, here in his bed.

And the wanting was like a drug, driving him half mad.

CHAPTER FIFTEEN

The following morning, Luke stepped out of his room and paused at Ingrid's closed door. Hearing no sounds from within, he moved on and found himself hoping she'd slept comfortably, knowing she was safe here.

When he entered the kitchen, he saw Ingrid sitting in the pretty alcove with Frank and Grace, talking quietly while enjoying coffee.

Yancy was removing freshly baked rolls from the oven. At the stove, old Mick was flipping flapjacks onto a platter. The two men were working side by side as though they'd done this all their lives.

"Good morning." Luke greeted the two men before snagging a mug of coffee and ambling over to where his grandparents were sitting with Ingrid.

"'Morning, Luke." Frank was grinning from ear to ear. "We've just been comparing stories about our families. Ingrid's grandfather came here just about the time I did.

Our paths crossed hundreds of times. But through the years, with family obligations and all, we lost touch. I only saw her father, Lars, a dozen times or so, and then usually when we were both in town for supplies." He looked over at Ingrid. "But I remember the pride in his voice whenever he spoke about his daughter. He thought the sun rose and set in you."

Her eyes were shiny at his words. "That means the world to me, Frankie."

Her easy use of Grace's term of endearment for her husband caught Luke by surprise. He glanced at his grandmother, who was beaming.

She touched a hand to Ingrid's shoulder. "It's been fun catching up on old times."

The back door slammed, and Lily trooped in with Burke, Colin, and Reed. The four shed their boots and paused to wash up at the big sink before stepping into the kitchen.

Lily's wild gypsy hair had been pulled back in a ponytail. Her shirt and jeans were faded and patched, but her face was wreathed in smiles.

"Where've you been, Li'l Bit?"

"Mucking Turnip's stall."

"But I said I'd do it."

"I told Reed I wanted to pay up. And he said I'm a..." She turned to the tall cowboy who was smiling down at her. "What did you call me?"

"An independent woman."

"That's right." Lily looked at her sister. "Ingrid says a woman who can pay her own way gets through life without owing anybody."

"Well said." Vanessa, who had just descended the

stairs beside her husband, Matt, gave the little girl a high five. "I can see that you and Ingrid will have no trouble living in today's world." She indicated the tray of drinks. "Would you care for some orange juice, Lily?"

"Thank you." Lily sipped, then looked over at Mick. "This is good. What did you put in it?"

Mick pointed at Yancy. "He squeezed the OJ. Ask him."

Yancy shrugged. "There's nothing in it. Just orange juice."

"But there's this good stuff in it." She ran her tongue over her upper lip, leaving an orange mustache.

"Oh." The cook grinned. "That's orange pulp. It falls in when I squeeze the oranges."

"You squeeze real oranges?" The little girl was clearly intrigued. "Why?"

"So you can enjoy fresh-squeezed orange juice." Yancy paused a beat. "You like it?"

"Yes. Will you show me how to squeeze oranges, Yancy?"

He couldn't hide his delight. "Later today we'll have our first lesson."

"Yay." She pumped a fist in the air before polishing off the glass of juice.

Vanessa, who had watched and listened in silence, broke into laughter before explaining. "The first time I tasted Yancy's orange juice, I sounded just like you, Lily. The only juice I'd ever had came from a plastic jug from my grocery store. I couldn't believe there were people who actually squeezed their own juice."

"And now she does the same for me," Matt said with a wink.

Luke and Reed put their hands to their throats in a gesture of gagging.

"Hey," Matt added. "Don't knock it until you've tried it."

"Having your juice served by a gorgeous woman?" Reed asked.

"Marriage." Matt chuckled at the looks that passed between his two brothers.

"But thank you both for referring to me as gorgeous." Vanessa dimpled.

"No question, Nessa. You haven't changed." Reed pointed. "It's my brother I'm worried about. Who is this mellow, old, married man? And what have you done with my wild brother, Matt?"

Matt simply chuckled. "These days, I leave all the wild stuff for Luke."

"Which is just the way I like it," Luke muttered.

"Breakfast is ready," Yancy announced.

The family gathered around the table and began passing platters of scrambled eggs, thick slices of ham, biscuits warm from the oven, and stacks of pancakes with maple syrup.

"Going to be a good day for chores," Colin announced. "The rain blew over, and the sun's coming out."

"What did you have in mind?" Burke cupped his coffee mug in his hands before drinking.

"Heading up to the hills to check on the herds." Colin helped himself to several pancakes and smothered them in syrup. After his first taste, he looked over at Mick. "Hey. These are good."

"Thanks." The old cowboy grinned. "I told Yancy I'm not in his league, but the few things I can make never get complaints from my girls."

"Or from me." Colin dug in while the others began outlining plans for the day.

After breakfast, Burke and the men headed toward the barn, ready to pack up the trucks before heading to the highlands.

Luke paused beside Ingrid. "Would you and Lily want to ride with us?"

At her hesitation, Grace remarked casually, "I was hoping I might have the girls to myself." She glanced at Nessa, Ingrid, and Lily. "Most days I'm outnumbered around here, and I thought it might be fun to take a day off from ranch chores and just have a girls' day."

Luke grinned before dropping an arm around his grandmother's waist and pressing a kiss to her cheek. "I'd say a girls' day is long overdue, Gram Gracie. Enjoy."

He turned to Yancy and Mick. "Care to ride along? Maybe you could bring enough supplies to surprise the wranglers with a barbecue."

The two men grew animated as they decided what to pack for the hills. An hour later the men were heading out in a caravan of trucks.

Ingrid watched Luke go, feeling a moment's indecision. She wasn't sure she'd be comfortable spending a day with women she didn't know. But since she was accepting the hospitality of this family, she thought it would have been rude to refuse. She would simply get through this as best she could.

Nessa seemed delighted at Grace's words. "Does this mean we might get a chance to visit your studio?"

"Oh." Grace gave an embarrassed laugh. "I can't imagine anything more boring than a visit to my studio. It's so crowded with stuff, I can barely move in there half the time."

"Now you're being modest." Nessa turned to Ingrid and Lily. "I'll bet the two of you are as excited as I am about seeing where Gram Gracie works."

"I . . ." Ingrid tried not to show her ignorance. "I'd love to see it."

"Well then." Grace started toward the mudroom. "We'll need boots and jackets. We've a bit of a walk to the barn."

Intrigued, Ingrid trailed along, while Lily caught Gracie's hand and skipped beside her.

Once outside, they passed the first barn and walked toward the second, smaller barn. As Grace shoved open the doors and switched on the overhead lights, Ingrid simply stared in silence.

The back wall of the building had been replaced with floor-to-ceiling windows, where sunlight streamed in, allowing a spectacular view of the hills and meadows outside. The rest of the walls were lined with tall shelves holding an assortment of photographs of every size and shape. Some were wrapped for shipping. Some were framed. Most were simply loose, stacked in piles on the floor and on tables.

Ingrid took her time circling the cavernous room, studying the photos, before she turned to Grace with a look of awe. "Oh my goodness. I can't believe I'm really in your studio and able to actually see your work up close. I've seen your photographs of mustangs since I was Lily's age. They're my absolute favorites. But I never dreamed I'd ever get to meet the famous photographer."

Grace beamed with pleasure. "Thank you. I'm so glad

you enjoy my photos. The mustangs that live in our hills are the great loves of my life. After," she added with a smile, "my sweet Frankie, of course."

Nessa dropped an arm around Ingrid's shoulders and kept her voice low. "I felt the same way the first time I was in her presence. And now, even though I'm still in awe of her talent, I think of her more than ever as Luke's grandmother."

"Luke was so casual about her."

"It's such a guy thing." Nessa laughed. "And such a Malloy thing. They figure everybody in the world already knows about their famous grandmother and great-grand-father, so they don't need to say a word."

"I guess I should have known that the Great One's daughter would find a way to express herself as beauti-fully as he did."

Overhearing, Grace nodded. "My father wasn't happy when I switched my college major from film studies to photography. But even then he believed that in time I'd use my love of photography to enhance a career in film. It never occurred to the great Nelson LaRou that a child of his could be anything other than a clone of the famous father."

Ingrid was clearly intrigued. "Luke told us that your father didn't approve of you living on a ranch in Mon-tana."

"Oh, he was horrified. The thought of his beautiful, tal-ented daughter throwing her life away on some cowboy in the middle of nowhere had him fit to be tied. Then, when his grandsons were born, he thought he might grace us with a visit. But he still wasn't sold on the idea of actually living on a ranch, until the day he had to make the critical decision to leave all that he loved in Hollywood and Connecticut to come and live with us permanently."

Ingrid's eyes went wide. "How long did it take for him to fall in love with this lifestyle?"

"Ha." Gracie laughed aloud. "I guess someday he'll let us know. In the meantime, he makes do, thanks to Yancy's excellent martinis and"—she turned to Lily with a grin—"fancy-schmancy meals."

The little girl joined in the laughter.

Ingrid crossed the room to a row of photographs of mustangs. "Do you mind if I look at these?"

"That's why we're here," Grace said simply. "Look all you'd like."

"Oh." Ingrid moved slowly along the rows of shelves, sighing over the spectacular photos. "I swear I can see them moving and hear the thundering of their hooves. You and your camera make them so alive. So real."

"Thank you." Grace stepped up beside her. "That's the nicest compliment you can give me."

Lily pointed to a smoke-gray mare, forelegs in the air, ears flattened. "I think I've seen her in our hills, Gram Gracie."

Grace nodded. "I'm sure you have. They come down from the hills in search of grass when the highlands are covered with snow. But often, in the summer, they graze for miles on the lush grass around the lower meadows."

"Ingrid and I always stop to watch whenever a herd of mustangs crosses our path." Lily's eyes took on a dreamy look. "I always think it would be fun to climb on the back of one of them and just race across a meadow like the wind."

"It's fun to think about." Ingrid tousled her sister's hair. "But it wouldn't be any fun to be tossed off one of those skittish animals. If they decided to trample you, you wouldn't have a chance to defend yourself."

Grace nodded. "It's taken me years to earn their trust. And some of them simply refuse to allow me to get close. But those that do are worth the effort." She pointed to a photo of a pure white stallion standing still as a statue on a distant hill, with snow swirling about him. "I snapped this picture more than two years ago, and I've never spotted him since. How I yearn to get close enough to study him and his herd, and to photograph him in all his many moods. I think he would prove a spectacular model."

Ingrid was studying the photo with interest. "I can't be certain, but I think..."

She let the words die, but not before Grace looked over at her. "You think what?"

Ingrid shrugged. "Just thinking out loud. I may have seen him not far from my ranch."

Grace's smile was radiant. "I know where my next photographic safari will take me."

An hour later they stepped out of Gracie's studio.

Grace adjusted her sunglasses. "Since the men will be gone the better part of the day, I think we'd be smart to head to town. We can shop a bit if you'd like and then have some lunch." She drew an arm around Lily. "And afterward, maybe we'll stop at I's Cream."

"Oh boy." Lily's eyes went wide. "Does that mean ice cream?"

"It does. Ivy has every flavor known to mankind. And a few nobody has ever heard of."

They climbed into one of the ranch trucks. With Grace at the wheel, they took off in a cloud of dust and laughed and chatted all the way to Glacier Ridge.

CHAPTER SIXTEEN

As the ranch truck rolled along the main street, Grace kept up a running commentary on the shops and their owners.

"That's D & B's Diner. That stands for Dot and Barb Parker. Twin sisters, though Dot claims to be older by four minutes, which she says makes her the boss."

Ingrid and Lily stared with interest at the pretty little white building, sporting black shutters and white polka dots.

"Oh," Ingrid said as a fact dawned. "The dots are for Dot?"

"Exactly." Grace and Vanessa shared a laugh. "Folks around here can tell the sisters apart because Dot's favorite clothes have polka dots. That's all she wears. But nobody complains about her choice of wardrobe, as silly as it sometimes looks, because she and her sister serve cowboy-sized burgers big enough that they boast nobody can eat more than one and the hottest chili in town."

Vanessa pointed to a pair of buildings across the street. "Matt told me this was originally a barbershop, and then the owner's wife added a women's beauty shop when she couldn't find any in town. Then they got the idea to add a spa."

"A spa?" Ingrid's brows shot up. "Does anybody from around here actually go there?"

Vanessa shrugged. "Not much call for a spa around here, but folks are intrigued by the idea. I've heard business is picking up since they added therapeutic massages to their menu. A lot of ranchers come in with aching backs and shoulder muscles and such, from all the tough ranch chores, and Dr. Anita at the medical clinic has begun writing prescriptions for massages, so it's considered medical instead of just vanity."

"Sounds reasonable to me." Ingrid pointed to the clinic. "You have a doctor here in town?"

"We do." Gracie nodded toward the medical clinic. "Actually two doctors. Old Dr. Cross has been thinking of cutting back on his practice, so he invited his niece Anita from Boston to come and share the workload. I understand she worked in the ER of one of Boston's biggest hospitals, and she was considered one of their best."

Vanessa added softly, "Dr. Anita happens to be not only a very good doctor, but also very pretty. A fact that hasn't escaped Colin's notice."

Grace swiveled her head to study her grandson's wife. "Has he said so?"

"Not a word. But I've seen the way he lights up whenever he sees her."

Grace put a hand to her heart. "Oh, now wouldn't that be grand? With all Colin's responsibilities since his brother Patrick died, I'd just about given up hope that he would ever find someone to settle down with."

"Oh, I don't think they're anywhere near that point, Gram Gracie. I doubt they've even said more than a dozen words to one another. But"—Nessa shook her head—"there's just a look that comes into Colin's eyes when he's around her that I've never seen when he's with anybody else. I may be reading too much into it, but I just have a hunch about it."

Grace smiled and patted her hand. "That's enough to give me hope, Nessa. And for that, I thank you."

They drove slowly until Grace pulled up to the curb outside a pretty little shop sporting a red-and-white-striped awning. The sign announced ANYTHING GOES.

"If you girls don't mind waiting," Grace called, "I need a new shirt." She touched a hand to the shirt she was wearing with her ankle-skimming denim skirt as she stepped from the truck. "Something along these lines, practical but with a feminine touch to it. Want to browse while I shop?"

They all climbed out and entered the shop, setting off a bell. A pretty young woman walked out of a back room, her face wreathed in smiles.

"Hello, Miss Grace. How nice to see you."

"Hello, Trudy. You know Matt's wife, Vanessa."

"I do. Hello again, Nessa."

The two shook hands.

"Trudy Evans, these are friends visiting the ranch. Ingrid and Lily Larsen."

"Hello. Welcome to my shop. Is there anything special I can show you?"

They shook their heads. Grace said with a laugh,

"We're going to browse, Trudy. Which means we intend to see everything before we're finished here."

"Well then, please make yourselves at home and let me know if I can help."

Grace made her way to a line of hangers displaying women's shirts. Within minutes she'd chosen a pale blue long-sleeved shirt with a delicate rose embroidered on the pocket.

While Vanessa stood in front of a mirror trying on wide-brimmed hats, Ingrid stopped at a display of baggy sweatshirts, and Lily crossed the room to stare at the array of girls' denim pants and jackets and an assortment of fancy boots.

Grace walked up behind the little girl. "See anything you like?"

Lily looked away. "No. I was just looking."

Grace held up a pair of jeans. "These look to be about your size. Why don't you try them on?"

"Oh, I don't think..."

The older woman was already rummaging through a stack of T-shirts. "Oh, look. You really have to try this on, too." It was pink, with vivid purple letters that read IN-DEPENDENT WOMAN. "Reed will be impressed, since he's the one who called you that."

The two of them laughed before Grace caught Lily's arm and led her toward the rear of the shop where a curtain hid a dressing room.

Minutes later Lily emerged in the jeans and T-shirt.

"Oh, they fit you perfectly," Grace called.

Ingrid walked over to study her little sister. "I have to admit they look a whole lot better than those old things you were wearing." She dug into her pocket to count her money.

Grace touched a hand to her arm. "You're not allowed to pay for a thing, Ingrid. This is my treat. In fact," she added, lowering her voice, "this entire day is really Frankie's treat. He insisted. He even gave me his credit card, with firm orders to spend his money."

Nessa ambled over, modeling a wide-brimmed hat in charcoal felt that perfectly matched the fitted charcoal denim jacket she was wearing. She managed to look both city-chic and country-casual at the same time. "What do you think?"

The others nodded their approval.

"It's too pretty to pass up," Grace called, while sifting through denim jackets in girls' sizes. She held one up. "Why don't you see if this fits, Lily?"

With a look of pure happiness, the little girl took it into the fitting room.

"Look, Ingrid." Nessa held up a pretty tee in deep teal. "This would look so great with your fair skin and hair. Want to give it a try?"

"No, thank you." Ingrid was actually backing away.

"Why not?" Nessa gave her an encouraging smile. "At least try it on."

"I'm more comfortable in... slouchy things."

"I've noticed." Nessa's smile grew and she thrust it into Ingrid's hand. "It's just a T-shirt."

Ingrid reluctantly walked to the fitting room just as Lily walked out, ready to model her entire outfit.

"Oh, Lily." Ingrid stopped in her tracks. "That's just perfect. You're going to be the prettiest girl in town."

Lily's eyes rounded. "You mean I can keep them?"

Ingrid couldn't hold back her smile. "Those clothes were made for you, honey. And since Gram Gracie insisted…"

"Oh boy." Lily danced around the shop, modeling her outfit for Grace and Vanessa.

Minutes later Ingrid pulled open the curtain to show off the tee. She actually crossed her arms over her chest and stared pointedly at the floor.

Nessa exchanged a look with Grace. "Who knew there was such a fantastic body beneath that baggy shirt?" She turned to Ingrid. "You really have to have that."

Ingrid stepped past the curtain, looking completely flustered. "Don't you think it's too"—she huffed out a breath—"too tight and revealing?"

"The only thing it reveals is the fact that you're a lovely young woman." Grace touched a hand to her arm. "Please let me buy it for you. The color is fantastic on you."

Ingrid caught sight of her reflection in a mirror across the room and felt her heart do a little dance. "It is awfully pretty, but..."

"And you deserve to feel pretty in it." Grace turned to the shop's owner. "Trudy, I think we've found what we came for."

"Will I wrap them, or would you ladies care to wear them and I'll wrap the clothes you were wearing when you came in?"

Lily caught her sister's hand. "Can I wear mine, Ingrid?"

"Absolutely. But I'll get my old..."

Before she could finish, Grace gave a firm shake of her head. "You're wearing that." She turned to Trudy. "You can wrap my new shirt and the clothes left in the fitting room."

"And these," Nessa added.

While Ingrid was busy admiring her little sister, Vanessa handed Trudy several T-shirts in deep shades of red, and yellow, and lime green.

At Grace's arched brow, she said softly, "They're the same size as the one Ingrid tried on, so I know they'll fit her. And the colors are fantastic."

Grace chuckled. "I have a feeling Luke will approve."

"All part of my plan," Nessa replied with a wink.

The shop owner rang up the sale, handed Grace her credit card, and then crossed the room to fetch the clothes they'd shed in the fitting room.

Minutes later they tossed the bag in the truck and began walking along the sidewalk, taking in the sunshine, waving at friends and neighbors who were out and about and pausing before each shop to peer in the windows.

At last they found themselves in front of Clay's Saloon.

Grace turned to the others. "This is the famous Pig Sty. We can eat here, or we can walk back to D & B's. Anybody have a favorite?"

Nessa was grinning. "The first time Matt took me here, I heard the name Pig Sty and was ready to put up with awful food and disgusting surroundings. But I have to tell you, it's a really fun, clean place. And Clay's pork meals are as good as Yancy serves." She leaned in to whisper, "Just never tell Yancy I said that."

The others laughed before Grace pushed open the door. "I think you've sold Ingrid and Lily."

The two sisters nodded as they followed her inside.

It was a typical lunch-hour crowd. Cowboys, in town for supplies, crowded the bar or sat in groups of three and four at the scarred wooden tables. Workers from the nearby small businesses made up the rest of the crowd.

The familiar voice of Willie, crooning about being on the road again, filtered through the chorus of raucous conversation and laughter.

A white-haired man in jeans and suspenders, his rolled sleeves revealing muscled biceps, stood at the grill, methodically turning pork chops while carrying on a running conversation with several grizzled cowboys seated on bar stools. From the jokes flying back and forth, it was clear that they were longtime customers.

"Hello, Clay."

At the sound of Grace's voice, his hand paused in midair and he made a courtly bow.

"Ms. Grace. Good to see you in town. How are you?"

"I'm just fine, Clay. I believe you know Matt's wife, Vanessa."

"Yes'm." He nodded in her direction.

"And these are guests of mine. Ingrid and Lily."

He gave them each a smile.

"What's on the menu today, Clay?"

Clay continued flipping chops on the grill as he went through the items available. "I have grilled pork chops. Stuffed baked chops. Pulled pork sandwiches on homemade sourdough bread. Pork chili. And pure pork hot dogs, also on homemade sourdough rolls. All served with a side of deep-fried onion rings or my special pork chili fries."

Grace turned to wink at the others. "They all sound wonderful. What's your pleasure?"

Vanessa opted for the pulled pork sandwich. Ingrid decided on the chili. Lily pointed to the foot-long hot dog.

And Grace ordered the stuffed baked chops, with a side of both onion rings and chili fries to be sampled by all of them.

"Careful, Ms. Grace," one grizzled old cowboy shouted. "Clay won't reveal what's in his stuffed pork chops. He calls it his mystery stuffing. We call it stuffing a la salmonella."

Above the laughter Clay asked calmly, "And to drink, ladies?"

"I believe I'm ready for a longneck." Nessa turned to Ingrid. "Join me?"

When Ingrid nodded, Grace turned to Lily. "Clay has root beer and lemonade. Is that right, Clay?"

"Right you are, Ms. Grace."

"Root beer," Lily called.

"And I'll just have ice water, Clay."

He nodded. "Find a seat, ladies, and I'll get that right to you."

Grace led the way to the rear of the room, away from the loud chatter of voices and Willie's crooning. She chose a booth in the corner, and the four of them settled in.

Minutes later Clay Olmsted was there with their drinks, followed shortly after with plates, bowls, and platters heaped with their orders.

They took their time, savoring the amazing flavors and remarking over the onion rings and chili fries.

Ingrid nudged Vanessa. "You were right. This isn't at all what I expected from the name Pig Sty. And even though you said it was clean and the food was good, you didn't do it justice."

"You realize it isn't really called the Pig Sty," Grace

explained. "It's called Clay's Saloon, but folks around here started calling it the Pig Sty, because Clay owned a pig farm before starting this business. He sold it and then bought a piece of land just outside of town, where he and his wife still raise hogs, but not nearly as many as he once did."

"And that's why all his recipes call for pork. He has an endless supply," Vanessa added.

Ingrid sat back, finishing her longneck with a wide smile. "I don't think I'll be able to eat again for a week."

"Me too." Lily took the last bite of her hot dog. Then, for good measure, bit into another chili fry. And another.

Ingrid shared a look with Vanessa and Grace, and the three of them broke into gales of laughter.

Lily looked around. "What's so funny?"

"You, honey." Ingrid reached across the table and squeezed her little sister's hand. "Should we get you another plate of chili fries?"

Lily gave it a moment's thought before shaking her head. "Now I'm full. That was so good." She turned to Grace. "Thank you for lunch. I haven't had root beer in forever."

"To a seven-year old, forever means at least a month or so." Ingrid was still laughing.

"Yeah." Lily nodded. "And I've never had a hot dog that big before." She stretched out her hands to show just how long it had been.

"That's because Clay's wife makes them at their little farm. Clay wanted them big enough to fit the long, sourdough rolls he bakes daily."

"So he's really a cook rather than a farmer," Ingrid remarked.

"And his wife is a better farmer than a cook." Grace laughed. "That's why they make such a great team."

Ingrid turned to Vanessa. "Did you and Matt grow up around here?"

Vanessa shook her head. "I grew up in Chicago. I work for a group of wildlife animal activists based in Washington, DC. I came to Montana to meet with Gram Gracie, but she was out on one of her photographic safaris, and she asked Matt to meet with me instead. But there was a problem. Matt was up at one of the range shacks, and after our meeting, a storm blew in and I was forced to spend the night." She looked over at Grace. "And the rest, as they say, is history."

Grace put a hand on Ingrid's arm. "I'm afraid she's left out most of the good parts of the story, but our family is delighted that they have their happy ending."

"And we continue to live it every day." Nessa's eyes went soft before she said, "You and Luke seem to have had an equally stormy meeting."

Ingrid's eyes crinkled with humor. "You could say that."

Grace's voice lowered. "I know Luke has a wild streak in him. And has had since he was just a boy. But I'd trust him with my life."

Ingrid nodded. "When I first met him, I saw only that wild side. But after a while, I started to see other things, too. He's generous. With his time. With his patience. With his energy. While he was at my ranch, he seemed to sense when one of us was at the end of our rope, and he quietly stepped in to give us some room to breathe."

Grace heard the change in Ingrid's voice and looked into her eyes in time to see them mist, for just a moment, before she blinked and the look was gone.

She put a hand on Ingrid's arm. "I know I'm prejudiced, but I happen to know that Luke is a good man. A very good man."

Seeing that the crowd had thinned considerably, they walked to the front of the room, where Clay was still flipping chops while carrying on a running conversation with his regulars.

"Good-bye, Clay, and thank you for a grand lunch," Grace called.

He gave a courtly bow. "My pleasure, ladies. You all come back. I hope you had a chance to recharge your batteries for the rest of the day."

Grace smiled and looped her arm through Lily's. "I don't know about the others, but I'm definitely recharged and reenergized."

CHAPTER SEVENTEEN

Grace turned in the direction of the hardware store, and the others trailed slowly behind.

At the door she paused. "Frankie told me he'd ordered a few things here. Care to join me?"

They followed her inside. While she walked to the counter to pick up the supplies Frank had ordered, the other three walked slowly around the store.

Nessa stopped to study an assortment of glass door-knobs. "These look just like the ones in my grand-mother's old Victorian house in Illinois."

"Oh, how pretty." Ingrid picked one up. "It's heavy. It feels like leaded glass."

"It is," came a voice behind them.

They turned to see Grace beside an elderly man with a walker.

Grace smiled at the others. "This is Melvin Hopkins Sr. He built this store. His son, Melvin Jr., runs it now, but as you can see, Senior is still very much involved in the products they carry." She indicated the young women. "Melvin, this is Matt's wife, Vanessa."

"Matthew got himself a beautiful bride," he said as he shook her hand.

"And these are our houseguests. Ingrid and Lily Larsen."

He gave Ingrid a look. "Was your daddy Lars?"

Both sisters nodded.

"A good man, your daddy. He was a regular customer here." He extended a hand to Lily, and then to Ingrid, meeting her dircct gaze. "I was sorry to hear about his passing."

"Thank you." Ingrid spoke for both of them, clearly touched by his kind words.

The old man returned his attention to the bin of knobs. "I started collecting those when I was just a boy. Now they've become the choice for a lot of young couples who want to bring back the glory of the old days."

Vanessa looked down at the light glinting off the glass knobs. "I know where I'm bringing Matt when we get around to building our house."

"I hope it won't be soon." Grace lay a hand on Nessa's arm. "Frankie and I so enjoy having you both with us."

"And we love being with you, too." Vanessa brushed Gracie's cheek with a kiss. "But Matt has always wanted to build a place on the North Ridge. It's really special to him, and to me."

"I know. And I completely understand. You deserve your own place, where you can start your family and make a home uniquely yours. But whenever you move, you know that Frankie and I will miss you both terribly."

"We'll be so close, you'll soon find yourself wishing we'd move far away."

"Never." Grace gave a vehement shake of her head.

Nessa glanced at Ingrid. "Maybe we'll hold off long enough for you to find some other permanent guests, so you won't be lonely."

Seeing where this was going, Ingrid smiled gently. "I have a ranch to run. I told Luke this was only for a night or two."

"Of course. But please don't blame us if we try to coax you to stay longer." Grace caught Lily's hand and began leading her back to the counter, where Frankie's order was bagged and waiting.

A short time later, after calling their good-byes to Melvin Sr. and Melvin Jr., they left the hardware store and started up the street.

"We can't leave town without having dessert." Grace pointed to the pretty little shop with a sign that read I's CREAM.

Lily read the words out loud. "I's Cream."

Grace winked at the others. "Say it aloud again."

"I's Cream. I's Cream." The little girl's eyes went wide. "Ice cream." She looked at Grace. "We're going for ice cream?"

"You bet we are." Grace caught her hand. "Come on."

"Oh boy." Lily's words sang on the air as the two skipped down the sidewalk.

Behind them, Ingrid and Nessa shared a giggle as Ingrid said, "I don't know which of them is more excited."

"Two kids in a candy store," Nessa remarked.

"Or in an ice cream shop." At Ingrid's words, they caught hands and hurried to catch up.

* * *

"Now this alone would be worth the drive to town." Grace licked the edges of her cone.

Nessa's eyes lit. "What in the world did you order?"

"A double-dipped Monster Chocolate Marshmallow Honeycomb Delight." Grace laughed like a girl. "How about you?"

"Mud Pie and Cookie Dough, with hazelnut topping."

"Ingrid?" Grace looked at the two sisters as they sat side by side on a smooth log, which rested on two massive tree trunks and served as a bench.

"Minc's Strawberry Cotton Candy and Jolly Cherry Cherub."

"Lily?"

The girl had to take a moment to lick away a drop that was about to fall from her sugar cone. "Once in a Blue Moon and Purple People Eater."

"Who would have believed blue and purple ice cream?" Grace gave a mock shudder. "I'm sure it tastes lovely, but those colors..."

Lily held out her cone. "Want a taste, Gram Gracie?"

The older woman laughed. "No, thank you. If I manage to eat all this, I'll be amazed."

"My money's on you," Vanessa said between licks of her ice cream.

As they sat in the sunshine, enjoying their sweet treats, they looked up when Nessa called, "Dr. Anita. How nice to see you."

A pretty young woman stepped out of the shop holding a cone of chocolate ice cream.

"Nessa. What a lovely surprise." She looked over. "And Ms. Grace. How are you?"

"Just fine, dear." Grace moved over to make room. "Will you join us?"

"Thank you."

As Dr. Anita sat, Grace added, "Dr. Anita Cross, these are guests of ours. Ingrid and Lily Larsen."

They smiled and greeted one another while keeping careful hold of their cones.

"How are things at the clinic?"

Dr. Anita rolled her eyes. "Busy. This is the first break I've had all day, and I thought I'd treat myself before the next go-round begins." She kept her gaze averted as she asked casually, "How is Colin, Ms. Grace?"

"Just fine, dear. He's currently up in the highlands with our wranglers."

"This has to be a busy time for ranchers."

Grace gave a small laugh. "I can't think of a time when we aren't busy. Whether it's calving in spring, or roundup in fall, or all the times in between, there's just never a lull in the activities."

Anita nodded. "It's the same for doctors. There just never seems to be enough time in the day."

Grace gave a knowing smile. "And still, despite all the demands on our time, we manage to live our lives. Sometimes, when Frankie and I look back, we wonder at all we've experienced. Birth, death. Laughter and tears. Good times, and some not so good that we'd rather forget. But here we are, still filling every hour of every day, and grateful for every minute of it."

Anita Cross polished off the last of her small cone before getting to her feet. As she did, she lay a hand on Grace's arm. "Thank you for the reminder that I need to take time for life while rushing through my busy routine." She glanced around at the others. "It was so good meeting you, Ingrid and Lily. And, Nessa, good seeing you again." In an aside to Grace she added, "Give my best to Colin."

"I will, dear."

Grace turned to watch as the pretty doctor hurried along the sidewalk toward the medical clinic.

She turned back to Vanessa. "I do believe I caught a glimmer of something in her eyes when she mentioned Colin's name."

Nessa gave a little cat smile. "You see? There's always hope, Gram Gracie."

The older woman returned her attention to the cone with renewed enjoyment. But she kept glancing down the sidewalk until the young doctor disappeared inside the doors of the medical clinic.

Dr. Anita Cross was pretty and bright and had an endearing personality. She probably also had half a dozen men standing in line in the hope of winning her hand. But that didn't stop Grace from wishing and dreaming.

As the ranch truck drew up alongside the back door, Ingrid spoke for all of them.

"Gram Gracie, I can't thank you enough for this day." She looked down at her new shirt, then at Lily's entire outfit. "Thank you for these beautiful clothes. And lunch. And ice cream. I can't remember the last time I did nothing except indulge myself."

Grace turned off the ignition and glanced at Ingrid in the rearview mirror. "And now I'll thank all of you. It was such a treat for me to have a girls' day. I've never done this before. Usually, when I go to town, I go with Frankie, or with Burke or one of my grandsons. I have to tell you, it's much sweeter doing it with girls."

Vanessa caught her hand. "Then we should make a pact to do this on a regular basis. And maybe next time we'll try Snips and Dips."

Grace held up her hands. "These old fingernails haven't seen polish since I was a bride."

"Then it's settled." Nessa turned to glance at Ingrid and Lily. "I see it as our duty to force Gram Gracie into having a manicure, pedicure, and massage."

"Only if you three promise to do it right along with me."

"A manicure? To shovel manure?" Ingrid looked horrified.

"Not only a manicure, but a pedicure as well," Nessa declared. "Think what a beating our poor feet take. Trekking up and down pastures. Locked in heavy work boots for days and weeks. Wouldn't it be fun to have your feet massaged with oils and your toenails painted a pretty shade of pink?"

Lily and Ingrid turned to one another with matching looks of amazement, as though they'd never even thought of such a thing.

But it was Grace who said, "You may have something there, Nessa. I do believe I've been mistreating my poor body for a lifetime. I just hope, if we decide to take you up on your suggestion, this old body doesn't go into shock."

The four of them laughed as they climbed down from the truck and carried their parcels through the mudroom and into the kitchen.

When Vanessa handed Ingrid her bag of clothes, the young woman jiggled the bag. "This feels heavy."

She opened the bag, and for a moment was speechless. Finally she lifted out the colorful T-shirts. "Whose are these?"

"Yours." Grace shared a knowing smile with Vanessa. "Once we knew your size, and how great you looked in that pretty teal shirt, we agreed that you needed a few more."

"Gram Gracie, I can't—"

"Too late. They're already bought and paid for. Now why don't you take them upstairs and, after a shower, decide which of them to wear this evening for dinner."

Ingrid pressed a kiss to the older woman's cheek and then walked over to do the same for Vanessa. "You two are very good at keeping secrets."

"Yes, we are." Nessa caught her in a hug. "Now I'm heading upstairs to shower and change."

The young women ran upstairs, with Lily and Grace following at a more leisurely pace.

When the men returned from the hills, they trooped up the stairs to shower and dress for supper. By the time they came downstairs, Grace and the girls were gathered in the sitting area of the kitchen, sipping their drinks and talking quietly.

Luke snagged a longneck from a tray on the counter and ambled over, stepping up between Reed and Colin to listen to Grace give a rambling commentary to Frank about their day.

Then he spotted Ingrid, her cap of fair hair curling softly around her face, eyes bright with laughter, a smile curving her lips. Frank moved, settling himself next to his wife and giving Luke a clearer view of Ingrid.

For a moment Luke forgot to breathe. Instead of her baggy shirt, she was wearing a tee of bright red, with a softly scooped neckline that revealed a hint of darkened cleft between her breasts. The material clung to her like a second skin, revealing that amazing body she'd always taken such pains to hide.

She lifted the glass of pale wine to her mouth and took a sip. Luke swallowed when she did and could have sworn he could taste her wine and, more, her lips. Just thinking about it had his pulse racing. Sweating, he lifted the chilled bottle to his forehead.

When he caught his grandmother staring at him, he couldn't help giving her one of those rogue smiles. Her own smile bloomed.

"I believe I'll have some ice water, Luke." Grace continued watching him as he turned away, then returned with her drink.

As he handed it to her, she said, "Gorgeous view, isn't it?"

He leaned close. "Yeah. And you're one sly woman, you know that?"

She managed to look every inch the prim-and-proper lady. "I do indeed."

CHAPTER EIGHTEEN

While the others took turns describing their day, Ingrid's phone vibrated in her pocket. When she lifted it and caught sight of the caller's name, she stood and made her way to the far side of the room, speaking softly.

Nadine's voice was high and shrill. "I drive all the way from Wayside, thinking I ought to look in on my family, and what do I find? An empty ranch. Nobody here. Where the hell are you?"

"We're staying with . . . friends."

"And Mick?"

"He's here, too."

"Do these friends have a name?"

At the fury in her mother's tone, Ingrid felt her heart drop to her toes. She glanced across the distance that separated her from the others, talking and laughing with such ease, and realized that the chasm between herself and them had just widened considerably. How could she have ever believed she had the right to be here with these good people?

"Well? Who are these so-called friends?"

Ingrid stepped into the mudroom, fearful that her mother's voice would be overheard during a lull in the conversation. "Luke's family."

"You're at the high-and-mighty Malloy Ranch?"

"What's that supposed to mean?"

"I've been asking around. According to folks in Wayside, the Malloy family is the closest thing Montana has to royalty."

"Nadine, that's not..." Ingrid sighed. There was so way she could describe or defend the decent, loving people she'd met here. "We'll be home first thing in the morning."

"Don't hurry back on my account." The conversation ended with an abrupt disconnect, followed by silence.

When Ingrid returned to the others, Luke put a hand on her arm. "Everything all right?"

"Fine." She couldn't meet his eyes as she added, "That was Nadine. She's"—she shrugged—"her usual self."

Luke hated the way the smile had been wiped from Ingrid's eyes. Leaning close, he whispered, "I've been wanting a chance to tell you how great you look."

Her frown deepened. The brief conversation with her mother had her in a defensive mood. "Is that a code word for *sexy*?"

"Miss Larsen, I'm shocked and appalled." He said it so sternly it took her a moment to realize he was having fun with her.

She gave his shoulder a quick punch. "Very funny, Malloy."

"But I had you going there for a minute."

"Only for a few seconds."

Luke was relieved to see her smile return.

When Yancy announced that dinner was ready, they gathered around the big table. Luke held a chair out for Lily, and then another for Ingrid, before taking the seat beside her.

Yancy had carved up several roasted chickens before arranging them on two big platters. He handed one to Frank at the head of the table and a second platter to Nelson at the opposite end. They, in turn, began passing them around, along with bowls of buttered mashed potatoes, tender garden beans, and sourdough rolls warm from the oven.

Old Mick took a taste and looked at Yancy. "I hope you'll give me this recipe."

Lily turned to stare at him. "Just so you're not thinking about cooking Little."

"Little?" Reed paused in the act of passing the rolls.

Lily dimpled. "Little is my pet chicken. I raised her from when she first hatched."

"A pet chicken?" Reed gave a quick laugh. "Does she sleep at the foot of your bed like a dog?"

Mick winked at Lily before saying to the others, "When Lily was four, Ingrid used to read stories to her every night. One of them was about Chicken Little and the sky falling. The next time a brooding hen brought her parade of chicks from the henhouse, Lily adopted the smallest one and named her Little. For a year or more she used to dress that chicken in doll clothes and push her around the yard in a doll stroller."

Lily smiled, remembering. "Until Little got too big and wanted to be with the other hens."

Reed looked around the table. "So, Little turned into Big?"

They all laughed. Even Lily joined in.

"And now," Mick added, "Little is way too old and tough to worry about ending up on anyone's table. That old pet is queen of the henhouse." In an aside he said to Yancy, "But I'd still like your recipe. This is the best darned roast chicken I've ever tasted."

"I'll write it down for you. Promise."

Yancy picked up a basket of rolls. "Who wants the few that are left?"

"I wouldn't want them to go to waste." Burke helped himself to one and passed the basket to Reed, who took two, and then to Matt, who took the last one.

Luke tried to shame Reed. "You should have left one for our company."

Reed held up a roll. "How about it, Ingrid? Lily?"

When the two sisters shook their heads, he raised a brow at Luke. "You really wanted this for yourself, didn't you, bro?" Before Luke could reply, he popped it into his mouth. Then, with a grin, said, "Oh, sorry. But I was afraid the sky was about to fall, and I wanted to save you from choking."

Around the table everyone was chuckling when the back door was thrown open with such force, it banged against the wall.

Luke, Reed, and Matt had already shoved back their chairs, prepared to do battle with some unknown intruder, when a figure stepped into the kitchen. A figure in tight, skinny jeans, fringed boots, and an off-one-shoulder top that exposed most of a lacy bra. Her red hair was piled on top of her head and held in place with a giant plastic clasp. The smell of her sweet perfume preceded her, drifting around her like a cloud.

Nadine put a hand to the kitchen counter to steady herself as she took her time studying the faces of all those at the table, before her gaze finally settled on Ingrid. "Well, here you are. I bet you weren't expecting to see me, were you?"

Luke's family turned to Ingrid.

In a subdued voice she managed to say, "This is my mother, Nadine Larsen."

Grace was the first to recover her composure. Pushing away from the table, she crossed the room and caught Nadine's hand.

"How nice to meet you. I'm Grace Anne Malloy."

In short order she proceeded to introduce all those around the table. The rest of the men, having recovered from their surprise, got to their feet.

"Nice to meet you all." Nadine waved a hand. "No need to stand on ceremony. I can see you're in the middle of supper."

Grace led her closer. "You'll join us."

Yancy had already brought a chair to the table, placing it beside Grace's.

"Don't mind if I do." Nadine settled herself at the table. "Something smells good."

"Roast chicken." Grace took her seat and held a platter, allowing Nadine to help herself. "And Yancy's mashed potatoes. Always a favorite around here."

Nadine took a spoonful before holding up her hands. "That's enough. I need to keep my girlish figure." She looked around the table. "I'll say this, Grace. You sure do have a bunch of handsome men in your family."

Grace gave her a smile. "Thank you. I have to agree with you."

Frank, watching as Nadine buttered a roll, remarked, "Ingrid said you were out. I assume you were with friends."

"Yeah." She shot a sly look at her daughter. "Friends. Just a nice, sociable evening. Or three," she added with a giggle.

She pushed aside her plate after just a single taste of everything.

Grace seemed surprised. "You're not hungry?"

"I ate earlier. With my . . . friends."

"Well then." Grace glanced across the table at Yancy. "I think we'll take our desserts and coffee in the great room."

He nodded. "You folks go ahead and I'll just cut up those pies cooling over on the far counter."

"Pie?" Luke's eyebrows shot up. "Fresh apple?"

"They are." Yancy's grin was quick. "Just for you, Luke."

As the family began pushing away from the table, Frank took Gracie's arm, leading the way to the great room, leaving the others to follow.

When Luke offered his arm to Ingrid, Nadine grabbed his other arm. "I'm impressed. Are the men in your family always such gentlemen?"

"We do our best." He stepped back to allow Nadine and Ingrid to enter ahead of him. When he turned, he saw Reed escorting Lily, who was more subdued than he'd ever seen.

He tugged on a lock of her hair. "What's wrong, Li'l Bit?"

"Nothing." She paused, then stepped back, signaling for him to wait with her.

When the others left the kitchen, she tugged on his arm to stoop down. The minute he did, she put a hand to her mouth to whisper in his ear, "Now that Nadine's here, does this mean we can't play cards?"

He knelt down and looked her in the eye. "Her presence doesn't change a thing." He saw the doubt and knew the little girl's fear wasn't just about playing cards. Though she was just a kid, she knew that her mother's behavior was out of place. Especially now that she'd had a glimpse of a different sort of family than hers. "As soon as we've had our dessert, I want my chance to beat you at Fish. Okay?"

Her eyes widened. "Okay."

He stood and took her hand. "Come on. I'm betting there'll be ice cream to go with that apple pie."

"We had ice cream today in town," she said as they entered the great room. The others looked up as she took a seat by the fireplace.

Nelson said, "You went to I's?"

She nodded. "When I read the sign over her shop, I didn't understand, so Gram Gracie told me to say it out loud a couple of times. As soon as I did, I got it." Her smile was back, blooming at the memory. "I's Cream. Isn't that funny?"

"It is. Not to mention clever." Nelson, charmed by the little girl's story, found himself getting into the spirit of the moment. "Why hasn't a dairy started calling its product Moo Juice?"

"Or," Reed put in, "why didn't a certain gifted director we all know and love call himself Art Tistic?" When the rest of the family erupted with a series of boos, he shrugged. "Hey. At least I tried. Can any of you do better?"

At his dare, everyone was tossing out clever names and titles, such as the new tailor in town calling himself "Lord And Taylor" and the veterinarian calling himself Hannibal the Animal Doctor, and the clinic's Dr. Cross calling himself Happy Not Cross. That, in turn, had the others teasing Colin about Dr. Cross's niece, Anita.

Though Colin refused to answer their taunts, he was grinning like a teen.

Yancy entered the room, shoving a trolley loaded with a carafe of coffee and mugs, along with slices of apple pie and a container of vanilla ice cream.

He held up an ice cream scoop. "Who wants ice cream on their pie?"

Minutes later, he began passing pie and coffee around. The family was full of compliments as they dug into their desserts.

"None for me," Nadine said as he paused beside her. "But I'll have one of those longnecks on that tray over there."

Yancy returned to hand her a cold beer.

She looked over at Lily, who had taken a seat as close to Ingrid as possible. "You get any closer, you'll be sitting on her lap."

Ingrid drew an arm around her little sister, who kept her head down, making swirls in her ice cream with her spoon.

To break the tension she could feel between the two sisters and their mother, Grace smiled at Nadine. "Now that we've had a chance to get to know your daughters, we're thoroughly charmed by them."

"Oh yeah. They're real charming." Nadine tipped up the bottle and drained it.

"Having only sons, I feel especially lucky to have spent the day with them. We had such fun, as I'm sure you've had through the years."

Instead of a reply, Nadine held up the empty bottle as a signal to Yancy, the way she would at a saloon.

He heaved himself out of the chair and brought her another.

"Thanks." She looked around at the others. "This is like having your very own butler. I could get used to this. All I can drink and handsome men for company."

In the silence that followed, Luke motioned to Reed. "I think you and I should challenge Ingrid and Lily to a game of cutthroat Fish."

Lily looked up. "What's 'cutthroat'?"

Reed stood and towered over her with a mock leer. "Be warned, little lady. You're about to find out."

"Oh boy." She turned to Ingrid. "Come on. Even if it's cutthroat, we can beat them."

The four gathered around a card table in the corner of the room, where Reed proceeded to shuffle the cards and deal them out.

While some of the family continued to make small talk, the rest of them gathered around the table to watch the action.

Nelson turned to Yancy. "Another fine dessert. You just keep on outdoing yourself, Yancy."

"Thank you, Great One. Ready for a nightcap?"

Nelson nodded and smiled a thank-you. Minutes later Yancy handed him a glass of fine brandy.

Seeing it, Nadine sidled over and pulled a chair close

to Nelson. "Now that looks good." She turned to Yancy. "I'll have what he's having."

The cook walked away and returned minutes later to hand her a drink.

"Why did he call you Great One?" Nadine asked.

Nelson stretched out his legs toward the warmth of the fire. "That's the nickname my grandsons gave me years ago, and it stuck." He looked at her. "Why do your own daughters call you Nadine?"

She smiled. "It sounds so much younger than Mom, don't you think?"

His expression hardened. "I can't think of a more beautiful name than Mom, or Mama, or Mother. There is nothing more important in this world than being a mother."

"Easy to say when you've never been one." Nadine polished off her drink in one long swallow and leaned her head back.

"But I had one. My own mother was one of the finest women I've ever known. Though she was a perfect lady, she allowed me the room to develop my talents, even though she understood nothing whatsoever about film-making and no doubt thought it a foolish waste of my time and talent. In fact, she…" His words trailed off when he realized that the woman beside him was snoring. Her chest rose and fell with each breath. Her mouth had gone slack, presenting a picture that was not at all flattering.

Seeing that her glass was about to spill its contents down the front of her shirt, he took it from her hands and set it aside.

He looked at his daughter. "Grace Ann, I believe our… guest needs a bed."

Frank and Grace hurried to either side of Nadine and gently got her to her feet. She never even awoke.

When Frank motioned toward the stairs, Grace shook her head. "She might wake during the night and, in her condition, get disoriented and take a fall. I think, Frankie, we'll put her in that small guest room beside the mudroom, in case she wakes and needs some night air."

"Good idea, Gracie Girl."

The two of them walked Nadine into the small room. While Frank held her by the arm, Grace turned down the bed linens, and together they eased her into the bed. After removing the fringed boots, Grace drew the covers over her.

Nadine hadn't once moved.

When they turned out the light and closed the door, Grace turned to her husband. "Those poor girls."

He nodded and said not a thing.

No words were needed. They had both seen more than enough to let them know something of what Ingrid and Lily had been going through.

CHAPTER NINETEEN

The card game lasted another hour, with Lily winning nearly every hand.

At first, Reed was giving Lily every opportunity to win. He would refrain from asking for something she'd already asked for, so she would have the upper hand. But after several losses, he realized the little girl didn't need his help. She was smart enough to win on her own.

When she won for the fifth straight time, he narrowed his eyes on her. "I think you've figured out the meaning of *cutthroat*, haven't you?"

She glanced across the table at Luke before her smile bloomed. "Luke told me."

"He may have told you what it means, but I don't think you needed his help to win at this game. You're killing me. It's a good thing we're not playing for money. You'd be the richest one in the room."

After watching the game, Matt and Nessa called their good nights and went upstairs to their suite of rooms. Colin did the same.

Yancy, Mick, and the Great One, discussing the finer points of gourmet cooking and exotic food, kept breaking into smiles at the teasing and laughter that erupted from the card players across the room.

Burke, sprawled by the fire, nursing a longneck, said to Mick, "That's music to my ears."

The old cowboy nodded. "I was just thinking the same. I haven't seen my girls this relaxed in a long time. Probably not since their pa died."

The Great One studied him. "You've been with them a long time?"

"Since before they were born."

"I'd say that makes them your girls."

"They'll always feel like mine," Mick said with feeling. "They're the only family I've ever had."

The Great One stifled a yawn. "Since Frank and Gracie went up to bed, I believe I'll do the same."

Yancy nodded. "My day starts early. I'll say good night, too."

Gradually Mick and Burke drifted off, as well, leaving the four to finish their card challenge.

Reed tallied the wins and losses. "Want to play one more?"

"Even three more wouldn't get you even," Luke said with a laugh. "I think we should call it a night."

Lily was too weary to disagree. But as she started up the stairs, she turned to call, "Thanks, Reed. I really enjoyed beating you."

"You realize you owe me a rematch."

"I can't wait." The little girl scampered up the stairs, trailed more slowly by her big sister.

Luke waited before shoving back his chair. He turned to his brother, keeping his voice low enough that he wouldn't be overheard. "Thanks. I know you'd have rather been doing anything tonight than playing Fish. But it meant a lot to Lily."

"I didn't mind. Really. I know it kept her mind off other things." Reed paused before adding, "Is her mother always like that?"

Luke nodded.

"Poor kid." Reed placed the cards in a box before setting it on a shelf and heading up the stairs. "'Night, Luke."

"'Night."

A short time later, as Luke passed Lily's room on the way to his own, he could hear the two sisters talking quietly. Ingrid's voice was low, soothing.

Lily was lucky to have a big sister like that. But, he wondered, while Ingrid was busy easing her little sister's fears, who could she count on to soothe hers?

Ingrid heard Lily's prayers and tucked her into bed.

Lily caught her sister's hand. "Wasn't that fun tonight?"

"Yes, it was."

"For a while I even forgot Nadine was here."

"Me too." Ingrid smoothed a hand over Lily's hair. "'Night, honey."

"'Night."

"If you need anything at all, let me know."

The little girl's eyes were closing. "I will."

Ingrid waited a moment at the door, watching as Lily slid ever so gently into sleep.

If only she could do the same.

She made her way to her own room and stepped inside, closing the door behind her. When she turned, she caught sight of Luke standing across the room, his back to her, staring into the darkness.

"Luke." Her hand went to her throat before she let out a quick breath. "Sorry, I wasn't expecting you to be here."

"I just wanted to make sure you were all right."

"Of course I am. Why wouldn't I be?"

He shrugged and stepped closer. "I thought having Nadine here might upset you."

"I'm not happy about it. But she's a fact of my life. I've had plenty of time to get used to it. But I'm sure it was quite a jolt for your family. I wish they hadn't been forced to see her like that."

She pushed past Luke and walked to the window, lifting her head to the night sky. "They were all acting so polite. So nice."

"They weren't acting. They *are* nice."

"I know that." She turned to face him. "But that just makes it even more awkward. After spending time with your family and seeing how kind they are, I can't help comparing them with what I've grown up with." She crossed her arms over her chest and studied the toe of her boot. "I felt ashamed tonight. And Lily did, too. I could see it on her face. That's not something I'm proud of. But the truth is, we don't belong here, Luke."

He put his hands on her shoulders and rubbed gently. "You've seen the way Gram Gracie reacted to having two more girls around. The rest of my family feels the same way. They all love having you and Lily here."

She struggled to ignore the little thrill that raced down her spine at his touch. "And I love them for that. But—"

"Shh." He lowered his face and brushed his mouth over hers.

It was the softest of kisses, but it had her hands gripping his wrists. "You know I don't—"

"Yeah. Sorry to break one of your hard-and-fast rules." His grin was quick. "But there's always been this devil inside me that just has to see how many rules can be broken."

Before she could respond, he dragged her close and covered her mouth with his in a kiss that had her forgetting everything but the hot sizzle of need.

His kiss was easy. Practiced. Hers was quivering. Awkward. The difference between them made her all the more wary. But she had to admit that she liked the taste of him. A purely male taste that had all her senses heightened. And more than anything, she loved the way it felt being touched and kissed by him.

Luke's hands tightened at her shoulders before gliding down her back and drawing her firmly against him.

Her arms found their way around his waist. Her breasts were flattened against his chest. A chest that rose and fell with every ragged breath. She was aware of his arousal, and she wondered at the way her poor heart soared at the knowledge.

"Now, isn't this nicer than playing Fish?"

He ran nibbling kisses down her jaw, then lower, to the little hollow between her neck and shoulder, sending the most delicious tingles along her spine.

"Is this where your mind was during the game?"

Without a thought to what she was doing, she angled her head, allowing him easier access.

He nibbled her earlobe, her throat, and all the while his hands, those clever, work-worn hands, were kneading her back, her sides, until they encountered the swell of her breasts. His thumbs began a gentle exploration that had her breath shuddering, before coming out in a long, deep sigh.

She pushed a little away. "Wait. Luke—"

"You want me to stop?"

"No." The word came out so quickly, it caught her by surprise. She quickly recovered. "I mean yes. I need...I need time to think."

She looked up into his eyes and saw the smile. "What's so funny?"

He shook his head. "Just giving you time to think. So?" He dipped his face to brush his mouth over hers.

At once the rush of sexual tension was back, stronger than ever.

She wanted, so badly, to just go with her feelings. But it was so contrary to every rule she'd set for herself.

What was happening to her? She hated this weakness in herself. She had probably inherited it from Nadine. This yearning to just let herself give in and enjoy the luxury of being held in a man's arms. Of being loved. But Luke wasn't just any man. He was so good at this, he made her believe that she was special. Cherished. Like some rare and beautiful treasure that he'd just discovered.

She ought to know better. As Nadine was fond of saying, if a man wasn't with the one he loved, he could always love the one he was with.

The thought was like being splashed with ice water.

She put a hand to Luke's shoulder. "I think I need some time. I can't think when you're holding me, kissing me."

"That's good." He let his fingers play through the short, silky strands of her hair, watching the way they settled around her face. "Sometimes you can overthink things. Maybe you should just go with your feelings."

"Like Nadine?"

The words had the effect of a slap across the face. The minute she said them, she felt him withdrawing.

She did the same, taking a step back. "I'm sorry, Luke. I warned you. I'm no good at this. You'd better go."

"I could stay. We could talk, if you'd like. Or"—he gave her one of those rogue smiles that did such strange things to her heart—"I could prove to you that you're a hell of a lot better at this than you think."

"It's late. Your family is nearby, and I wouldn't want them to overhear us."

"Is that what this is about?"

"No." She gave a quick shake of her head. "This is about me. I want you to leave now."

"Okay." He framed her face with his hands and stared down into her eyes. "Take all the time you need. I want you to feel safe with me, Ingrid. And comfortable. I want you to trust me, and trust yourself."

"Maybe that's the problem. I'm not sure I'll ever be able to trust myself. At least where men are concerned."

"I'm not just any man."

"I know that." Her tone softened. "Thank you for understanding, Luke."

He smiled. "You're welcome." He kissed the tip of her

nose. "But just so you understand, this isn't over. I want you. And whether you're ready to admit it or not, you want me. Whenever you come to terms with that, we'll take this to the next step."

She pushed free, breaking contact. "You're so sure of yourself."

"I'm sure of what I'm feeling." He winked. "And I'm even more certain of what you're feeling, even if you're not."

"This doesn't change a thing, Luke. First thing in the morning, Mick and Lily and I are heading home."

His easy smile turned into a frown. "What about the gunman?"

She shook her head. "I'll just have to be more cautious. I'll carry a rifle with me everywhere, but I'll also carry on as I did before. I have a ranch to run or I'll lose it. I can't afford to let some mystery man dictate my life. And I can't just stay here, feeling pampered, and pretend I don't have any obligations."

He gave her a long, considering look before slowly nodding his head. "Okay. If that's your decision, I won't try to talk you out of it. But just so you know, I'll be going with you."

"This isn't your fight. And don't say you owe me for saving your life. You've already more than repaid me for that."

"Then let's just say I'm doing this for my own selfish reasons."

"Which are?"

"Ask my family. They'll tell you I just can't resist a good down-and-dirty fight." He added with a smile, "Or a pretty woman in trouble."

He opened the door and walked out without a backward glance.

Ingrid closed the door and leaned against it, crossing her arms over her chest, deep in thought.

On the one hand she was grateful that Luke was willing to stand beside her in her fight. There was no one she would rather have watching her back.

But now that she'd met his family and learned their history, she found herself caring as much about them as she did her own family.

What right did she have to allow him to risk his life for her?

Allow? The word had her suddenly smiling as she began undressing. That wasn't a word that could be used in the same breath with Luke. He didn't ask permission for anything. He lived life on his own terms.

How she envied him that freedom.

She lay in bed, eyes pressed firmly closed, her mind working overtime. Though she tried to concentrate on the things she needed to do when she returned to her ranch, the image of Luke holding her, kissing her, kept intruding on her thoughts.

She found herself wishing with all her heart that she could just let go of all the hard-and-fast rules she'd set for herself and simply indulge in the pleasure he offered.

She fell asleep dreaming of things that, if she were awake, would have had her blushing.

CHAPTER TWENTY

Ingrid could hear the hum of voices as she approached the kitchen. Now that she'd become familiar with Luke's family, she could make out the low tones of Luke's brother, Matt, and the more cultured voice of his bride, Vanessa. She heard Yancy and Mick on one side of the room, and Frank and Grace talking with Luke, and Reed joining in. What was most surprising to her was Lily's voice, high-pitched with excitement. She'd thought her sister was still asleep. She hadn't even heard Lily leave her room.

The minute Ingrid stepped into the room, Lily dashed over to catch her hands. "Guess what? Gram Gracie is taking me on one of her safaris."

"Now, Lily," Grace was quick to add, "our agreement was that you'd accompany me only if your sister says it's all right."

Ingrid glanced across the room, where Luke was

lounging against the counter, watching and listening with a look of amusement. "I don't know." She looked from Luke to his grandparents. "Do you think it's safe?"

Frank set aside his mug of coffee. "Darlin', I'm betting Lily will be safer with my Gracie Girl than in her own bed. The wranglers and I will see to it."

"Will you come with us, Ingrid? Please?" Lily danced up and down, still clinging to Ingrid's hands.

Ingrid drew her sister close. "I can't, honey. I'm planning on returning to the ranch today. I was hoping..." She saw the pleading look in Lily's eyes and gave a sigh of defeat. "But you don't need to come with me. I can't think of anything more exciting than spending time with someone who shares your love of both photography and wild horses. As long as you promise to do everything Gram Gracie asks you to, I...I guess I'm fine with it."

"Oh boy." Lily hugged her sister before racing across the room to do the same with Grace. "We're going on a safari." She looked up into the older woman's face. "When do we leave?"

"In about an hour. As soon as you pack your things, and we take time to enjoy Yancy's fine breakfast."

Lily started out of the room, then hurried back. "What should I pack?"

"Everything we bought in town. A pair of jeans and a T-shirt. A jacket, hat, and comfortable walking shoes. I'll take care of the bedrolls."

"Bedrolls. Will we sleep in a tent or outside?"

"Outside, unless it's raining. Then we'll sleep in the back of my truck." Grace started laughing. "It wouldn't be a good trip if we didn't get to sleep out of doors at least once."

"Oh boy." Lily's voice trilled on the air as she dashed from the room and raced up the stairs.

Frank was grinning from ear to ear. "Gracie Girl, doesn't this remind you of someone else?"

Nessa kissed his cheek before turning to Ingrid. "He's talking about me. The first time I went to the highlands with Gram Gracie, I was so excited, I thought I was in heaven."

"She's not kidding." Matt put his arms around his wife and drew her back against him. "I think that's what sealed the deal on our relationship. Nessa fell in love with those mustangs the minute she laid eyes on them. And the rest, as they say, is history." He brushed a kiss across his wife's neck. Such a simple thing, but to those watching, it felt deeply intimate.

Ingrid happened to glance at Luke at that moment and felt her cheeks color. She could almost feel his arms around her in that same way and knew, by the look in his eyes, he was feeling it, too.

"Well, then." She drew in a deep breath. "I guess I won't worry about Lily. I'll just let her go and see if she returns from the hills a changed little girl."

"From the things she's said about 'her' herd, I can almost guarantee it," Grace said as Yancy called them to breakfast. "She can't wait to photograph them, and she confided in me that she really wants to try my zoom lens so she can get up close the way I did"—Grace pointed to a framed photograph hanging in an alcove—"in that picture."

"I know what she'll be asking for when her birthday rolls around." Ingrid had a sudden thought. "Isn't Nadine up yet?"

"Up and gone." Yancy turned from the oven. "The others had just left to do some barn chores when she helped herself to some coffee and whiskey and said she was headed out."

"Did she say where?"

He shrugged. "If she did, I don't recall."

Minutes later Lily hurried into the kitchen with her backpack stuffed. She set it carefully in a corner of the mudroom before taking her place at the table beside her sister.

As she began to nibble scrambled eggs and steak, she suddenly looked over at Grace. "Oh. What will we do for food? Will we have to fish in a creek?"

"Don't you worry. We may plan on roughing it, but it's not all that primitive." Grace nodded toward their cook. "Yancy will see that we won't go hungry."

He pointed to the plastic pouches, all neatly labeled and stacked in a metal container. "If you decide to stay in the hills for a month, you won't run out of food."

Lily's eyes went wide. "Could we? Stay for a month?"

Frank started laughing. "Not on your life. I can't stand to be apart from my Gracie Girl as it is. If you're gone more than a week, I'll find you both and drag you home."

"Or you could stay up in the hills with us, Grandpop."

The old man's eyes watered just a bit at her easy use of his name before he leaned over to tousle her hair. "I could be easily persuaded to do just that, Lily darlin'. I might decide to stay with both of you."

Around the table, the others listened in silence and smiled.

Ingrid gave Lily a fierce hug, closing her eyes for a moment before letting her go.

Lily climbed up to the passenger side of the truck, where Grace sat at the wheel. She lowered the window and waved until they were out of sight.

While the others made their way to the house or the barns, Ingrid remained, staring at the cloud of dust.

Luke took her hand in his. "She'll be fine."

"I know." Ingrid managed a weak smile. "But I keep thinking about all the things that could go wrong. An angry mustang stallion. A lightning strike during a sudden storm. A fall, far from civilization. A—"

"Has she ever left you before?"

Ingrid lifted her chin. "This isn't about me, Luke."

"That's right. We were talking about Lily." He gave her a heart-stopping grin. "But I'm just asking."

"This is the first time she's ever gone anywhere without me."

"She's going to have the time of her life." He put an arm around her shoulders and drew her close. Against her ear he murmured, "And her big sister will survive."

She couldn't help laughing as she pushed away and punched him in the arm. "You're being mean."

"I'm being honest. This will do you both good. And if Lily is serious about photography, she couldn't have a better teacher than Gram Gracie."

Ingrid slowly nodded. "I know. I still can't believe that the photographer of Lily's favorite photo is your grandmother."

"Small world." He nodded toward her ranch truck parked near the porch. "Looks like Yancy wants to make sure you have enough provisions for a year."

Ingrid caught her breath at the boxes being loaded by Yancy and Mick into the back of the truck.

"Is that all food?"

Luke chuckled. "You saw what Yancy sent along on the safari. I'd say he and Mick conspired to double that amount before you head home."

As they walked closer, Mick turned to her. "You ready, girl?"

She nodded. "I'll just say my good-byes and get my things."

Mick held out the keys to Luke. "You want to drive?"

"You drive." Luke headed toward the barn. "I'll be right back."

Minutes later, with Mick behind the wheel, Ingrid walked down the back steps and tossed her overnight bag into the passenger side of the truck before turning to hug each member of Luke's family, including Yancy. "Thank you for all that food, Yancy. It will certainly save poor Mick from having to tolerate my cooking."

"That's what he said."

The two shared a laugh before she turned toward the truck.

Before she could climb inside, Luke roared up on his Harley. He tossed her a helmet and indicated the spot behind him. "Climb on."

She stood a moment, staring in disbelief. "You can't be serious."

"Oh, he's serious, all right." Reed slapped his grandfather on the back. "I wondered how long it would take before Luke got the itch."

"Well, I don't have an itch to ride on that thing with him." Ingrid turned to Luke's family, none of whom seemed surprised to see him waiting for her to make up her mind. "Aren't any of you going to tell him he's crazy?"

"Oh, we all know that." Matt winked at his wife, who was covering her laughter with a hand over her mouth. "What we want to know is whether you're as crazy as my brother."

Vanessa added, "Nobody can be that crazy, Matt."

Ingrid turned to Colin. "You strike me as the sensible one. Am I taking my life in my hands by riding with him?"

"I guess you'll never know unless you try." Colin leaned close to add, "It's true that Luke's always been wild and crazy. But I'm betting he won't be taking any chances with you onboard. I'm thinking he considers you precious cargo."

Precious cargo.

Ingrid drew in a breath before accepting the helmet from Luke's hand. To his family she explained, "I know. Just call me crazy."

Then, with a shake of her head at her own foolishness, she settled herself behind him on the Harley and wrapped her arms around his waist. With a wave, he revved the engine and they took off in a roar. Mick followed more slowly in the ranch truck.

"You okay back there?"

"I'm fine." And, she realized, she was.

After the first mile or so she learned to take the dips and curves of the road by following Luke's movements. When he leaned left, she did the same. When he straightened, she would relax her hands a bit. But she kept her arms firmly around his waist, feeling a sense of being anchored.

Anchored.

She could get used to this.

The press of her body to his. The fresh breeze cooling her face, despite the heat of the helmet. The amazing feeling of flying as they sped along a smooth track. The dizzying blur of movement when they crested a hill and, seeing no one for miles, opened up and soared.

Every once in a while he would point to something, and she would be alerted to a herd of deer or elk, heads lifted, watching in silence as they rolled past.

She'd driven these roads and trails for a lifetime, but suddenly she was seeing them in a brand-new way. Without the encumbrance of a truck, she felt small and insignificant amid the towering hills and buttes.

It was, she realized, an experience like no other. She felt part of the scenery. She felt free. And wildly exhilarated.

When the motorcycle started up a steep dirt trail, she tightened her grasp around Luke's waist and pressed her face to his shoulder.

He turned his head slightly. "You're going to love this." Each word seemed to vibrate inside her head as they reached the top.

For a moment they were on level ground. But without warning they began a sudden descent, racing headlong down a steep hill at breakneck speed. It was more thrilling than any roller-coaster ride.

There was no time to react as the road raced past them in a blur of movement. Minutes later they were once again on a level stretch of road, moving at a normal rate of speed.

"How're you doing?"

"I'm loving it."

And she was. Though she should have been terrified, there had been no time for fear. It dawned on her that the presence of this man had made all the difference.

Colin had said she was Luke's precious cargo. If that was true, he was equally precious to her. She had somehow learned over these past weeks to trust him. Completely. She had the sense that, without a doubt, no harm could come to her as long as she was with Luke Malloy.

Was that the same as love?

The question flashed into her mind with such clarity, she was forced to suck in a breath.

Could it be? Was it possible for someone like her, who had vowed to never trust a man with her heart? Was it possible to love a man she'd known for such a short time? A man who was everything she wasn't?

Where she'd always been cautious, straightforward, Luke was fearless, jumping in where even angels wouldn't tread.

Yet here she was, having the time of her life on a dangerous vehicle, without an ounce of fear.

Because of Luke.

A wide smile split her lips, and she raised her arms above her head while giving out a shout of pure joy.

As they rolled up to her ranch, he brought the Harley to a halt and stepped off before taking her hand and helping her.

They both removed their helmets and listened for a moment to the silence around them.

He took the helmet from her hands. "Was that a victory shout-out?"

She couldn't stop the laughter that bubbled up. "Yeah. My version of the happy dance."

"I guess that means you're not sorry you gave up the truck in favor of this?"

"Not sorry at all. Oh, Luke, I loved every minute of it."

He was looking at her with such intensity, she knew he was going to kiss her. She actually lifted herself on tiptoe, barely able to contain herself as she placed a hand on his shoulder.

At that moment the old truck wheezed up behind them and came to a stop.

Luke leaned close to whisper, "Hold that thought. Sooner or later we're bound to find some time alone."

"You two crazy bikers going to stand there all day, or give me a hand with this food?"

At Mick's challenge, they turned and made their way to the back of the truck. But as they hauled the parcels inside, they kept exchanging knowing smiles.

Ingrid found herself tingling with a wild sense of anticipation at the thought of what was to come.

CHAPTER TWENTY-ONE

As Ingrid carried in a box filled with food packets, she began reading the labels aloud. "Roast beef. Fried chicken. Stuffed pork chops. Garlic mashed potatoes." She glanced at Mick. "We'll be eating like guests in a five-star hotel."

He chuckled. "Without paying a five-star price."

Ingrid unpacked the boxes and handed the packets to Mick, while he loaded them into the freezer.

Luke walked in with another box and set it on the table.

Ingrid was beaming. "This was so sweet of Yancy."

"He's a sweet guy."

"So is your family. All of them. I still can't believe your grandmother invited Lily to go on one of her photographic safaris."

He began unpacking the second box. "You should have heard Nessa when she returned from her first time up in the hills. She couldn't stop raving about the experience. The herds of mustangs. The chance to sleep under the stars. The fact that she was so far from civilization. For a city girl, it was pure heaven."

"Lily may be pure country, but I think she'll feel the same way. Just being in the presence of a woman she admires is such a treat. And then there's the chance to learn all about the techniques of photography that none of us could ever help her with. I'm betting she'll be in little-girl heaven."

Luke tugged on a lock of Ingrid's hair. "Yes, but will her big sister survive?"

Ingrid blushed. "I'm trying to stay positive."

"And doing a damned fine job, girl. You're not used to sharing Lily with anyone." Mick closed the freezer and wiped his hands on a kitchen towel. "Now the biggest decision we have to make today is which packet I should open for our dinner." He looked at the two of them. "Anything in particular you craving?"

"Nothing I can say out loud." Luke covered his words with a cough.

Ingrid colored. "Your choice, Mick."

"Okay. I'll surprise you."

Luke looked out the window. "I don't see Nadine's truck."

Ingrid's smile faded. "I guess, after the show she put on for your family last night, she isn't ready for the quiet ranch life yet. She's probably gone back to Wayside." She turned toward the door. "I need to get busy with chores. First I'll tackle the barn, and then I'm going to ride to the hills and check on the herd."

Luke kept his tone casual. "We'll both tackle the barn

chores, and then we can check on the herd together and still get back in time for supper."

"Thanks, Luke." Ingrid's smile returned. "Okay. I'll see you in the barn."

When the door closed behind her, Mick put the kettle on before turning from the stove. "That was smooth, son. I'm guessing you intend to see she's never alone."

Luke's tone hardened. "You got that right."

"Then you believe that shooter didn't make a mad dash out of town?"

"Who knows? He could be lying low. He could even be gone. But what I do know is this: He's a coward, who used the cover of darkness to shoot at an innocent woman. That sort of lowlife doesn't usually give up."

"Then how do you plan on keeping her safe? You can't be everywhere."

Luke managed a lazy smile. "Neither can he. But if I'm at the right place at the right time, he won't get a second chance."

"It's such a relief to see my herd still standing."

Ingrid and Luke kept their horses to a steady pace as they moved among the cattle.

They'd tackled the hard, never-ending barn chores before riding across the hills. In the heat of the late afternoon their shirts were plastered to their skin, their hair damp beneath their hats.

Spotting a calf that seemed to be favoring one leg, Ingrid slid from the saddle. Kneeling in the grass, she began to probe the animal's leg.

Luke studied her, wishing he had his grandmother's skill with a camera. Whether wielding a pitchfork or tending one of her herd, she moved with all the grace and poise of a dancer.

He sat back, enjoying the way her faded denims molded every line and curve of her backside. The fitted tee she'd bought in town provided him with a clear view of the body she'd always kept hidden inside those baggy tops. Her hair, cut in a haphazard manner, fell in damp wisps around her face.

As she worked, Luke couldn't keep his eyes off her. She did everything with quiet competence. From mucking stalls to hosing down the barn floors, from spending hours in the blistering heat to checking out her herd, she moved with both authority and competence, two traits he admired.

Of course, if he were being honest, it wasn't admiration he was feeling. It was lust, pure and simple.

He watched the darkened trail of sweat along the back of her shirt and had a vision of his hands following that trail. With every movement she made, he felt his throat go dry and his temperature climb.

If he thought she was beautiful in those trademark baggy shirts, she was dazzling in these new, skin-hugging tees.

"Ready to head back?" He remained in the saddle, watching as she finally pulled herself up on her horse's back.

"I guess so. There doesn't seem to be any discomfort in the leg. I think he was just feeling frisky and missed a step."

He couldn't keep the grin from his lips. "Yeah. Feeling frisky can do that to a guy."

With a last look at the herd, she turned her mount

toward home with a smile. Their horses moved easily across a meadow alive with wildflowers.

As they splashed through Glacier Creek, Luke shot her a sideways glance. "That water looks mighty tempting. Care to go skinny-dipping with me?"

"Oh, you don't know how tempted I am."

At her words, his hopes soared.

She lowered her voice. "But Mick will have supper ready, and it wouldn't be fair to keep him waiting on his first day home with all that fancy food to choose from."

"Oh, I don't know about that." Luke slid from the saddle to drink, allowing his horse to do the same. "We wouldn't be that late."

Ingrid stared longingly at the cool water.

To add to her temptation, he caught a handful of water and tossed it at her. "Can't you forget your schedule for a little while and just play?"

"Oh. You want to play?" Without warning, she was out of the saddle and into the stream, kicking a spray of water in his face.

A sexy smile curved his mouth as he wiped water from his eyes. "Lady, you just sealed your fate."

He made a dive for her, but she evaded him and sent another spray of water his way. She almost managed to run away, but he caught her ankle and she dropped face-first into the water.

She came up sputtering, only to find him standing over her, wringing out his soaked shirt, dripping a steady stream of water on her head.

She wiped at her eyes before making a grab for Luke. His reflexes were quick, but his foot slipped on a submerged log and he fell backward. Ingrid was on him in a flash, ducking his head below water when he tried to surface.

With a shout, he wrapped both arms around her and dragged her under with him.

They came up laughing. But as they continued wrestling, each fighting to topple the other, their laughter suddenly died in their throats when Luke lowered his head and captured her mouth.

For a moment Ingrid pushed back, eyes wide with surprise. Then, without a word, she wrapped her arms around his neck and kissed him with a hunger that caught them both by surprise.

They lingered over the kiss, taking it deeper, then deeper still, until they were both struggling for breath.

With his chest heaving, Luke nibbled the corner of her jaw. "Lucky thing we have all this nice, cold water. Otherwise, at least one of us would have gone up in flames." He stared into her eyes. "For a woman who doesn't like to be kissed, you really seem to have mastered the art."

"Thanks." Her voice was a purr of pleasure. "I thought I'd give it a try."

"Let's try it again." He lowered his face, his lips moving ever so slowly over hers, tasting, teasing, until, on a sigh, she wrapped her arms around his waist. When her hands came in contact with his naked flesh, she paused for a heartbeat before sighing and giving herself up to the purely sensuous feelings that curled along her spine.

When she came up for air, she touched a hand to his cheek. "That's nice. I do like kissing you, Luke."

"That's good to know. Because I intend to do a whole lot more of it."

He dipped his head and took her mouth. The kiss spun on and on until their breathing grew strained and their hearts were pumping.

He reached for the ends of her damp shirt. When his fingers fumbled, she surprised him by slipping her hands beneath his and quickly tugging it over her head.

He stared down at her with a look of pure male appreciation. "Oh, lady. Now you've done it. If a kiss is an invitation, getting half naked is a royal command."

He gathered her close and kissed her with a depth of passion that had them both struggling for every breath. "You know I want you, Ingrid," he said with a raw voice. "But you need to tell me if I'm misreading…"

She pressed a finger to his lips. "Yes."

He went very still.

She smiled then. A sly, woman's smile. "Yes, Luke. I want the same thing you want."

"Oh, God." On a moan he scooped her up and strode to the shore, laying her down in the grass and stretching out beside her.

There were no words between them as he dragged her close and nearly devoured her in a kiss so hot, so hungry, it rocked them both.

She responded, pouring herself into every kiss, every touch, with a passion that had them rolling in the cool grass together, hands clutching, mouths seeking as they kicked off their boots and shed their jeans.

Seeing her reaching for the fasteners of her bra, he whispered, "Let me help you out of—" In his haste he tore it from her. "Sorry. I didn't mean to…" He shook his head. "I want to be gentle, but…"

"I'm not some delicate flower, Luke." She framed his face with her hands and smiled. "I'm just a woman."

"Never call yourself *just* a woman. You're the most beautiful"—he closed his hands over hers and leaned in to kiss her—"most dazzling woman I've ever known. And you've got me so tied up in knots..."

Against his lips she murmured, "I think we should untie those knots."

His look was fierce. "Oh, the things I want to do with you."

She touched a finger to his lips. "Stop talking and show me, cowboy."

It was all the invitation he needed.

His big hands moved over her, touching her with a reverence he hadn't even known was possible. He moved calloused palms along the smooth trail of her back, the flare of her hips, and then up her sides until his thumbs found the swell of her breasts.

When she sighed with pleasure, he lowered his mouth to nibble and tease until she writhed and nearly sobbed from the exquisite pleasure.

On a growl, he showered her with deep, wet kisses and frantic touches. He explored every inch of her body with lips and tongue and fingertips, hungry to show her all that he was feeling.

No longer hesitant, Ingrid followed his lead, moving her hands over his muscled torso, pausing to follow the line of corded muscles. Her fingertips trailed the flat planes of his stomach, causing him to tremble. But when she moved her hands lower, he sucked in a breath before stilling her movements. "Oh, baby. I thought I could wait. But I'm so hot..."

Aware that she'd gone still, he froze. "I didn't mean to scare you. I'll wait as long as you need me to. Just tell me you want this, too." For a moment he couldn't breathe. His heart forgot to beat. "I don't want to hurt—"

She stopped his words with a long kiss that had all his breath backing up in his throat. Against his mouth she whispered, "You're doing it again, Luke. Talking. Just show me."

They came together in an explosion of passion that staggered him.

Ingrid reared up, her aroused body taut as a bowstring, her arms circling his neck, as he felt himself sinking fully into her. He tried to slow the storm inside him, but he had no control left.

He began moving with her, climbing, his heart pumping, body slick with sheen.

The world around him had narrowed to this place, this moment, this all-consuming need. If the skies had opened up, if the herd had stampeded and threatened to crush them beneath their hooves, he couldn't have stopped.

A desperate need inside him, like a beast fighting for release, had been waging a terrible war, and now free, it took over his will. He was helpless to do more than ride the passion.

"Ingrid. God, Ingrid!"

The words were torn from Luke's throat as he began racing, climbing, frantic to reach the very pinnacle of the mountain. As the climax slammed into him, he could feel himself touching the very center of the sun before shattering into thousands of hot, blistering fragments.

* * *

They lay in the cool grass, waiting for the world to settle.

Luke's face was buried in the hollow of Ingrid's throat. His breathing was as ragged as her pulse beat.

"You okay?"

She responded by touching her palm to his cheek and a murmured, "Mmm."

"I was rough."

"Hmm."

He lifted his head to stare down at her. "I hurt you."

"No." She smiled.

"Ah. She speaks." That had him relaxing. He nibbled the corner of her lips. "You don't have to say a word. I'll do all the talking."

"Mmm."

"Do you know how long I've wanted this? Just this. With only you."

Her eyes snapped open and she focused on him. "Since you first saw me?"

"Wait. How could you know? Have I already told you?"

She moved her head languidly from side to side. "I just know. It was the same for me."

He looked thunderstruck. "Are you kidding? I thought you could barely tolerate me."

"Yeah. Barely. I spent a lot of time fighting it. But honestly? First glance, and I was gone."

She saw the look of pure male pleasure on his face before glancing skyward, where the sun was already beginning to dip behind the hills. "We'd better go. Mick will be waiting."

"Wait. I want to talk about this."

"We can do it later."

"Later? Like later tonight?"

She merely smiled, like a woman harboring secrets.

Luke got slowly to his feet before helping her to stand. He drew her into the circle of his arms and kissed her. "I hope you'll agree to round two tonight."

"You make it sound like fight night."

"More like wrestling. You're strong for a woman. I like that. Round two later?"

She tried for a cool look before breaking into a laugh. "How can I resist such a sexy request? I wouldn't miss it for the world."

"Oh, thank you, God." He kissed her again before handing her the soaked clothes that lay in a heap on the banks of the stream. "And maybe tomorrow we can try actually skinny-dipping instead of water war."

"We can try. But I think I know how it will end." She had to struggle into the wet clothes that now fit her like a second skin.

She sat in the grass to put on her boots before pulling herself into the saddle. Then, with Luke beside her, they headed down the hill and toward the barn.

Inside, as they unsaddled their horses and turned them into a corral, Luke gave her a long, knowing smile. "I hope Mick can have dinner ready as soon as we've showered. I can't wait to get you upstairs and see what other moves you know."

"I'm betting you have a lot more than I do."

In his best imitation of an old codger he muttered, "Just so you know. I'm more than happy to share whatever knowledge I have with you, little lady."

"And I'm more than happy to take you up on that, cowboy."

They were both laughing as they made their way inside, where the kitchen was perfumed with the most amazing fragrances. Then they hurried upstairs to shower and change, eager to get through the evening so they could continue their newly discovered love fest.

CHAPTER TWENTY-TWO

That was amazing, Mick." Luke sat back, sipping coffee, feeling on top of the world.

"Thanks to Yancy." The old man helped himself to a second slice of Yancy's chocolate layer cake and topped it with ice cream. He looked at Ingrid and Luke, who had spent the entire meal smiling and darting glances. "Want seconds?"

They both shook their heads.

"Then I may have to eat your share, too." With a satisfied grin, Mick began to eat slowly, savoring every bite. "Girl, your pa loved chocolate cake more than any man I've ever known."

Ingrid's smile grew. "Probably because nobody ever baked him one. The only chocolate cake he ever had came from that little grocery in Wayside."

Mick nodded. "And it never tasted like this."

Luke circled the table, topping off their cups. "That's because those things are full of preservatives."

Ingrid shot him a look. "Well, listen to you. How would you know about such things?"

He gave her a wicked smile. "Lady, there are so many things you don't know about me."

"I'll bet you can't wait to fill us in on the real Luke Malloy." She turned to Mick. "Get ready for the big reveal."

Luke replaced the coffeepot and sat down beside her, stretching out his long legs. "The fact is, most of what little I know about such things I learned from my brother Reed. Ever since he was a teen he's been obsessing about all the harmful foods we ingest. Right now he's raising a herd of cattle that's been, from birth, completely hormone and steroid free."

Mick paused, his fork halfway to his mouth. "How can he keep an entire herd healthy without drugs?"

"It's a lot of work. He has to be really vigilant. One virus could wipe out his herd in a single season. But he figures it's worth the effort. An Italian beef supplier has given him a limited contract, to test the market. If they like the numbers, it could become a huge success for our ranch."

Mick turned to Ingrid. "You remember when your pa thought about that very thing?"

She shook her head. "I don't remember. How long ago was that?"

He thought a minute. "I guess it was just about the time you were getting ready to leave for college. He was moping around, missing you even before you left. Then he sat me down one evening and started laying out his plans for a new breed of cattle."

Ingrid watched the old cowboy's eyes. "Was it a solid plan?"

Mick nodded. "It was a good idea, but like so many of Lars's plans, there was no follow-through. He got sidetracked by having to deal with Nadine's wild side, and the fact that without you, he'd have to be both ma and pa to Lily. After a while, it was like everything else he ever planned. Life got in the way, and his plans fell flat. And then, without warning, Lars was gone."

"Sounds like he was a man ahead of his time," Luke remarked.

Beside him, Ingrid had gone strangely silent at the mention of her father's passing.

"Reminds me of another time, when Lars and I were riding across the southern ridge of his land and he mentioned that a mining company had approached him about taking some soil samples." Mick grew thoughtful. "They were pretty sure there were valuable minerals on his land."

Luke smiled. "Lots of ranchers make more on mineral rights than they do on cattle. Did Lars pursue it?"

The old man shook his head, remembering. "Lars always figured he'd take care of things tomorrow."

"We all do." Ingrid's voice was subdued. "We think we'll live forever, and if we're good enough, and work hard enough, we'll see all our dreams come true."

Hearing the thread of pain in her words, Luke caught her hand. "There's nothing wrong with that."

She stared at their joined hands. "You don't strike me as being a fool, Luke."

"You think it's foolish to believe in happily-ever-after?"

"That's for Lily's storybooks." She tugged her hand free. "I'm a realist. If life has taught me anything, it's this. The selfish takers of this world walk all over the good and kind and decent people who believe in playing by the rules."

He leaned over and planted a kiss on the corner of her mouth. "You're a hard-hearted woman, Ms. Larsen. Someday Prince Charming will come along and force you to admit how wrong you've been." He stood and walked to the sink. "In the meantime, I'll let you use your amazing talent to dry the dishes I'm about to wash. It's the least we can do to thank Mick for this meal."

Mick grinned as he picked up his cup of coffee and started toward his room. "I'm hoping to watch another rerun of *Perry Mason*. Good night, you two. After all this food, I'll be lucky to stay awake past the first commercial."

When his door closed, Luke winked at Ingrid as she stepped up beside him, towel in hand. "I thought we'd never be alone. How fast can you dry?"

She shrugged. "I guess that depends on how fast you can wash."

He wiggled his brows. "Five minutes tops. Then I'm getting you upstairs, all to myself."

After turning out the lights, Luke followed Ingrid up the stairs. Once there he pressed her against the wall, kissing her like a man starved for the taste of her. She responded with a hunger of her own.

"I thought dinner would never end." He ran wet, nibbling kisses down her throat.

She sighed and angled her head, giving him easier access. "I thought you were fascinated by all Mick had to say."

"Honestly?" He fumbled with the buttons of her shirt. "I can't remember a thing he told us."

She started to laugh, but it turned into a little gasp as his mouth trailed the swell of her breast, covered by the merest wisp of silk.

When he tried to tug it free, she whispered, "Luke Malloy, if you rip another bra, I'll soon run out of underthings."

"That wouldn't be the worst thing."

"You're impossible." She put her hands to his chest, but instead of pushing him away she found herself tangling her fingers in the front of his shirt to drag him closer.

Against her throat he muttered, "I want you out of these clothes."

"You're also impatient."

"I am when it comes to you, woman." He picked her up and started down the hallway. "Your room or mine?"

Before she could say a word, he strolled past her door and continued to the room at the end of the hall. Instead of setting her down, he merely nudged the door open with his foot, then kicked it shut behind them.

He lowered her to her feet and slid her shirt from her shoulders before reaching a hand to the snaps at her waist. She did the same for him, tugging his shirt over his head before unsnapping his jeans. Then he unhooked her bra and dropped it to the floor with the rest of their clothes.

"That's better." He ran his hands across her shoulders, then down her arms, gathering her close enough to feel her flesh against his. A smile warmed his voice. "Oh yeah. Much better."

She moved one booted foot up his leg. "I need to get out of these."

"Yeah. Leave it to me." He eased her down on the edge of the bed and sat beside her, nudging off his own boots and slipping out of his denims. Then he surprised her by kneeling before her to slide off her boots and jeans.

In the darkened room, illuminated only by a spill of moonlight through the window, he ran his rough, calloused palm along her leg to her thigh before bending close to press a trail of kisses.

"Luke..."

When she put a hand to his shoulder, he stopped her. "Earlier today, I promised you I'd make up for being too hot and frantic. Now that we have all night, this is for you, Ingrid. For both of us. Long and slow and easy."

He took his time, exploring her body with lips and tongue and fingertips, until her body shuddered, and they were both mad with need. He lifted her to the center of the bed and lay down beside her. His rough hands moved over her, surprisingly gentle, like a whisper of silk. His kisses followed. Soft, gentle kisses that had her sighing with pure pleasure.

"You're so beautiful."

"I'm not." The words spilled from her lips before she could think.

"Why would you say that? If you've ever looked in a mirror, you have to know how you look."

"I don't bother much with a mirror. I've no use for one."

"Then you've never seen what I'm seeing."

"What do you see, Luke?"

"A beautiful woman who tries so hard to hide that beauty so she won't become like her mother. It's why you cut off all your hair. Why you try to hide your body." He kissed her mouth when she started to protest. "But you can never be like Nadine. She's a selfish child. And you're a woman. A beautiful, generous woman who puts her own needs aside to care for those who matter to her."

He ran a trail of kisses down her throat. "I want to be one of those who matter to you, Ingrid."

"You are." Her words were muffled against his temple.

He gathered her so close he could feel her heartbeat inside his own chest. And though his passion threatened to overtake him, he'd do anything to give her all the pleasure she deserved.

Once again, his caresses slowed. His kisses gentled as the never-ending chores were put aside. For this night, the danger that threatened was also forgotten.

Now there were only the long midnight hours of leisure that lay ahead. And the knowledge that they could uncover all the hidden pleasures they'd so long anticipated.

As their kisses deepened, and their touches grew more demanding, they lay steeped in glorious feelings that lifted them above anything they'd known. Not just pleasure, but need. A quiet, desperate need that had their bodies slick with sheen, their hearts pumping in anticipation.

"Luke. Please. Now."

At her soft plea, he moved over her with deliberate care, entering her and holding back as she welcomed him. Every movement, every thrust was slow, deep, measured.

"Luke. Oh, Luke, I can't stop. I can't..." Her words died as she was lost in the unbearable pleasure.

Even now, with his passion building, his heart pounding, Luke waited until he felt her reach the very top of the mountain and slip over to the other side before allowing himself to give in to his own shuddering climax.

For the longest time they lay, still joined, as their world slowly settled.

When at last he could move, he framed her face with his hands and looked down into her face.

She smiled up at him.

No words were needed as she wrapped her arms around his waist and clung to him.

He moved his weight off her, gathering her close.

"That was..." She sighed, letting the sound express what she was unable to put into words.

Against her temple he murmured, "Sleep awhile."

She had already gone limp in his arms, her breathing soft and steady.

He watched her, loving the way she looked in his arms. His woman.

The thought caught him by surprise before he smiled.

She was his. He didn't know quite how it had happened, or when she'd gone from just another rancher to this amazing, beautiful creature who'd captured his heart. Or how pure lust had morphed into something much more.

He'd always prided himself on his freedom. From rules. From doing all the ordinary things other men did.

Yet here he was, thinking about permanence, and settling down, and happily-ever-after.

Prince Charming he wasn't. The very thought had him

grinning again. But he did intend to let her know that there was such a thing as a happy ending. Her cynical little heart might not be ready to accept it quite yet, but he would just have to wear her down until he made a believer of her.

CHAPTER TWENTY-THREE

Ingrid felt the mattress shift and looked up to find Luke facing her on the edge of the bed, holding two mugs.

"Coffee?" She breathed deeply before sitting up. "Oh, Luke."

"Yeah. I thought we could both use some caffeine." He handed her a cup before settling in beside her.

She drank gratefully before glancing toward the window, to see clouds drifting past a full moon. Caught up in the heady excitement of their newly discovered freedom, they'd barely snatched any time to sleep. Instead, they'd loved in the dark with a passion that left them both breathless.

"Only a few hours left until morning."

"Is that disappointment in your voice?"

She chuckled. "Sorry. But if I'm going to be honest, I have to admit that I hate to see this night end."

"About that honesty of yours . . ." He looked at her. "Yesterday, by the creek, you said I had you at first glance."

She looked down. "I was hoping you'd forgotten."

"A guy doesn't forget an admission like that. Why did you act like you could barely stand me?"

She cupped her hands around the mug. "I guess it was a survival tactic."

"Survival?"

She drank, then set the mug on a nightstand beside the bed before looking at him. "I vowed I'd never be like Nadine."

He gave a snort of derision. "You couldn't be if you tried."

"You've said that before, but it isn't so. I saw the moves she made on you. And I was jealous. And that jealousy made me afraid that I'd do something stupid."

"You mean liking me would be stupid?"

"No. Yes." She blew out a breath. "It's complicated. When you started paying attention to me, I was afraid I'd find out that you pretended to like me so you could get close to Nadine."

"Has that happened before?"

She nodded. "I brought home a . . . friend from college to meet my family over spring break. The next day I caught him coming out of her room."

"What did your father have to say?"

"I didn't tell him. I ordered Roger to leave. He was gone within the hour, and I told my dad that he'd had a family emergency."

"And Nadine?"

"She left later that day with a smug, satisfied grin. Knowing Nadine, she probably arranged to meet him again in Wayside."

"Oh, baby." Luke set down his mug and gathered her into his arms. Against her temple he murmured, "Roger

Whatshisname was a damned fool. In fact, the biggest fool in the world."

Ingrid sighed, wrapping her arms around his waist. "I hope I'm not just as big a fool."

He drew a little away to look down into her face. "What's that supposed to mean?"

"I saw that same smug look on Nadine's face that night she came out of your room. I don't want to ask, but—"

"No."

At the harshness of his tone she blinked. "No? You mean don't ask?"

"That's exactly what I mean. Don't lower yourself to ask. Not now. Not ever." He put a finger beneath her chin and tipped up her face, forcing her to meet his steady gaze. "There may be a lot of fools in this world attracted to someone like Nadine, but I'm not one of them. The only woman I see is you, Ingrid. The only one I've seen since being in this house is you. Only you."

She took in a long, slow breath. And then, without a word, offered her trembling lips to him.

He took them with a hunger that caught them both by surprise.

"You brought more coffee?" Ingrid shoved wispy hair from her eyes before sitting up.

"Yeah. Along with some food." Luke climbed into bed and set a plate of toast and cold roast beef between them. "I've burned more energy during this night than I would in a week rounding up cattle."

A look out the window showed the first faint smudges of dawn coloring the horizon.

Ingrid touched a hand to Luke's arm. "I wish we could hold on to this night."

He held the beef and toast to her lips for a bite. "But think about the fun we can have by day. Or have you forgotten about skinny-dipping?"

That brought a smile to her eyes. "Oh, I haven't forgotten."

"Good. I hope this turns into one long, hot, sweltering day. We could make it last for hours."

"I think you're getting spoiled."

"If so, you're the one who spoiled me." He leaned over to indulge in a long, lazy kiss. "For any other woman."

"Am I supposed to feel guilty?"

He set aside the plate to drag her on top of him. Against her mouth he growled, "Not guilty. Just thoroughly satisfied, woman. Because that's how you've made me feel."

And then there were no words as they took each other on a slow, delicious ride of pure pleasure.

Luke and Ingrid were laughing together as they stepped into the mudroom to wash after their morning chores.

"'Morning, you two." Mick opened the oven and retrieved a tray of biscuits when they entered the kitchen. "Sounds like you were having fun out there."

"Luke boasted that he could clean more stalls."

Luke stood back grinning. "I guess you showed me."

Mick looked from one to the other. "So I guess you won that bet, girl."

"Of course I did."

"And Luke got to lean on his pitchfork and watch you do the bulk of the work."

"And it was a damned pretty sight to behold." Behind her, Luke winked.

Ingrid turned in time to see it. "You conned me."

"You can't blame a guy for being a guy."

At that, both Luke and Mick burst into laughter.

Instead of her usual irate response, Ingrid joined in while playfully punching Luke in the shoulder. "And here I thought I was being so smart."

Luke reached up and smoothed a lock of her hair from her eyes, and the two of them shared a smile.

Mick's look sharpened.

He set out a plate of scrambled eggs and another of crisp bacon and toast. "You two heading up to the herd again today?"

"Later." Luke held the plate toward Ingrid before helping himself to the food. "But first, we have a chore to see to here."

Ingrid shot him a questioning look. "A chore?"

He took his time tasting the eggs, the bacon, the toast. "I'm hoping you'll give me a haircut."

"A . . ." She lowered her fork to stare at his head. "A haircut? Why?"

"It's hot. I'm tired of dealing with it. It's time for a change."

Mick was grinning. "Amen to all of that."

Ingrid looked from Mick to Luke. "All right. But I'm wondering how you'll look without that ponytail."

"I guess you'll find out." Luke turned his attention to his breakfast, soon helping himself to seconds.

"You've got yourself a healthy appetite, son." Mick topped off their coffees.

"Yeah. I burned a lot of calories—" Luke stopped himself before adding, "out in the barn."

Ingrid shot him a sideways glance and covered the laughter that bubbled up by coughing behind her hand.

Mick placed the coffeepot on the stove and returned to his seat at the table. "Maybe I'll join you two up in the hills. Looks like a good day for a ride."

Luke swallowed back the groan that threatened before pushing away his half-filled plate. "Looks like I wasn't as hungry as I thought."

"That's all right, son." Mick dug into his food. "You'll have plenty of time to work up another hunger for some of Yancy's Fancy Chicken by tonight."

"Yeah, I will." Luke carried his dishes to the sink. "I'll get started on washing up here."

Ingrid joined him, picking up a towel. "Where do you want me to cut your hair? Upstairs in the bathroom?"

He shook his head. "I don't think you want all this hair on the floor up there. I think I'll just haul a chair outside and you can cut it in the yard."

"Good idea, son." Mick drained his coffee and sat back. "I think I'm going to enjoy watching this."

Luke took off his shirt and draped a bath towel around his shoulders before taking a seat in the yard.

Mick settled himself on the back stoop to watch as Ingrid stepped outside with a mirror, comb, and scissors.

Luke reached a hand to the elastic holding back his hair. Once free, his hair fell to his shoulders.

Ingrid ran a comb through it, and Luke gave a humming sound.

She paused. "Something wrong?"

"No. That feels good."

She leaned close, so Mick couldn't hear. "Why are you insisting on me doing this?"

"The truth?" He turned his head, keeping his voice low. "I don't like the idea of my hair being longer than my woman's."

My woman.

Her heart took a hard, quick bounce before the smile touched her lips, and then her eyes. "Really?"

"Yeah." He closed a hand over hers. "Now get on with it, woman."

She shoved the mirror into his hand. "Use that tone again and I just might shave your head."

He laughed and turned away.

She approached the job hesitantly, snipping a few strands of hair, pausing to watch as they drifted to the grass. With each snip she could feel Luke watching her in the mirror. Each time their gazes met and held, she felt a tiny shiver of heat along her spine. Despite all that they'd shared, it seemed strangely intimate to be cutting his hair.

Before long she got so caught up in the task, she found herself taking bigger clumps of hair and cutting, then cutting even more.

She indicated the mirror. "Well?"

"Shorter."

She cut more, then more. And finally, using an extension cord that snaked all the way from the mudroom, she used the electric trimmer to shave his sideburns and the back of his neck.

Mick ambled over. "Now that's a man's haircut, son. You look like you just stepped out of BillyBob's barbershop in Wayside."

Ingrid arched a brow. "I'll take that as a compliment, Mick. Luke? What do you think?"

He studied his reflection in the mirror before giving a nod of approval. "Perfect."

He stood and removed the towel, shaking the hair from it. Tossing it over the back of the chair, he leaned close to press a kiss to the top of her head. "You're hired."

She stepped back, feeling the heat on her cheeks. "Thanks. Did I do as good a job as Yancy?"

"Better. But I'd appreciate it if you keep that our little secret." He picked up the chair and carried it inside. When he did, Mick followed.

Luke set the chair by the table and picked up his shirt.

Mick cleared his throat. "There's something I'd like to talk to you about before you and Ingrid head back up to the hills."

Luke tucked his shirt into the waistband of his jeans before turning. "I thought you were coming with us."

"I thought so, too. But I'd like to ask you something first."

"I'm listening."

"You and Ingrid." Mick was staring intently. "Since she has no one else to care about her, I'm asking. I'm thinking something has changed between you. Is that so?"

Luke nodded. "I think you already know the answer. And for your information, you're not the only one who cares about her. She matters to me, Mick. She matters more than my own life."

Mick cleared his throat. "Thank you for your honesty, son. And you're right. I did know. I could tell just by looking at the two of you. But I wanted to hear it from you. I'm glad for you. And glad for her, too." He ducked his head before adding, "She's a loner. Doesn't let folks get close, 'cause of her ma."

"Yeah. That's why I intend to take great care of her feelings. They're special. She's special." Luke turned toward the door. "I think it's time we headed up to the herd." He turned to Mick. "You coming?"

The old man shook his head. "I think it's way too late for me to play chaperone. Since the day's half over, I'll just stay here. You two go ahead."

"We'll be home in time for supper." Luke strolled out.

Mick stood at the back door and watched as Luke conferred with Ingrid before she led two saddled horses from the barn. She and Luke pulled themselves into the saddle and started up across a meadow.

The sound of their easy laughter trailed on the summer breeze, warming the old man's heart.

CHAPTER TWENTY-FOUR

Luke walked to the corral, where Ingrid stood holding the reins of their horses.

She glanced behind him. "Where's Mick?"

"He decided to stay here." Luke took the reins from her and held them while she mounted.

"How did you talk him into that?"

Luke handed over her reins before pulling himself into the saddle. "He said he figured it was too late to insist on going along to chaperone."

She laughed, until she realized he wasn't kidding. "Chaperone? Why would he say that? Unless..." Her jaw dropped. "You told him about us?"

Luke met her wide-eyed stare. "No need. Mick's a smart guy. He figured it out by himself. But when he asked me to confirm or deny it, I figured he deserved the truth."

As she digested his words, she looked dismayed. Then,

slowly, her smile bloomed. "I bet Mick appreciated your honesty."

"Yeah. He feels responsible for you."

She flicked the reins and started off at an easy pace. "Through everything that's happened in my life, Mick's been my rock."

"He's a good guy. And you deserve some good guys in your life." Luke reached over and caught her hand. "I hope I'm one of them." The flare of heat was instantaneous. "I'll race you to the herd."

"You're just a glutton for punishment, aren't you?" With a quick laugh, she yanked her hand back and spurred her horse into a run.

For several moments Luke held his mount still as he drank in the sight of her. She poured herself into this simple challenge as she poured herself into everything. Full out. Nothing held back. She made love the same way.

She was simply magnificent.

She stirred his heart.

She owned his soul.

"The herd, at least what's left of it, is growing sleek and fat on this grass. I could look at them for hours." Ingrid slid from the saddle to examine yet another cow.

"I get it. But I'm growing impatient to go skinny-dipping. Come on, woman. This sun is hot."

She shielded the blinding sunlight from her eyes and looked up at him. "My, my, cowboy. I didn't realize you had an impatient streak."

"I didn't, either, until I met you. You should know that not all this sweat is from the sun. I get overheated just looking at you. I hope you're going to take pity on me soon."

She couldn't help laughing at his frown. "Okay. The herd's fine. Let's get to that stream." She pulled herself into the saddle and nudged her horse into a run.

Halfway down the hill, Luke passed her, and by the time she reached the banks of the creek, he was already slipping off his boots and tearing aside his damp shirt.

He tossed a bar of soap in the grass. "Last one in gets to wash my back."

"That's not fair…"

He shucked his jeans and waded into the water before turning and watching as she stripped down and made a mad dash into the water.

Luke's eyes narrowed as the water lapped at her hips, then her waist, and finally, as she reached his side, the water spilled over her breasts.

She held up the bar of soap. "Okay. You won. Turn around and I'll wash your back."

His grin was quick and dangerous. "Thanks. But all of a sudden winning or losing doesn't mean half as much as enjoying the view."

At her questioning look, he explained. "The most perfect woman in the world just stepped out of her clothes and into my arms. Baby, that's a view that will never get old."

He dragged her close and poured himself into a kiss.

Against his mouth she whispered, "If I'd known it meant so much to you, I'd have taken more time. Want to see my imitation of a model's walk?"

"Models can't hold a candle to you." He lowered his head, running hot kisses down her throat, then lower, as his mouth closed around one slick nipple.

She shivered and ran her hands over the corded muscles of his shoulders and down his back. Still holding the soap, she left a trail of suds everywhere she touched him.

He kissed her again, slower, softer. She returned his kisses with a hunger humming with need.

His gaze sharpened. "You in a hurry?"

"No. Yes."

At her admission his arm encircled her while his other hand moved between them until he found her. He kept his eyes steady on hers as he began to stroke.

She gasped and her eyes widened as wave after wave of pleasure rippled through her.

She was wonderful to watch as, lost in the moment, she reached a hand to his shoulder and clung as she rode the feeling until she reached a shuddering climax.

For a moment her eyes closed and she wrapped herself around him. With a smile of triumph he lifted her and started toward shore.

With her legs around his waist, arms around his neck, she buried her face in the little hollow between his neck and shoulder.

For the space of a heartbeat, he paused. "You know what you're doing to me, woman?"

"It's the least I can do after what you did for me."

"That was just the opening act." He continued walking to the shore, where he lay her down in the grass.

His eyes were hot and fierce as he lay beside her and gathered her close. "Now for the main event."

There were no words as they came together in a blaze of passion that put the sun to shame.

"I've never had a day that could compare with this." Ingrid lay in the circle of Luke's arms.

"You've never gone skinny-dipping?"

"Of course I have. Alone," she admitted. She leaned up on his chest to smile into his eyes. "I mean I've never taken a day to just...play."

He gave her a lazy smile. "Lady, you're the perfect playmate. Any time you want another day off, I'm your man."

"Yes, you are. My big, strong man." She played with the hair on his chest. Her tone grew thoughtful. "When I first met you, I thought you were"—she paused, searching for the right phrase—"too quick with a joke, and too good-looking, to be anything but a tumbleweed. I figured you'd be gone the minute you were strong enough to stand without falling over. I certainly never intended to trust you. And especially with my"—she looked up to find him watching her—"heart."

He reached up to frame her face with his hands. "Thank you." At her raised brow he added, "For trusting me enough to say the words. I know that isn't easy for you."

Their kiss was soft. Sweet. As though sealing a very special bond.

The sun burned hot overhead. The summer breeze whispered over their heated flesh. The sound of the stream rushing over rocks formed a background of music that seemed to match the rhythm of their sighs.

As their kiss deepened, it exploded into something much more. Heat. Hunger. And a yearning of the heart that needed to be answered.

This time, as they came together, they savored each kiss, each touch, like lovers who knew they had all the time in the world to explore this newly discovered passion. And intended to make every moment count.

* * *

Luke and Ingrid held hands as their horses ambled across the high meadow toward home.

"Still worried about Lily?" Luke asked.

A laugh escaped Ingrid's lips. "I can't believe I'm admitting this. I haven't given her a single thought today."

Luke grinned. "I guess you had other things on your mind."

"Naughty things."

He couldn't help laughing. "Sorry. That's not the way I see it. But then, your naughty is really nice."

"I think you're a bad influence, cowboy."

"Or a good one. It all depends on your point of view." He squeezed her hand. "I hope Mick has supper ready. It just dawned on me that I'm hungry." He shot her a sideways glance. "Probably all those calories I've been burning."

She studied his toned body. "I guess that's one way to stay in shape."

"The best way." He withdrew his hand. "Come on. One last race to see who gets home first."

As he nudged his horse into a run, Ingrid drew back on the reins for a moment. Did he realize he'd just called her place home?

She didn't want to take the time to mull it over. It might have been a slip of the tongue. Or it might be that her place had become as special to him as it was to her.

Either way, right now she needed to get there first. There was still time to beat Luke. It just wasn't in her nature to ignore a challenge.

* * *

Mick looked up as they stepped into the kitchen. "You two have been gone a long time. The herd all right, or have more of them gone missing?"

"The herd's fine." Luke rolled his sleeves. "It's so hot, we couldn't resist a dip in the creek."

Mick shot him a speculative look before turning to Ingrid. "That so?"

Her cheeks turned a becoming shade of pink before she inhaled the wonderful fragrance coming from the oven and tried to change the subject. "Are you baking bread?"

"Just heating up rolls." The old cowboy grinned. "To go with Yancy's Fancy Chicken."

At the sound of a truck's engine, they glanced out the window.

Seconds later they gathered around the back door as Lily bounded toward them, trailed more slowly by Grace and Frank.

"Oh, Lily." Ingrid hugged her little sister fiercely. "I've missed you. How was your very first safari?"

"It was so much fun. But first I have to tell you..." Her words were forgotten as she stared at Luke, eyes wide. "You cut off all your hair."

"Well, actually it was Ingrid who did the cutting."

"Why?"

He shrugged. "I asked her to."

"Why?"

Another shrug. And then a lazy smile. "I figured it was time."

"More than time, sonny boy." Frank was grinning from ear to ear. "Don't you agree, Gracie Girl?"

His grandmother was studying him with a critical eye.

She touched a hand to his face. "Oh, Luke. With your hair short, you're the image of your father."

"There's nothing you could have said that would make me happier than that." He bent to kiss her cheek. "I consider that the ultimate compliment, Gram Gracie."

Ingrid closed a hand over her little sister's shoulder. "What were you about to tell me?"

"Oh yeah." Lily turned to Frank and Grace, who were smiling broadly. Her voice was high-pitched with excitement. "It's the reason why we're home early. While we were up in the hills, we found our missing herd, Ingrid."

CHAPTER TWENTY-FIVE

Y ou found our herd?" Ingrid could barely contain her surprise. "Where? When? Are they injured? Are they safe? Are they all accounted for?"

Lily turned to Luke's grandmother. "You tell her, Gram Gracie."

The older woman took up the story. "On the trail of our herd of mustangs, we came up over a rise and spotted, far below in a valley, a large herd of cattle. As far as we could tell, there were no wranglers around to tend them. They appeared to be on their own and isolated from any other herds. It was then that we realized we were on Bull Hammond's property."

At the mention of Ingrid's neighbor, Luke swore.

His grandfather surprised him by saying, "Hold on, sonny boy. I was just as upset as you when we checked their brands and realized they were part of Ingrid's herd. I figured I'd report that thieving crook to the sheriff the minute we got phone service. We'd just started driving them back toward Ingrid's place when Bull himself rode out and demanded to know why we were crossing his land with cattle. When we explained what we'd found and showed him the brand, he was shocked."

"You mean, he pretended to be shocked? That lying—"

Luke started to speak, but his grandfather held up a hand. "Now maybe Hammond's a really good actor, but he has me convinced. He seemed genuinely surprised to see those cattle on his land. When I confronted him with what I suspected, Hammond said he had nothing to do with the herd's disappearance."

"Then how did they end up on his property?"

"He didn't have a clue. It's all pure speculation, of course, but he suggested they could have simply wandered off, each one following the leader, and then found themselves stranded in a deep ravine with lush grass and a meandering creek and no reason to leave."

Luke was staring at his grandfather as if he'd just grown a second head. "And you believe that?"

The old man shrugged. "Like I said, Hammond seemed as surprised by this as we were."

"What else could he say when he was caught red-handed?" Luke plucked his cell phone from his pocket and dialed the sheriff's number before repeating what he'd just learned.

A minute later he announced to the others, "Eugene said he and Archer will be out here first thing in the morning. But to add weight to what Hammond told you, the sheriff assured me that nobody else in the county has reported the loss of any cattle. Ingrid's herd is the only one affected. Not that it proves Hammond's innocence, since he still seems to be the one who would benefit the most from Ingrid's loss. But the sheriff will make that determination when he's had time to look into this further."

Ingrid turned to Frank. "Where are my cattle now?"

"Back on the hill with the rest of your herd."

She gave a deep sigh. "Oh, wouldn't it be wonderful if this nightmare is over?"

"That doesn't explain..." Seeing Lily's questioning look, Luke felt a wave of self-annoyance and bit back the rest of his words.

They'd taken such pains to keep the dangerous facts as far away from the little girl as possible, and now in his anger, he'd almost revealed that gunshot through Ingrid's window.

Lily turned to Frank. "Is Ingrid right, Grandpop Frank? Are all our troubles over?"

Frank gave her an encouraging smile. "I don't know, darlin', but this gives us some hope. And at this point we'll take all the hopeful signs we can get."

For all his upbeat words, the old man exchanged a silent admonition with his grandson.

Seeing it, Grace tried for a further distraction. "Oh my, Mick. Something smells amazing."

"That would be Yancy's fine food." Mick grinned. "Ever since our return from your ranch, we've been eating like kings." He motioned toward the table. "Supper's ready, and there's enough for everyone. I'd be proud to have you join us."

While Lily and Grace and Frank washed up in the mudroom, Mick added three more place settings at the table.

"Perfect timing," Luke muttered to his grandfather as he returned to the kitchen.

"When have you ever known me to miss a meal?" The old man winked.

They gathered around the table and began passing trays of chicken and potatoes au gratin, a salad of field greens, and dinner rolls warm from the oven.

While they ate, Lily regaled them with all she'd seen while in the wilderness.

"We found a herd of mustangs. And we took lots and lots of pictures." The little girl turned. "Didn't we, Gram Gracie?"

"We certainly did."

Luke offered the basket of rolls to his grandmother. "Did you find your long-absent white stallion?"

"Unfortunately we didn't."

Lily broke in. "But we found a spotted black-and-white one, and he didn't even run away when he saw us. Did he, Gram Gracie?"

"No, he didn't. I told Lily that sometimes he looked tame enough to be a saddle horse posing for our camera. But whenever I'd get too complacent, he would prove to us just how wild and free he really is."

Lily turned to her big sister. "Wait 'til you see my pictures, Ingrid. Gram Gracie let me use her telephoto lens and even her wide-angle lens, and I'm going to help her frame some of them for you." She put a hand to her mouth. "Oh, I wasn't supposed to say anything about that. It's our secret."

Ingrid gave her little sister a gentle smile. "Well, then, I guess I'll just have to forget you ever said that."

"Good. 'Cause I'm saving it for your birthday."

"When would that be?" Luke asked.

"Next month." Lily spooned more potatoes onto her plate before digging in. "And now that we found the missing herd and I've got a special present, it's going to be the best birthday ever." She turned to Ingrid. "Isn't it?"

"You bet."

Under the table, Luke caught Ingrid's hand and squeezed. The two shared a look.

Seeing it, Frank and Grace exchanged a look of their own.

"…and we slept in bedrolls under the stars." Long after Frank and Grace had taken their leave, and Ingrid led Lily upstairs to say her prayers and get ready for bed, Lily was still recounting every detail she could recall of her safari with Ingrid, while Luke lounged in the doorway. "And we hiked up one side of the mountain and down the other, and Gram Gracie said I'm the best safari partner she's ever had, next to Matt's Nessa. She said I never get tired and I never complain when it gets too hot or too cold. And I love the herds of mustangs as much as she does. And besides, I love taking pictures as much as she does. She said I'm a natural photographer. She called me gifted. And…" She paused a moment to catch her breath.

"It sounds as though this trip was even better than you'd hoped it would be." Ingrid turned down the blanket and waited until Lily climbed into bed.

"It was. And you know what was the best?"

"Let me guess. Either getting photography tips from an expert or coming across our herd on your way back." Ingrid bent down to kiss her good night. "Which was it?"

Lily wrapped her arms around her sister's neck and

hugged her fiercely. "It was pretending that Gram Gracie was my very own grandma, and that Grandpop Frank was my very own grandpa, and that I could go places with them my whole life."

Luke stepped back into the shadows, unwilling to let Ingrid and Lily see how deeply those words affected him while he wiped at a speck of dust that made his eyes water.

"I love you, Ingrid. And I missed you."

"I love you, too, Lily. And I missed you something awful."

"I'm glad you had Luke here while I was gone. 'Night, Luke," Lily called.

"'Night, Li'l Bit."

Her smile deepened. "That's something else I missed. I missed having you call me that."

Composed, he poked his head in the doorway. "Then I'll have to say it twice tomorrow."

The sound of her giggles had his smile returning.

When Ingrid walked out of the room, he caught her hand. For a moment she simply rested her head on his shoulder, sighing deeply, before stepping back.

He pressed a kiss to her cheek, which still bore the dampness of tears. "It's nice to have her back home."

"Yeah. I was thinking the same thing." As they made their way down the stairs, she added, "Now I can breathe."

Ingrid, Luke, and Mick were enjoying their longnecks in a rare moment of quiet in front of the fire.

Luke turned to the old foreman. "You think Bull Hammond hid the herd in that ravine?"

Mick shrugged and tipped up his bottle. "Don't know

what to make of it. But I'm thinking a man would be pretty foolish to steal a neighbor's cattle and think he could keep them hidden for long."

Luke frowned. "It's no secret I don't trust him. Still..." He took a drink before setting aside his beer. "The fact that he didn't have any wranglers keeping them in place has me second-guessing myself. If I stole someone's cattle and hid them somewhere, I'd make damned certain they'd stay hidden."

"That's the problem I have with this." Ingrid stood and began to pace. "Even during roundup, with plenty of wranglers to keep watch, there are always strays that manage to break free of the herd and wander off track. Up there in the hills, with no one around to chase after them, if one old cow made a break for it, who's to say the rest didn't just blindly follow?"

Luke watched her pace. "Are you thinking that the disappearance of your herd isn't connected to the gunshot through your window?"

She paused. Sighed. "I don't know what to think anymore. None of this makes sense."

Mick rubbed at a spot between his eyes. "Don't forget all those other incidents. The range fire. Tippy." He saw Ingrid blanch and softened his tone. "And then there's the other gunshot. The one that caused the mustangs to stampede. The gunshot that brought Luke here."

Luke caught Ingrid's hand, causing her to pause in her pacing. "At least that one ended up being a good thing."

She managed a smile. "Yes. But at the time, I was scared to death."

"You've got a funny way of showing fear, woman."

His words had Mick chuckling. "He's got you there,

girl. You dragged him in here in such a temper, it was like unleashing the wrath of God."

"I thought he'd been the one who fired that shot. I figured he wasn't going to survive the night. And then, when he did, I thought he was such a pain in the..."

"Go ahead. You can say the word."

"I was going to call you a pain in the neck."

"Sure you were."

That had them all forgetting their tensions and bursting into laughter.

Ingrid settled down on the sofa beside Luke and helped herself to a long pull on his beer before handing him back the bottle. As their fingers brushed, they shared a secret smile.

"I'm just glad Eugene Graystoke will be here tomorrow to sort it all out." Luke stretched out his legs toward the warmth of the fire. "I'm still not convinced that Hammond is innocent. I saw the fury in his eyes when he accosted you in the barn. He was a man on a mission. And after that scene, half your herd just up and disappeared. And now they're found on his land. If that doesn't point to guilt, I don't know what does."

Mick stared into the flames, his tone thoughtful. "There was bad blood between Lars and Bull, though I never knew what caused it. Lars always played his cards close to his vest." He eased himself up from his easy chair and picked up the empty bottle. "I'm turning in now. I'll say good night."

"'Night, Mick." Ingrid blew him a kiss.

"See you in the morning," Luke called.

When they were alone, Luke passed his beer to Ingrid, who took a sip before passing it back to him. He drained it before linking his fingers with hers. "Ready to head up-stairs?"

She nodded.

At the door to her room she paused. "I think I'd better sleep in here tonight."

"Okay. I get it. Lily's back." Luke reached around her to turn the knob.

When he remained in the hallway, she wrapped her arms around his neck and drew him inside her room before kissing him.

He gave a shaky laugh. "It's a really mean thing, to kiss me like this and then send me on my way."

"Who says I'm sending you away?"

"I thought..." His smile grew. "You want me to stay?"

"Not the night. Lily has a way of slipping into my bed when something wakes her. But I'd love it if you'd stay awhile."

"Just to rub your back or something?"

She laughed. "It's the 'or something' I'm hoping for."

He gathered her close and kissed her until they were both breathless. Against her mouth he whispered, "Woman, that's the kind of invitation I just can't resist."

CHAPTER TWENTY-SIX

I'll dispose of this." After finishing morning chores, Luke reached for the handles of the honey wagon and easily pushed it out of the barn.

When he returned, Ingrid and Lily had already peeled off their work gloves and were hanging their pitchforks on hooks along the wall of the barn.

They looked up when the sheriff's car rolled up, trailed by a second car driven by his deputy.

The two men stepped out and approached the barn.

"'Morning, Ingrid." Sheriff Graystoke touched the brim of his hat. "Lily. Luke."

Behind him, his deputy, Archer Stone, merely nodded a silent greeting.

Where the sheriff was stocky, with broad shoulders and a slightly bulging middle, his deputy was trim and walked with a swagger. Eugene Graystoke's uniform was rumpled and well-worn. Archer Stone's was crisp, his badge polished to a high shine.

"Bull Hammond showed me where your cattle were found." The sheriff flipped a page in his dog-eared notebook. "Then we followed the route back to your property, where your herd is summering. It's a direct path from there to Hammond's ravine."

Luke's eyes narrowed.

Before he could say a word, Ingrid touched a hand to her sister's shoulder. "Why don't you go inside, honey, and let Mick know we'll be in for breakfast in a few minutes?"

"Okay." Lily skipped away.

When she was gone, Luke's voice was low with a growing anger. "Are you saying, after a simple interview, you believe Hammond when he denies having anything to do with this?"

Archer stepped up beside the sheriff, his eyes narrowed on Luke. "Watch your mouth, Malloy."

"I'll let you watch it for me." He directed his words toward the sheriff. "What are you saying?"

Eugene kept his tone level. "I understand your frustration, Luke. I'm saying it's not impossible to make the case that Ingrid's cattle wandered away and found themselves in that ravine on Hammond's land."

"They wandered away from the rest of the herd and then just stayed there?"

"With enough lush grass and an endless supply of water in that stream, why would a herd make an effort to leave? Especially since they were surrounded by steep hills. It would have been much easier for them to wander in than to wander out."

"And this is the end of it?" Luke's tone was pure ice. "You're just going to walk away and give Bull Hammond the benefit of the doubt?"

"That's enough." Archer reached out a closed fist toward Luke, and Eugene slapped it back, shooting his deputy a flinty look.

"I know tempers are flaring. Let's not add fuel to the fire."

He turned a resigned look toward Luke and Ingrid. "My hands are tied. Unless there's a way to prove this was a deliberate act, carried out to cause harm, I can't do anything more than watch and wait."

"You mean wait until the next incident? Like the range fire that destroyed Ingrid's entire wheat crop? Like the death of her herding dog that looked suspiciously like poison? Like the shot fired that caused a herd of mustangs to stampede and nearly kill me?"

"That's right, Luke. And all of them without a shred of evidence to back up any claim that they were done with malice."

"And the shot through her bedroom window? Was that an unexplained incident, as well?"

"That's an entirely different thing. It's clear that was no accident. That one was a deliberate act of violence. And I intend to continue to pursue any and all leads."

"How many leads do you have so far?"

"Just one. Hammond claims to have been at the diner in Wayside at the time of that shot. Four of his wranglers backed up his claim. But I haven't had a chance to interview Lon Wardell yet."

"Forget Wardell." Archer Stone glanced at Ingrid before asking loudly, "What about Nadine Larsen?"

Ingrid's eyes betrayed her pain before she looked away.

Eugene said, "I haven't interviewed her, either."

Luke drew an arm around Ingrid's shoulders. "Thanks, Sheriff."

Ingrid seemed to pull herself together. "Would you two like to come inside for coffee?"

"Sorry, no time." Eugene touched a hand to the brim of his hat. "Archer and I will be on our way, ma'am. You know to call me if anything at all happens."

"Yes, thank you."

Ingrid stood beside Luke as the two police officers settled into their vehicles and drove off in a cloud of dust.

When they were gone, Ingrid turned to Luke, eyes blazing. "How dare the deputy hint that Nadine could have fired that shot."

"I know it hurt you. And I admit that I wanted to put my fist in his face. But I guess we have to accept that everyone is a suspect."

She shook her head emphatically. "Not everyone. Not Nadine."

"And why not?"

Her mouth was a thin, tight line of denial. "She may be guilty of a lot of things, but she would never try to kill me."

Luke realized with horror that she was dangerously close to tears. But was it from anger at what Archer had suggested? Or fear that the deputy could be right in his suspicions? From the look in her eyes when the question had first been posed, it was clear it had never occurred to her that Nadine would be a suspect. In truth, it hadn't occurred to Luke, either.

Banking his own emotions, he caught her hand and experienced a deep well of tenderness as he drew her close.

Against her temple he muttered, "Come on. We both need food."

"Great breakfast, Mick." Luke polished off his third cup before getting up from the table. "Let's do the dishes, Li'l Bit. You wash, I'll dry."

"Okay." Lily deposited her dishes in the sink and turned on the taps.

When Ingrid started to push away from the table, Luke stopped her with a hand to her shoulder. "Relax. We've got this."

Her smile returned. "All right. Then I guess I'll head to the barn to saddle up. I want to see my herd."

"I'll go with you as soon as we finish here." Luke turned to Lily. "Want to ride along?"

She shook her head. "I promised Mick I'd show him some of my pictures from the safari."

Ingrid paused at the back door. "When do I get to see them?"

Lily gave a mysterious little smile. "You have to wait until your birthday."

"You mean I can't see any of them?"

The little girl shrugged. "Maybe. I guess I can show you some, but not all. That would spoil my surprise."

"I can't believe I have to wait a month to see what Mick will see today." Ingrid was muttering and shaking her head as she left the house.

In the kitchen, Luke turned to Lily. "You've really got her going, Li'l Bit. I hope those pictures are worth it."

"Wait 'til you see, Luke." Lily's smile was radiant. "She's going to love her birthday surprise."

* * *

Ingrid and Luke reined in their mounts at the top of the hill and stared around with matching looks of appreciation.

"Oh." Ingrid let out a long, slow breath. "It's so good to see my herd together again. I really thought they were gone for good."

"Yeah." Luke remained on the perimeter of the herd as she urged her horse into the very center of the milling cattle.

She dismounted and led her mount as she walked among them, the look on her face telling him more than any words just how relieved she was feeling.

Nearly an hour later she returned to his side, where he stood holding the reins of his horse.

He reached over and took her hand. "I can tell you're feeling much better."

"I am." She gave him a bright smile. "I'm still not quite ready to believe Bull was telling the truth." She looked up into his eyes to gauge his reaction. "But I have to admit there's a possibility they just wandered off."

"Okay." He squeezed her hand. "I'll take that into consideration, though I'm still suspicious. It's hard for me to declare that hothead Hammond innocent. What about the other incidents?"

She shook her head. "I don't know. A part of me wants to believe they were just a coincidence. But in my heart, I know better." She glanced at their joined hands. "I'm so glad you're here with me, Luke. But I know you're neglecting your own ranch. How much longer can you afford to stay?"

"As long as it takes." He gathered her close and pressed his mouth to her temple. "Until all of this is resolved, I'm not going anywhere." As they mounted, he indicated the stream in the distance. "Got time for a quick dip?"

She laughed. "Will we get any swimming in?"

"Probably not. But if nothing else, we'll get in some hot exercise."

"Hot? You just said the magic word." She urged her horse into a run. Over her shoulder she called, "Win, lose, or draw, it's definitely time for you to scrub my back, cowboy. And then we can both cool down."

As they drew near the house, Luke caught the reins of Ingrid's mount. "You go ahead inside and I'll unsaddle these two and turn them into the pasture."

"Thanks." She slid from the saddle and started toward the back door.

Inside, she washed up at the sink before stepping into the kitchen. "I'm back, guys…"

She stared around with a puzzled look. The kitchen was empty, the table clear. There was nothing on the stove or in the oven. The usual tantalizing scents were absent.

She poked her head in Mick's room off the kitchen. "Hey, sleepyhead, it's dinnertime. Wake—"

His bed was empty.

"Mick! Where are you?" She raced toward the parlor. Seeing it empty, she hurried up the stairs and stepped into Lily's room, which was also empty. Alarmed, she ran down the stairs and out to the barn.

Luke was just rounding the corner of the barn, carrying the saddles toward a stall. Seeing her in the doorway, he frowned. "I had to haul feed and water to the pasture. You need to remind Mick and Lily about their chores—"

He caught the look on her face and let the saddles drop. "What's wrong?"

"The house is empty."

"Maybe Mick and Lily needed something in town."

"The truck is still parked by the back door. Besides, if they were leaving, even on horseback, they would have left me a note."

"Maybe you missed it."

She was shaking her head. "Mick wouldn't leave without leaving me a message. Oh, Luke, I'm—" Her words died as she caught sight of a booted foot sticking out from one of the stalls.

Seeing the direction of her gaze, Luke raced to the spot.

"Oh, no. Mick." She dropped to her knees beside the still form of the old man, who lay in a pool of blood.

At the sound of her voice, Mick's lids flickered and he struggled to sit up. With a moan he fell back.

"Don't move, Mick. Thank heaven you're alive. You took a nasty fall. How did this happen?"

Luke dropped down beside her as Mick struggled to get the words out. "Hit. Shovel. Wardell..." Mick touched a hand to his bloody head. "Grabbed...Lily."

"Lily? Where? Why?" Terror had Ingrid by the throat. She could barely get the words out.

The old man moaned, before his eyes flickered, then closed.

"Mick." Ingrid clutched at the old man's shoulders. "Tell me where he's taken Lily. Please."

Luke touched a hand to Mick's throat. "His pulse is feeble. Probably shock. We can't move him. I need some blankets."

"But Lily—"

"You looking for the brat?" A whispered voice had both Luke and Lily frozen as a muzzle of a pistol was pressed against the back of Ingrid's head. "She's right over there."

When Luke made a move to get to his feet, he was hit so hard it sent him crashing into the side of the stall, causing the wood to splinter and fall, revealing Lily, bound and gagged, in the adjoining stall. As Luke struggled to get his bearings and stand, a shot rang out, and he felt a river of blood begin to spill from his arm as it dropped helplessly to his side.

Ingrid let out a bloodcurdling scream.

"That's just a taste of what I've got in store for you, Malloy."

While Luke shook his head, trying to clear his vision, Lon Wardell's voice echoed off the walls of the barn. "You move a muscle, cowboy, and your woman's dead."

CHAPTER TWENTY-SEVEN

Luke watched in amazement as Ingrid spun toward Wardell, landing a fist in his midsection.

"Why you..." Instead of disarming him, it made him even more furious. He brought the pistol across her temple, dropping her to her knees.

Before she could clear her vision, her arms were twisted painfully behind her back and her wrists bound with plastic restraints. Wardell forced her to her feet and shoved her toward her little sister.

Blood trickled from a cut on Lily's head. Tears flowed freely down her face, but no sound came from her mouth, because it had been taped shut.

Once there, Ingrid was knocked to the straw and her ankles tightly bound.

"Oh, honey..." Ingrid attempted to soothe Lily, but her words were halted by a second blow to the head that had her moaning in pain.

"Not one word. You hear me?" Wardell stood over them, his face twisted into a mask of fury. "The brat tried talking, and I taught her a lesson. You can learn from that, or you can learn the hard way." He gave a shrill laugh. "Your choice, girlie."

Ingrid bit down hard on the cry that threatened to escape her lips.

"Now that you understand the rules..." Wardell sat on a bale of straw, holding the pistol in one hand, while tilting a bottle of whiskey to his lips. "Isn't this cozy?"

As Luke struggled to tear off the sleeve of his shirt, he kept his gaze firmly on Wardell.

"Look at that. A Boy Scout." The gunman seemed to be enjoying Luke's clumsy attempt to stem the flow of blood.

Once Luke ripped the sleeve free, he wrapped it tightly around the gunshot wound, using his teeth to help tie a knot. As he fumbled with it, he managed to slip his cell phone from his shirt pocket. He knew he couldn't look at it, or it would draw Lon's attention. Instead, he blindly ran his finger down the list of favorites. Knowing many of his family could be in the hills, with no service available, the only ones he could count on were Yancy and the Great One. He pressed the speed dial, hoping he'd counted correctly. Hoping they were home, or at least in an area of phone service. As he buried the phone beneath a layer of straw, he prayed whoever answered would persist in listening long enough to realize the importance of what he was hearing.

Desperate to hide any sounds that might give away what he'd done, Luke decided to risk it all by shouting, "Why don't you tell us why you're doing this, Wardell?"

He knew breaking the code of silence would bring their attacker's wrath down on him, but it was the price he was willing to pay in order to keep Wardell's focus off Ingrid and Lily and to keep him talking to mask whatever sounds would be made by the phone.

"Weren't you paying attention, Malloy?" Lon got to his feet and looked over at Luke. Seeing the tourniquet he'd fashioned, he threw back his head and laughed. "Well now. You really are a Boy Scout, aren't you? A pity I'm not one of those do-gooders." He took aim with his pistol. "Let's see what the Boy Scout can do with this." With a swagger, he walked closer and shot point-blank into Luke's leg, sending up a fountain of blood.

Across the room, Ingrid let out a scream and struggled frantically against her restraints.

Wardell turned away and ambled back to the bale of straw as though he'd done nothing more than take a stroll.

Through a haze of blinding pain, Luke fought to remain conscious as he tore away the rest of his shirt and struggled to wrap the gaping wound.

"Now, where was I?" Lon downed another slug of whiskey before twirling the pistol like a professional gunslinger.

It was clear that he was enjoying his newly discovered sense of power. "All those good citizens who refer to me as some stupid down-and-out drunk ought to see the three of you. I guess we know who holds all the cards now.

"Oh yes. The reason I'm here." A slow, dangerous smile curved his mouth as he turned his attention to Ingrid. "You're going to sign over your rights to the cattle on this ranch. And if you do it nice and clean, I'll do the same to you. Give me any trouble, I'll shoot the brat just like I shot your lover boy. And I intend to shoot him a lot more times before I put him out of his misery. But if you're a good girl, I'll kill the two of you with the first shot, sparing you a whole lot of pain and misery."

Yancy was having a fine day. Earlier he'd picked fresh strawberries from his garden beside the house, and now he was baking Miss Grace a glorious torte, which he intended to layer with mounds of whipped cream and sweet strawberries. In his mind he could already see her smile blooming when she took her first bite.

"If you could spare a few of those berries, Yancy, my boy, I'd be grateful."

At Nelson's words, the cook looked over with a quick grin. "Says the man with the famous appetite. When's the last time you ate only a few of anything, Great One?"

"You've got me there, Yancy." The old man patted his stomach. "But I've discovered a yearning for fresh strawberries ever since I saw you washing them earlier."

"I figured as much." Yancy gave a warm laugh. "That's why I set aside a bowl just for—"

The ringing of his phone had him glancing toward the kitchen counter, where he'd set it earlier. "I'll just get this and then I'll fetch those strawberries."

"Or you could let it ring and get the strawberries first."

Yancy was still chuckling when he picked up the phone and glanced at the caller ID. "Hey. Hello, stranger." To Nelson he mouthed the word *Luke*.

Walking toward the refrigerator, he opened the door while asking, "When are you bringing those pretty little Larsen sisters back for another visit?"

He took out the covered bowl of berries he'd set aside for Nelson. When he straightened, he looked at the phone. "That's odd. No one's there..." And just as he was about to disconnect the call, thinking the wires were crossed, he heard a strange, muted sound coming from the phone. It sounded like a man's voice, distant, raspy. He couldn't place the voice, but it sounded angry. And then he heard a sound that had him going rigid with shock.

It was, without a doubt, a gunshot—followed by a woman's scream.

Sheriff Eugene Graystoke's day had gone from bad to worse. After that scene with Luke and Ingrid Larsen, he'd hoped for some good news. But now, as he did a follow-up on Lon Wardell, his mood darkened.

According to the bartender at Barney's in Wayside, Wardell had been on a weeklong bender, after his usual drinking companion, Nadine Larsen, had walked out on him following a bitter argument. By the time Lon left, after running out of money to pay his enormous bar tab, there was murder in his eyes. Even the toughest cowboys who frequented Barney's had backed off, knowing he was running on a very short fuse.

Eugene figured he'd warn Ingrid and then start looking for Nadine, just in case Wardell tried to hit her up for money. Though Ingrid had defended her mother, the sheriff had his doubts. In his years on the job, Nadine's name had appeared on too many drunk-and-disorderly complaints to count. But even a tough woman like Nadine, who could hold her own against most cowboys, deserved protection from a mean drunk like Wardell. There was no telling what he'd do when liquored up.

When his phone rang, Eugene pressed the speaker button on his dashboard. "Sheriff Graystoke here."

"Sheriff." Yancy's voice sounded breathless. "I got a call from Luke's phone, but he never said anything."

"Butt dialing." Eugene managed a quick laugh. "Happens all the time. My wife hates it when I do that."

"No. Listen. This was different. I heard a voice I didn't recognize. And then a really loud report like a gunshot and a woman screaming."

"You sure about that?" Eugene hit the brakes. "I know you and Nelson have a fondness for Hollywood drama, Yancy."

"That we do. I can't deny it. But I'm so convinced of what I heard, I'm calling the family as soon as I hang up with you."

"Now, Yancy—"

"There's trouble at the Larsen place, Sheriff. I feel it in my gut. Just as surely as I feel Luke was trying to get a message out. Okay. I've warned you. I'm hanging up now."

Eugene heard the click and then sudden silence.

He dialed the state police headquarters to report the gunshot and to request backup. Though he hesitated to call out the troops on what might be a false alarm, Yancy Martin wasn't the only one to trust his gut feeling. Eugene's told him this could be really serious.

As he turned his vehicle in the direction of the Larsen ranch and floored the accelerator, he punched the number for his deputy.

When he heard Archer's voice, he said, "Get hold of Nadine Larsen. Tell her to steer clear of Lon Wardell until he sobers up. Then get on out to the Larsen ranch.

It may be nothing, but I've got a report of a suspected gunshot."

Lon walked around the cavernous interior of the barn, obviously searching for something. While he walked, the others watched him with looks that ranged from terrified to thoughtful.

Poor Lily was trembling, probably as much from shock as fear. She'd been forced to witness Mick's assault, and then the attack on both her sister and Luke. The gunshots, the blood, the pain glazing Luke's eyes, had her traumatized.

Next to her, Ingrid leaned over to press a trembling kiss to her cheek, as if to offer a measure of comfort, but the painful bonds restricted movement.

Luke kept his gaze fixed on Wardell, watching for any opportunity to take him down. Though he knew the chances were slim, since he would no doubt fall on his face the moment he tried to stand on his badly injured leg, he was determined to try. He was troubled by the amount of blood he'd lost. If he didn't act soon, he could lose consciousness. But he was even more troubled by the fact that Mick seemed to slip in and out of consciousness. The old man had taken a powerful blow to the head. A blow that could cost him his life if he didn't get medical help soon.

Wardell picked up a flat piece of wood from the splintered stall and dropped it next to Ingrid. "Here's your desk, girlie."

At her blank look he snarled, "You're going to sign over your rights to your cattle. I call this my declaration of independence."

He withdrew a wrinkled paper from his pocket, along with a pen. He dropped it on the wood and gave an imitation of a smile. "But you can think of it as your last will and testament."

Sheriff Graystoke's vehicle pulled up in Ingrid's driveway and parked behind her battered truck. Minutes later Archer Stone's truck arrived. By the time he stepped down, Eugene was beside him.

"You get hold of Nadine Larsen?"

Archer nodded.

"Where'd you find her?"

"She didn't say. But from the static, I'm thinking she was driving. Maybe she's on her way here." Archer looked around. "Awfully quiet to be a crime scene."

"Yeah." Eugene looked up in annoyance at the sound of a plane's engine. While he and his deputy watched, the Malloy plane circled the area and came in for a quick landing behind the barn. Minutes later Frank, Grace, Yancy, and Nelson made their way toward the house.

"You didn't waste any time." Eugene's voice was accusing.

"Neither did you, Sheriff." Frank nodded toward the back door. "Anybody home?"

"I haven't checked. We just got here." Eugene waved a hand to his deputy. "Go ahead and knock."

While they stood watching, a parade of Malloy Ranch trucks pulled up. One after the other, the doors opened, revealing Matt and Nessa, Colin, Burke, and Reed. All of the men were armed.

Archer returned to the others. "No answer."

"I guess we'll start checking the buildings one by one."

Eugene pointed to the house. "A couple of you go inside. I want every room inspected. Archer and I will start on the barn..."

The sheriff's words died in his throat at the sight that snagged his attention.

Lon Wardell was framed in the barn doorway, his muscled arm wrapped around Lily's neck. In his hand was a pistol pressed to her temple.

Tears were streaming down her cheeks, mingling with the blood to form a river of red staining the pretty denim shirt Grace had bought her in town. She was so small and vulnerable, so completely at the mercy of this madman, the sight of her tore at all their hearts. Nessa clutched her husband's arm and stifled the cry that lodged in her throat.

Lon's voice broke the stunned silence. "One by one, you'll walk over here and drop your weapons before stepping into my office." He smiled at his little joke. "If anybody tries anything stupid, I'll blow the kid's head off. And you can all watch, knowing you were the reason for her death."

He dragged Lily backward, causing her to gag, and waved his pistol drunkenly. "Move it. Or the kid pays."

CHAPTER TWENTY-EIGHT

Hearing Grace's sob, Frank Malloy put an arm around his wife's shoulders as he dropped his rifle and walked with her into the barn.

"Sit against the wall." Lon waved his pistol, and the two slumped down.

Lon turned to Nelson, being assisted by Yancy. "Move it, old man. First, your weapons."

"We are unarmed." Nelson's imperious tones were an odd contrast to Lon's slurred words.

"If you're lying, I'll blow the brat's head off." To prove his point, he jammed the pistol against her temple.

Matt, his eyes as hard as flint, held Nessa's hand as he tossed his rifle to the ground and joined his grandparents along the wall.

Next came Colin, Reed, and Burke, all silent and scowling as they deposited their weapons before joining the others.

The sheriff and his deputy walked in last, their grim faces betraying their outrage at being ordered about by this drunken cowboy.

Lon studied the pile of weapons before breaking into a smirk. "Well, now. Looks like I could hold off an army with all this firepower. I thank you all kindly for adding to my arsenal."

He gave Lily a shove, sending her sprawling headfirst into the straw beside her sister.

"Oh, Frank." Grace squeezed her husband's hand as she took in the horrifying scene. Mick barely conscious. Luke bloody and glazed with pain. Ingrid and Lily bound hand and foot, their pretty young faces smeared with their own blood. "This is like some terrible nightmare."

"Hold on, Gracie Girl." Frank drew her close. "Where there's life, there's hope."

She closed her eyes, and her family knew she was silently praying.

"Why are we here, Wardell?" In an effort to keep this man talking as long as possible, Eugene Graystoke's voice bounced off the walls and ceiling of the barn.

"We're here to celebrate my inheritance." Lon lifted his whiskey bottle in a salute before taking a long pull.

"What is it you inherited?" Eugene glanced at the others, then at the pile of weapons, and they nodded their understanding of his unspoken signal to watch for any opportunity to retrieve their guns and stop this before it turned into a slaughter.

"Didn't you hear?" Lon chuckled to himself. "Old Lars Larsen loved me so much, he considered me like the son he always wanted. And since all he had were a couple of worthless daughters and a drunken whore for a wife, he wanted to make sure I was put in charge of his ranch."

At his harsh words, Lily started crying again, and because of her bonds, all Ingrid could do was lean close to whisper words meant to soothe.

Luke felt a wild rage burning inside at the pain. Not his own pain, but the pain this drunk was inflicting on all the people he loved.

The people he loved.

He stared around, filling himself with the images of his grandparents, his great-grandfather, his brothers and sister-in-law, his uncle Colin, the ranch foreman Burke, who was as much family as the others, and Yancy, a sweet man who had been reborn because of them. He studied old Mick, so still and lifeless. And finally a tearful Lily and Ingrid, stoic even in the face of such violence.

He knew, without a doubt, that he was about to risk his own life for theirs. But his life no longer mattered. What mattered was that he could create enough distraction to give the others a chance to act. And if he died, at least his death wouldn't be in vain.

He gathered himself, forcing aside the pain radiating from his arm and leg all the way to his head and throbbing with an almost unbearable ache that nearly blinded his vision.

He didn't need to stand for any length of time, he told himself. He just needed to summon enough strength to make a mad dash to that bale of hay and force Lon Wardell to shift his focus for an instant. It could create enough of a distraction to help the others retrieve their weapons and take down this monster.

He moved his body, testing his strength. Closing his fingers around the rail of the stall, he pulled himself to a kneeling position and then made a valiant effort to stand.

Outside the barn, a car's brakes screeched, sending gravel spitting.

All heads turned to the doorway as Nadine raced inside, screaming and swearing at the top of her lungs.

Seeing her, Wardell made a grab for Lily, holding her in front of him like a shield.

"You liar! You no-good, cheating, scumbag liar!"

She flew at Lon like some kind of whirling dervish, shoving Lily aside before pounding his chest with her fists, her long painted nails scratching at his eyes.

"You promised me you'd never hurt my girls. And look at them." She turned, tears in her eyes at the sight of Lily and Ingrid, bound and bloody. "Now you'll have to answer to me, you filthy, lying piece of—"

"Shut up, you slut. I'm doing this for you as much as for me."

"For me? You'd hurt my girls for me? You've always known they were off-limits. You knew that, and you came here anyway? You swore it wasn't you who caused that wildfire. You said you'd swear on your mother's grave that you didn't poison old Tippy or fire that gunshot at the mustangs. You're a liar. A cheat. But this is one thing you won't get away with, you disgusting piece of—"

A gunshot echoed and reechoed around the barn.

Nadine's body stiffened. The fist she'd been shaking in Lon's face dropped to her side. Without a word she began to slide to the floor in slow motion.

For a moment Lon seemed unable to process what he'd

done. He simply stood there, gun in hand, watching in a drunken fog as she fell.

It was all the distraction Luke needed. Though he wasn't certain his wounded leg would support his weight, he made a flying leap across the distance separating him from Wardell.

Seeing him, the others sprang into action, grabbing up weapons and circling Luke and Wardell.

The sound of another gunshot had Ingrid screaming as Luke fell back, blood streaming like a river from his chest. For a moment Luke lay as still as death, and his entire family seemed suspended in time and space, unable to move.

Then he got to his knees, shaking his head to clear it. Before Wardell could fire again, Luke was on him, trading punches, fighting desperately to take control of his pistol.

The others circled around the two, preparing to shoot if they could get a clear shot at Wardell.

Hearing the sound of helicopters landing, Eugene Graystoke turned to his deputy. "Let the state boys know where we are."

Archer Stone dashed out the door.

As an army of sharpshooters raced inside, taking up positions, Luke gave a blow to Wardell's jaw that had his head snapping back.

Still holding his pistol, Wardell looked around at the assault rifles aimed at him. All the fight seemed to have left him. He grasped Luke's shoulders. "I want to make a deal, Malloy."

"A deal?" Luke swore. "The only deal you'll get is prison. I hope you die there."

"But I know something you'll want to hear."

Luke shook his head. "There's nothing you could say that would matter in the least."

"I know something you don't. Something I was sworn to keep secret about the night your parents died."

At his words, Luke's head came up sharply.

Across the barn, his family members riveted all their attention on the man who had just offered them the most tantalizing words ever spoken.

With a fierce oath, Luke grabbed Wardell by the front of his shirt and twisted. "Tell me what you know. Tell me now."

"Not without the promise of a deal." Wardell lifted both hands and shoved him backward with all his strength.

In that instant, seizing their only opportunity for a clear shot, a deafening volley of gunshots rang through the air.

Wardell, pistol in hand, fell to the floor.

Through a blinding mist of fury, Luke looked around at the line of sharpshooters, including the sheriff and his deputy. "Why the hell did you shoot? He wanted to tell me something. Something important."

"He was threatening you with a gun, Luke." The sheriff holstered his weapon and started toward Luke.

Luke's arms shot out like a prizefighter, holding him at bay. "You heard him, Eugene. He said he knew something about the night my parents died."

"He was playing for time, Luke. That's what men do when they run out of options."

Luke was shaking his head, unable to hear anything except the loud buzzing in his brain. He'd been so close. So close...

He turned to his brothers. "You heard him. He knew something."

Matt and Reed caught him as he began to fall to the floor.

He knew he was losing consciousness, but he managed to say, "Get help for Mick and Nadine. They've been hurt badly. And see if Wardell is alive. We need to know what secret he's been keeping."

"We'll see to it." Colin directed a medic toward the old cowboy, who remained, silent and still, in a pool of blood in the hay.

The sheriff turned to his deputy. "You've known Wardell since your teens. What do you make of this?"

Archer Stone shrugged. "You can know a man for a lifetime and not really know what goes on in his head."

Grace hurried over to Lily and Ingrid, cutting their bonds, before trying to lead them outside to safety.

"No." Ingrid pushed away and hurried to kneel beside her mother. Finding a pulse, she shouted and Lily raced over, followed by Frank, Grace, Nelson, and Yancy.

"Hold on, Nadine." Ingrid caught her hand. "The police are here. They'll take you to the clinic."

"Not . . . going to make it." Nadine's eyes opened, and she stared at her two daughters. "Hurts too bad."

"Don't say that. You're going to live, Nadine." Lily was crying.

"Don't call me . . ." She paused and looked up at Nelson before trying again, marshalling all her energy to say what she needed to say. "A very smart man once said Mother was the most beautiful name in the world. Would you . . . would you mind calling me Mama just once?"

The two sisters looked at each other in amazement.

Lily started to speak. "But you said—"

Ingrid closed a hand over her little sister's to stop her. "All right. If that's what you want, Mama."

Nadine managed a weak smile as she turned to Lily. "Now you. Please."

"Mama." Lily's lips trembled. "I . . . love you, Mama."

"Oh, my sweet girls. I never thought I'd hear that. Look how many years I've wasted. I'm so sorry. Can you forgive me?"

"There's nothing to forgive." Ingrid touched a hand to Nadine's cheek. "You're home now, Mama."

A medic walked over and began to check her vital signs. She pushed his hand away. "Don't waste your time, sugar."

She reached out, grabbing hold of her daughters' hands, twining her fingers with theirs. "If I could do things over . . ." Ever so slowly her fingers relaxed their grip and her hands went slack.

The burly medic touched a finger to her neck before glancing at the two grieving sisters. "I'm sorry. She's gone."

Ingrid and Lily were joined in their grief by the others who gathered around, forming a circle of love as they continued holding their mother's hands.

Ingrid left Lily kneeling beside their mother, with Grace watching over her, while she went in search of Luke, who had already been placed on a gurney. One medic was inserting an intravenous tube while the other covered him with a blanket and prepared to take him to a helicopter.

Seeing him, so still and bloody, had tears springing to her eyes. She caught Luke's hand. "Please don't die, Luke."

His eyes opened. He gave her one of those dangerous smiles. "Didn't you know? Only the good die young."

"Oh, Luke." Sobbing, she buried her face in his neck.

"Hey now." He wrapped his good arm around her. "Are all those tears for me?"

"Some." She swallowed. "The rest...Nadine...my mother is dead."

"Oh, baby." He brushed a hand over her hair, seeking to offer comfort. "She was the one who saved us. You know that, don't you?"

"No. It was you. You were so brave. So..."

She sniffled against his neck before straightening as the medics made ready to lift his gurney.

"Wait." He motioned them to move back a pace. "You need to get to the clinic." Ingrid started to step back, but he caught her hand and held her fast. "If your mother hadn't come rushing in like a crazed grizzly protecting its cubs, we'd all still be hostage to that madman. Whether she planned it or not, whether accidental or deliberate, she turned out to be a true hero. I want you and Lily to hold on to that thought."

Fresh tears started falling, and Ingrid didn't bother to stop them. "Thank you for that, Luke. And for...everything."

He gave her another smile before calling to the medics, "Okay. Let's get me out of here." He squeezed her hand. "I'll see you at Glacier Ridge. Last one there has to scrub my back."

Despite her tears, she found herself smiling as the medics carried his gurney to a waiting helicopter and loaded it aboard.

In a whirl of sand and gravel, the copter lifted off and disappeared across the sky.

CHAPTER TWENTY-NINE

The state police crime unit was methodical as its members swarmed over the barn and ranch, bagging evidence, photographing anything that could be useful for their files.

After giving video statements, the family was allowed to leave.

A convoy of ranch trucks and police vehicles left the chaotic scene at the Larsen ranch behind as it snaked along the highway and through the town of Glacier Ridge.

Grace and Nessa opted to ride with Ingrid and Lily, patiently encouraging them to open up about all that had happened and offering comfort as the reality of their situation began to sink in, and their grief bubbled to the surface.

"Is Nadine...Mama really dead?" Lily kept asking.

"Yes, honey." Ingrid had her arm around her little sister's shoulders, feeling the tremors that rocked her body.

"Is Luke going to die, too?"

Grace closed her eyes against the pain.

Seeing it, Nessa was quick to reassure all of them. "Luke said himself that he's too tough to die."

"Nadine...Mama was tough."

"Yes, she was." Ingrid gathered her closer.

"But she died."

The words were muffled against Ingrid's chest, and she was forced to absorb a sudden jolt at the realization of all that had happened. Even now, she couldn't quite take it all in.

"Here we are." Nessa was relieved when their truck pulled up to the emergency entrance of the Glacier Ridge Clinic.

The women climbed from their vehicle and walked into another scene of complete chaos.

The Malloy men were already there, milling about the waiting room, asking endless questions of Agnes, the assistant to the Cross doctors, and demanding admittance to the examining room.

"Gracie Girl." Frank Malloy hurried over to hug his wife. "She won't tell us a thing about Luke's condition, or Mick's."

A pretty, dark-haired young woman in a white lab coat said, "Because, until now, she didn't know."

"Dr. Cross."

As she stepped into the outer room, the entire mob of people gathered around her, shouting questions.

"How is Luke? Is he alert?"

"Does he require surgery?"

"What about Mick? Will he recover from that blow to the head?"

She held up a hand and gave a quick shake of the head,

sending dark curls dancing around her face. "Luke is being prepared for surgery to remove the bullets. Mick is now awake and alert, but we'll keep him overnight for observation. I would suggest that, since you've all been through a terrible ordeal, you return to your homes and you can have a visit with the patients later."

When nobody moved, she glanced over their heads until she spotted Colin on the perimeter of the crowd.

He was staring at her in that quiet, thoughtful way she'd come to know. Of the entire Malloy family, he was the only one who was quiet and reserved. Traits she found admirable, especially at a crazy time like this.

Seeing the question in her eyes, he shook his head, causing her lips to curve in the merest hint of a smile. "Or, if you insist on staying, I suppose you could take yourselves off to D & B's Diner or Clay's Pig Sty. By the time you've eaten, both Luke and Mick should be ready to receive visitors."

Instead of doing as she'd suggested, they seemed to dig in. Now silent, arms crossed over their chests, faces stern or thoughtful or determined, they stared past her toward the doors leading to the patient rooms.

"Or..." Resigned, she sighed. "Maybe I could have Agnes show you to the surgery waiting room, where I can meet with you postsurgery and fill you in on how Luke's operation went."

They moved like a giant swarm toward the doors, and Agnes, the clinic's receptionist, wisely pushed the button to admit them, then led them down the hall and into a comfortable room equipped with TV, Internet connection, and several vending machines, as well as freshly brewed coffee. But one Malloy stayed behind.

"Doctor. Anita."

Anita paused at the sound of Colin's voice. "Yes?"

He managed a smile. "Thanks for your kindness."

She gave a small laugh. "It wasn't kindness. It was wisdom. I'm not prepared to go to war with a family as intimidating as yours, so I decided to make an executive decision that would please everybody and free me to get on with my surgery."

He arched a brow. "You'll be doing the surgery?"

"Does that worry you?"

He shook his head. "I'm glad." Then he flushed. "I mean, I trust your uncle. Old Dr. Cross has been our doctor for a lifetime." Colin touched a hand to her shoulder. "But I'm glad you're taking care of Luke."

She smiled before stepping back. "I'll make a complete report to you and your family as soon as the surgery is over."

While Colin watched, she stepped through the open doors and disappeared along a corridor leading to the sterile inner sanctum of the small-town clinic.

Luke lay in bed, pleasantly sedated, as an IV tube dripped fluids into him and a machine monitored his vitals.

He looked around at the sea of faces staring at him. The Great One in an armchair, with Yancy standing beside him. His grandparents, holding hands. Matt standing directly behind Nessa, his arms around her waist. Reed and Colin and Burke at the foot of the bed, looking somber.

Closest to the bed were Ingrid and Lily. Both of them had stitches at their temples, covered with gauze. Both were gripping his hand, and it seemed to him that their breathing was in sync with his. Each time he breathed in, so did they. Each time he exhaled, they did the same. He struggled for a way to put them at ease.

"Does it hurt?" Lily seemed very worried about his level of pain.

"Not right now, Li'l Bit. They've got me on too much happy juice to feel a thing."

"What's happy juice?"

"Some kind of painkiller," Ingrid whispered.

"Oh."

The Great One glanced around at the others. "Dr. Cross said the bullet in your leg went clear through."

Luke smiled. "I guess that's a good thing."

"I'd say so. And she said the bullet didn't tear through anything vital, like bone or ligaments, so the healing should go smoothly."

"So I'll be able to dance?"

Ingrid seemed surprised by his question. "I don't see why not."

He shot her one of those wicked grins. "That's great. 'Cause I couldn't dance before this."

The others laughed. Ingrid continued clutching his hand like a lifeline, until he could no longer feel his fingers.

He glanced around until he caught his grandmother's eye. "I'm feeling a little sleepy. Must be all this happy juice. Would you mind if I just close my eyes for a while?"

Taking the hint, Grace began herding the others from the room. "We'll all go back to the ranch, now we know you're in good hands. But we'll be back first thing in the morning." She turned to Ingrid. "I'd feel better if you and

Lily would stay at our place. At least until Mick is strong enough to go home. You shouldn't be alone right now."

Very gently she eased the little girl away from Luke's side, took her hand, and led her toward the door.

Before Ingrid could respond, Luke said, "As long as Lily's in good hands, maybe you could stay in town for a while. I think I could persuade Dr. Anita to get you a tray. Maybe even a bed."

She was shaking her head. "I couldn't—"

Burke stepped up beside her. "I was thinking I'd hang out in town. Maybe grab a beer and a sandwich at the Pig Sty before heading back. If you'd like a visit, I could drive you back later."

Luke shot him a look of gratitude.

Ingrid nodded. "I guess...as long as you're staying, and I'm not making extra work for anybody..." She turned to Luke. "You're sure I won't be in the way? You have to be exhausted."

"I'll sleep better knowing you're here."

She turned to Burke. "All right. It looks like I'll be coming back with you later." She hurried to the door to kiss her little sister. "Will you be okay with Gram Gracie?"

Lily nodded and tightened her grip on Grace's hand.

As the room emptied out, Ingrid returned to Luke's bedside and took his hand in hers. "Are you sure you're feeling up to this?"

In answer, he drew her down for a slow, leisurely kiss. "That's all I needed." He kissed her again, lingering over her lips until her smile returned. "Now I know I'm going to be fine."

* * *

The lights in Luke's room had been dimmed. Agnes had wheeled a recliner into the room and positioned it beside Luke's bed so that Ingrid could lie beside him without disturbing the tubes and wires leading to the monitor.

Both of them had been covered with warming blankets, to fight any lingering shock to their systems.

Snug, warm, content, they lay holding hands.

Luke turned his head to study Ingrid's face. "Feel like talking about Nadine?"

"No. It's all too fresh."

"Yeah. I get it. But whenever you feel like talking, I'll be here to listen."

"Thanks. Luke?"

"Hmm?"

"Did we really live through this?"

"I guess we did. Although"—he chuckled—"the way I'm feeling right now, maybe I've died and gone to heaven." He pretended to pinch himself. "Let's see. There's not a sound in this place, except for that annoying monitor. No drunken gunman. No blood. And I'm lying beside the most beautiful woman in the world, who could very well be my angel." He lifted her hand to his lips and pressed a kiss to her palm before closing her fingers around it. "Let's sleep on it, and figure things out in the morning."

Long after he'd fallen asleep, Ingrid lay with her hand in his, watching the steady rise and fall of his chest and thinking it was the most glorious thing she'd ever seen.

If they weren't in heaven, this was the closest thing to it. Lily was safe and secure in the loving circle of the Malloy family.

Mick was awake and alert, and Dr. Anita had assured

her that he could be discharged in the morning, as long as he agreed to return in a week for another X-ray.

Nadine...Mama...had been the catalyst to saving all of them.

How could Nadine have been attracted to a monster like Lon Wardell?

Attracted?

A poor choice of words. Nadine hadn't been so much attracted as addicted. She hadn't been able to stay away from his type. Hard-drinking. Hard-living. A loser.

But she'd redeemed herself by one unselfish act of love.

Love.

An image of Luke, charming, laughing, ducking her head beneath the water of the creek as they swam naked together, played through her mind, easing her pain, soothing her spirit. That man had a way of making her forget every hardship she'd ever endured. He was fun, funny, irreverent, fearless.

And here she was, after surviving impossible terror, calmly lying beside the man she loved.

The man she loved.

Were there any sweeter words in the world?

At last, exhausted beyond belief, she gave in to the need to sleep.

Hours later, when Burke stopped by to see if Ingrid was ready to leave for the ranch, he found Ingrid and Luke sound asleep, each wearing matching smiles.

With a nod of approval, he silently let himself out.

CHAPTER THIRTY

A convoy of ranch trucks moved slowly along the ridge of the meadow, abloom with wildflowers.

When they came to the small gravesite, the Malloy family stepped out. Wearing somber black pants and string ties, the men lifted a simple pine box from the back of Ingrid's battered truck.

Sheriff Graystoke was there, offering an apology that his deputy wouldn't make it, since one of them had to handle the duties back in town.

Bull Hammond rode up on the back of his dappled mare, his face dripping with sweat, his cheeks red from the sun. He dismounted and yanked off his hat before mopping his face with a handkerchief.

The Reverend Townsend from Glacier Ridge Church stood beside the open grave, flanked by Mick, Ingrid, and Lily.

The men removed their best Sunday hats and bowed

their heads as the minister spoke the words over the casket.

"We will be judged, not only by the way we choose to live, but by how well we love. No greater love is there than this: that a man would lay down his life for another. This day we send our sister Nadine to her eternal rest. May she sleep in the knowledge that her generous action resulted in the safe return from certain death of those she loved."

As Mick and Burke lowered the casket into the ground, Ingrid picked up a handful of dirt and scattered it on the lid. Lily, clutching a handful of wildflowers she'd picked, dropped them and watched as they fluttered down to cover the top of the box.

The others stood back respectfully while sand was shoveled and the grave was mounded with fresh earth. Then, with a word to the minister, and hugs to Ingrid and Lily, they walked to their trucks, giving the two sisters a chance to say their private good-byes.

When they finally turned away from the grave, Luke caught their hands and walked between them to Ingrid's truck. He helped them settle inside before taking the wheel.

"That was a nice service."

Ingrid nodded. "I'm grateful that Rev. Townsend would come all this way. He suggested a funeral in town, but I knew that wasn't something Nadine...Mama would have wanted. Besides, the only ones who will grieve her loss are right here."

Luke squeezed her hand. "Yancy's preparing a lunch."

She looked over. "We're driving to your ranch?"

He shook his head. "Yancy and the Great One are at your place."

"Poor Yancy. I bet he can't find any of the utensils he needs."

"Don't worry about Yancy. That man travels with half the kitchen in the back of his truck."

As they pulled up to the house, the others were standing around the back porch, sipping longnecks.

Reed handed a bottle to Luke and another to Ingrid, while Grace walked up to Lily with a frosty glass of lemonade.

It was the Great One who lifted his martini in a toast. "Here's to Nadine, who learned the wisdom of motherhood and the power of true love."

Ingrid shot him a grateful smile before lifting her glass to say softly, "To Mama."

To save space, Yancy had set the food out in buffet style. Along the kitchen counter were platters holding thick slabs of roast beef, as well as mounds of whipped potatoes, hot rolls, and a salad of garden lettuce, tomatoes, cucumbers, and peppers, all dressed with Yancy's famous vinaigrette. For dessert there were slices of carrot cake with dollops of freshly whipped cream.

The Malloy family and the few guests took over the entire house. While some snagged chairs at the kitchen table, others ambled into the parlor to sit at the game table or even on the lumpy sofa, while the rest stepped outside to eat in the shade of the back porch, where Yancy had covered an old log picnic table with a cheery red-and-white-checked cloth.

Spotting Ingrid and Luke standing off to one side of the porch, Bull Hammond walked over.

"I hope I'm not intruding."

Ingrid smiled and shook her head. "I'm glad you came, Bull. I'm sorry for the things I'd been thinking when all this trouble was happening."

"Please don't apologize. I'm not proud of the way I behaved. I guess, after years of feuding with your father, I forgot how to be a neighbor."

Ingrid seized on a single word. "What was the feud about?"

Bull flushed. "It's hard to remember now. I guess it started over some cattle that wandered into my hayfield. And then it escalated over the years, until every little slight became a giant insult." He fidgeted and cleared his throat. "I'm really sorry about you losing both your ma and pa. Ranching's hard enough with the proper help, but it's almost impossible on your own. I admire what you've managed to do, and I want you to know that my offer to buy your land still stands. I've always wanted to enlarge my holdings, and this place would be perfect. I could rent out your house to a tenant farmer and get not only an income from him, but also have extra help during calving season and roundup." He paused before adding, "But I'll understand if you want to hold on to it. Whatever you decide to do, I want you to know I'll respect it."

"Thank you, Bull." She offered a handshake. "I need some time. Whenever I make a decision, I'll let you know."

"That's fair enough." He shook hands with Luke and made his way to where he'd tied his horse.

When Rev. Townsend took his leave, followed by the sheriff, Grace and Frank walked up, hand in hand with Lily.

"We're hoping you and Lily will spend the night."

Ingrid smiled at her little sister, who looked so comfortable with these two people. "What would you like to do, honey?"

"I'd like to go with Gram Gracie and Grandpop Frank. Yancy said he's going to teach me to make peanut butter drops tonight."

Luke put a hand over his heart. "I haven't had Yancy's peanut butter drops in months now. Wait until you taste them, Li'l Bit. They're the best."

"Better than his chocolate chips?"

Luke leaned close. "Don't tell the Great One. You know how he craves his chocolate chip cookies. But I swear Yancy's peanut butter drops are the best in the world."

The little girl's eyes went wide. "You hear that, Ingrid? Can I please go?"

"Of course."

"And you, Ingrid?" Grace put a hand on her arm. "I'm hoping you and Mick will agree to stay the night, too." She glanced toward the barn. "I don't like thinking of you staying here yet. It's all too soon. Too fresh."

Mick ambled over. "I've already told Burke I'd be happy to go, but only if you're going, too, girl. You can't be alone here tonight."

As she was shaking her head, Luke interrupted. "I think this is the perfect time to invite you to go riding with me. And when we're done, I'll take you back to my place, or if you want to be here, I'll stay." He shot a grin at his grandparents. "Just so she's not alone, you understand."

"You're being too noble, sonny boy." Frank chuckled. "And not at all subtle." He turned to Ingrid. "It's your call, honey."

She thought a moment before saying, "Why don't we

go for that ride, and then I'll decide whether to come back here or go to your place."

"Fair enough." Luke winked at Lily like a conspirator, and she winked back before he followed Ingrid into the house to lend a hand with the cleanup.

When everything was in order, and the long line of ranch trucks had rolled away, Luke took the dish towel from her hand.

"You've done enough for today. Time to go riding."

They walked out the door. When Ingrid started toward the barn, Luke stopped her with a hand on her arm. "You ready to walk on the wild side?"

He pointed to his Harley, parked near the back porch. When she nodded, he handed her a helmet before putting on his own and climbing aboard.

Ingrid climbed on the back and wrapped her arms around his waist. He revved the engine, and they took off across a sloping, flower-strewn meadow, up the side of a hill, and down into a valley lush with grass.

As they rode, Luke kept turning his head to make silly comments, until Ingrid was laughing so hard, she had tears in her eyes.

Happy tears, she thought. On such a day, it seemed impossible that she could be filled with so much joy.

"Playtime," he called, and Ingrid was yanked from her reverie at the banks of the creek.

"Today? Luke, are you serious?"

"Woman, today is the perfect one for skinny-dipping." He pointed to the sky. "Look at that broiling sun. Look at that blue sky, without a cloud around. The day begs for a dip in cool water."

And they did. Laughing and pouncing on one another,

swallowing half the creek with their antics. Chasing and catching, hugging, and loving on the banks of the stream, feeling like the only two people in the world.

Her heart as light as air, Ingrid lay in the cool grass, pressing soft, moist kisses to Luke's throat. "I could stay here like this all night."

"Mmm. Me too. Except it gets really cold when the sun goes down in these hills. We might want to get dressed and chase the sunlight."

"If you say so." She slipped into her clothes and climbed on the back of his motorcycle.

As they sailed across rolling hills, she leaned close. "Where are you taking me?"

"To my secret hideaway."

They came up over a ridge, and he pulled over to enjoy the view. Below them lay a series of gently sloping meadows that seemed to fold one over the other for as far as the eye could see.

"Where are we?"

"This is Malloy land. One of my favorite places. It's where I come when I want to get away from the whole world and refresh my soul. It's my sacred retreat."

She was looking at Luke with a dazed expression. With a smile, she touched a hand to his forehead. "Who are you, and what have you done with that irreverent, silly guy named Luke Malloy?"

He laughed with her. "I know. I don't get serious about too many things. But this is my own private heaven. Someday I plan on building my home here." He took her hand. "What do you think of it?"

"It's breathtaking. I can see why you love it."

"Can you?"

She nodded.

"Don't be polite. I'm being serious. Do you really love it?"

"I do. It's amazing."

He sighed. "Good. I want you to share it."

She looked slightly dazed. "What do you mean?"

"I want you to share all this with me. I love you, Ingrid. I want you to share my life with me."

Because she didn't speak, he felt the need to say more. "I don't want to scare you off, dumping this on you so soon. I know you've just been through a really traumatic event. The attack. Losing your mother."

"Luke..."

He shook his head. "Just so you know, you can sell your ranch or keep it. You can live here with me, or I'll put it all on hold until a time when you're ready. Whatever choice you make, I'll respect it, as long as you're willing to let me be part of your life." His tone lowered. "I realized, when I thought I might lose you, just how important you and Lily had become. I can't imagine life without you. Either of you."

Tears sprang to her eyes, and he was quick to lift his thumbs to wipe them before framing her face and staring down at her. "Sorry. It's too soon. I should have—"

She put a hand over his. "Don't say another word. Just kiss me so I'll know I'm not dreaming."

"You're definitely not—"

She stood on tiptoe to press her mouth to his. And as the kiss spun on and on, she wrapped her arms around his neck and whispered, "Yes. Yes. Oh, yes."

He let out a long sigh before kissing her with a fervor that had both their heads spinning.

Against her mouth he whispered, "You've just made me the happiest man in the world."

The ringing of his cell phone shattered the moment. He pulled it from his pocket and muttered, "This is a fine time for the service to work. It almost never works up here."

He looked at the caller ID and handed the phone to her.

She heard Lily's voice happily chirping, "Well? Did he ask you? Did you say yes? Is Luke going to be my big brother?"

At the startled question in Ingrid's eyes, Luke gave her one of his most charming grins. "Sorry, baby. I had to share it with her. After all, she's going to be part of this, too."

"Oh, Luke. I ought to be really annoyed with you for letting her in on a secret you were keeping from me, but including Lily is just so sweet." She handed him the phone. "She's waiting for my answer."

With his eyes steady on Ingrid's, he spoke into the phone. "Li'l Bit, she said yes. Yes. Yes."

To the sound of the entire family cheering in the background, he gathered Ingrid into his arms and kissed her again, while letting his cell phone drop to the grass.

And then there were no words as they came together in a dance of love as old as time.

EPILOGUE

The sticky heat of late summer had given way to fresh autumn breezes. Soon it would be time to bring the cattle down from their lush highland meadows to winter in the more protected fields of home.

Luke had finished mucking stalls before loading his Harley into the back of one of the trucks. With his chores completed, he headed into the house to shower and change.

He was tucking his shirt into his waistband when a knock sounded on his bedroom door.

Reed's voice called, "The Great One's getting restless. It's time to pay a visit to the gravesite before heading over to the Larsen ranch. You've got five minutes, and then Matt and I have orders to carry you if necessary."

Laughing, Luke opened the door. "I can still walk."

"Your bride will be glad to hear that. Now get a move on."

The two brothers descended the stairs and slammed out the back door.

They made their way up the sloping meadow, where Nelson, Frank, and Matt had already gathered. Luke looked around. "Where are Gram Gracie and Nessa?"

"The women left for Ingrid's hours ago."

Luke shook his head. "Women and weddings."

Matt grinned. "Yeah. Tell me about it."

Frank passed around tumblers of Irish whiskey and the four generations lifted them as he offered the first toast. "To Patrick and Bernie, who left us far too soon. But this day, I have no doubt they're watching with great joy."

They solemnly drank.

Nelson cleared his throat before saying, "To my beautiful Madeline, who is smiling down on us this day and loving every minute of it."

They drank again.

Reed lifted his glass. "I should be toasting myself, since I'm the only one here who's managed to avoid the marriage trap. But since it's Luke's day..." He turned to his brother. "To you, bro, for at least having enough sense to fall for a gorgeous woman who's your equal in all things." Shaking his head, he added, "Though what she sees in you is beyond comprehension."

Luke good-naturedly tousled Reed's hair before they drank.

"And finally," Matt said, "here's to us. Family always. And always room for one more."

They drank, then tipped their hats at the graves before heading down the hill to climb into their trucks for the drive to Ingrid's ranch.

* * *

A long table had been set up on the back porch of Ingrid's house. It was covered with a white linen cloth and lined with a dozen chairs, each tied with a giant white bow.

Yancy and Mick were busy putting the finishing touches on the wedding lunch, which consisted of prime rib of beef and twice-baked potatoes, along with a salad, fresh corn from the garden, and a wedding cake baked by hand and decorated with fluffy white frosting. In the place of honor in the center of the cake were two figures. Instead of the traditional bride and groom, these two sported simple Western attire and helmets, while seated on a motorcycle.

Mick studied the figures. "You've managed to capture them perfectly, Yancy."

The cook gave a nod of appreciation. "Thanks, Mick. I'm pretty proud of this creation."

"You should be. Luke and Ingrid are going to love it." The old man turned away. "Time to get myself ready to give away the bride. I'll be back in a few minutes."

As Mick disappeared into his room, Yancy strolled out the back door to check on last-minute items.

Mick looked up from the stool where he was polishing his boots. As Ingrid stepped into the kitchen, all he could do was stare. She was dressed in a white sundress that fell to her ankles in a swirl of cotton and lace. Cap sleeves fluttered at her shoulders. On her feet were simple strappy sandals.

"Well, don't you look…" He struggled to find the words.

"I know it's not the usual. Luke and I agreed to keep it casual."

"Girl, that may not be a wedding gown, but you look every inch the beautiful bride."

He glanced at her freshly cut hair, which fell in fine wisps around her cheeks. "Guess I figured now that the big day was here, you'd let your hair grow."

"It's easier like this. Besides, Luke loves my hair short."

His eyes crinkled with humor. "Girl, that man would love you with no hair at all."

She was surprised by the sudden urge to weep. Instead, she wrapped her arms around Mick's neck. "Isn't it wonderful that someone like Luke could love me so much?"

He patted her hand. "Luke's a smart man. He knows a good woman when he sees her, thank the Lord. He wasn't about to let you get away."

Ingrid sniffed, deeply affected by his words, and turned away.

He watched her as she walked to the window to peer at the parade of Malloy vehicles pulling up to the back porch. "Is Lily ready?"

Ingrid gave a dreamy smile. "I think she's been ready since dawn. Wait 'til you see her. She went to town yesterday with Gram Grace, who went all out on my little bridesmaid."

"Think she'll outshine the bride?"

Ingrid laughed. "I hope so. She's so excited about her first-ever wedding."

They both turned to the doorway when the object of their discussion stepped through.

"Well?" Lily twirled, showing off the pale pink dress with a full skirt gathered here and there with darker pink bows. On her feet she wore glittering pink ballerina slippers that sparkled in the sunlight. Her usual tangle of waist-length hair had been tamed into shiny dark waves that spilled down her back and were tied off her face with pink ribbons.

Behind her stood Grace and Nessa, who had spent the better part of an hour fussing over the little girl's hair and dress.

"You do good work," Ingrid called.

"Do you like it? I know you said I could wear denim, but Gram Gracie and I found this, and ..." Lily twirled in front of her sister.

"I love everything. The dress, the shoes, and oh my, your hair."

Lily dimpled. "And you look prettier than ever."

"Thank you." The two sisters hugged.

Hearing voices outside, Lily danced toward the door before turning with a look of pure bliss. "Luke's here."

In an aside, Grace said to Ingrid and Nessa, "You'd think she was the one getting married."

They laughed before Ingrid said, "In a way she is. Luke's been so sweet about including her in all the plans. And she's so excited about gaining this big family."

"Not nearly as excited as we are." Grace pressed a kiss to Ingrid's cheek. "Now I have two more females to counter all that testosterone."

Lily's excited voice called from outside, "Hurry, Ingrid. Rev. Townsend is here."

Arm in arm, Grace and Nessa started toward the back door. Grace blew Ingrid a kiss. "That's our cue to leave you and Mick alone in here."

As they walked outside to join the rest of the family,

Mick turned to Ingrid and offered his arm. "Come on, girl. Time to get you hitched."

"Oh, Mick." As Ingrid tucked her arm through his, she leaned over to press a kiss to his leathery cheek. "I'm so glad you're going to be staying at the Malloy Ranch while Luke and I are gone. I feel better knowing you're there if Lily should feel homesick."

"Girl, in case you haven't noticed, Lily's already adopted all of them as family." He patted her hand. "She'll be fine. I'll be fine. As for you, I don't have a worry in the world. You're one strong woman. And you're about to marry the only man I know who's your equal."

As they walked into the sunlight, Lily picked up two nosegays and handed one to Ingrid.

"What's this?"

"Luke brought them."

Ingrid looked up to see him standing at the top of the hill, dressed in a white shirt and string tie, his freshly cut hair slightly mussed, his smile causing her heart to start those funny little flips.

"Now remember," Lily said, enjoying her role immensely. "I go in front of you. Just follow me, okay?"

Ingrid couldn't stop the smile that curved her lips. "Okay."

They walked slowly up the hill until they came to the spot where the minister stood in front of their mother's grave, where a pretty stone marker had been added.

Flanking the minister was the entire Malloy family.

As she'd been instructed, Lily took the flowers from her sister's hand and crossed over to stand next to the others. Mick kissed Ingrid's cheek and then placed her hand on Luke's arm before stepping aside.

Instead of turning toward the minister, Luke closed a hand over hers and stared down into her eyes. "The words we're about to say will make it legal. But I want you to know I've been yours since I woke up on that lumpy sofa and got my first look at you. If ever a woman grabbed my heart and owned it, it's you, babe."

Ingrid blinked back the tears that had welled up out of nowhere to embarrass her yet again. "I love you so much, Luke Malloy, it scares me."

He draped one strong arm around her shoulders and gave her that famous smile. "After what we've been through, nothing should ever scare you again, woman. Now let's do this together."

Together.

The very word had her lifting her head and turning with him to face the minister.

As Rev. Townsend led them through their vows, Ingrid and Luke couldn't stop smiling and staring into each other's eyes.

Afterward, as they accepted congratulations from the family and hugged and kissed each one, they floated on a cloud toward the house and the lovely lunch prepared by Mick and Yancy.

They were sipping champagne, after yet another toast, when Lily approached with a tissue-wrapped package.

"Want to open my gift?"

As Luke and Ingrid began tearing off the wrapping, Lily said, "It was going to be your birthday present. And now, since you got married on your birthday, I wanted it to be for both of you."

They studied the framed photograph of a herd of mustangs grazing in a mountain meadow. Several mares had their foals beside them. The stallion stood watch on a rocky promontory, like a king surveying his kingdom. The entire scene was perfectly captured.

"Now that's just about as professional as it gets, Li'l Bit."

At Luke's words of praise, the little girl beamed. "Gram Gracie showed me how to"—she hesitated, then repeated the lesson she'd learned from Grace—"frame a shot so that all the elements are in proportion."

"Spoken like an apt pupil." Luke dropped a kiss to her cheek.

Ingrid gathered her close and kissed the top of her head. "I love this. And when Luke and I build our house, this will have the place of honor. And someday, I'll brag to everyone about my little sister who became a world-famous photographer."

Lily was fairly bursting with pride. "Is it all right if I go on a safari with Gram Gracie and Grandpa Frank while you and Luke are away?"

Ingrid glanced at Grace before saying, "Honey, we'll only be gone for a few days. But I think a photographic safari would be just the thing."

With her fist pumping the air, Lily hurried inside. A short time later she emerged, wearing jeans and a T-shirt and carrying her backpack.

Luke shook his head before leaning toward Ingrid. "And you were worried she might miss you. You think she's just a tad impatient to get started?"

Ingrid gave him a blinding smile. "She's not the only one."

Inside, Yancy and Mick finished up the last of the cleanup before loading the serving dishes into boxes they stored in the back of a truck.

With hugs all around, the family began the drive back to the Malloy Ranch.

When they were alone, Luke and Ingrid stood awhile, sipping the last of the champagne and watching the sun dip below the hills.

Luke framed her face with his hands for a long, leisurely kiss. "Ready to change and start on our fancy honeymoon?"

With a laugh, she led him inside. A short time later, dressed in faded denims and T-shirts, they climbed aboard his motorcycle and headed toward the hills.

"First stop, the stream," he called over his shoulder. With a roar of engines, he shouted, "And I promise, no matter who reaches the water first, I'll scrub your back."

"And after that?"

"Probably wild sex."

"Promise?"

"You bet. And then we're going to wander like tumbleweeds. Stop whenever we want. Make love as late as we please. Babe, as long as we're together, it doesn't matter where life takes us."

Ingrid wrapped her arms around his waist and pressed her face to his shoulder. As the wind took her hair, Nadine's face appeared in her mind, and her tears mingled with her laughter.

Oh, Mama, she thought. *We all had such a rough road. But I'm leaving the past behind and starting the first day of the rest of my life.*

As they soared and dipped, her laughter grew. Who

would have ever believed that a bearded stranger, who'd looked more like a shaggy beast than a rancher, would turn into her Prince Charming?

With this wild, unpredictable rogue in her life, she was absolutely certain she would never again be sad or afraid or lonely. For with Luke Malloy, all of life would surely be the adventure of a lifetime.

Ranch Chili (Mick's Fire)

- 3 pounds sirloin—cubed
- 1 large onion chopped
- 3 jalapeno peppers stemmed, seeded, chopped
- 3 cloves garlic, peeled, crushed
- 6 tablespoons chili powder
- 1 tablespoon ground cumin
- Salt
- Pepper
- 3 large tomatoes peeled, seeded, chopped
- 1 can beer
- 2 ounces tequila
- 4 cups beef stock

In a large Dutch oven, heat oil over high heat. Add meat and stir until no longer pink. Lower heat to medium and add onions, peppers, garlic, and chili powder. Stir several minutes before adding cumin, salt, and pepper. Add tomatoes and stir. Add beer, tequila, and beef stock and simmer for 2 to 3 hours until the meat is fork tender.

Serve with bowls of chopped green onions, shredded cheese, sour cream, hot sauce, and thick slices of sourdough bread.

Cowboys love it.

You will, too.

The town's resident ladies' man, Reed Malloy, is always on the hunt for his next conquest. But when Reed meets beautiful Ally Shaw and her adorable son, Kyle, this wild cowboy aches to settle down...

A preview of *Reed* follows.

PROLOGUE

Glacier Ridge, Montana—Twenty Years Ago

Hey now, Frank." Burke Cowley, white-haired foreman at the Malloy Ranch, caught his boss, Francis X. Malloy, storming out of the big, sprawling ranch house shared by four generations.

From the look on Frank's face, it was the final straw in a winter that had been filled with tragedy, with the shocking accident on a snowy road that had taken the life of his son, Patrick, and Patrick's beautiful wife, Bernadette, leaving three sons without their loving parents.

"Where are you going in such a hurry?"

"Reed's missing."

"What do you mean, missing?"

"Yancy called him down for supper, and he never answered. Matt and Luke went looking for him. So did Gracie. They searched the house while Colin and I went through the barns. He's nowhere to be found. Colin said the last time he saw Reed he was saddling up old Nell, but that was hours ago. Damned fool kid said he just wanted to be left alone. Colin thinks he was heading up to the range shack on the North Ridge, since that's the last place Reed spent with his pa."

"And Colin couldn't stop him?"

"He tried. You know how hotheaded Reed can be. He dug his heels into Nell's rump, and that horse took off like it had a burr under the saddle."

"Hold on. You're not thinking about heading up there now?" Burke held up a hand. "You can see the blizzard heading this way."

"You think I'm blind?" Frank Malloy's eyes burned with a terrible, raging passion. "I've already buried a son. I'm not about to lose a grandson, too."

"You get inside. I'll go." The ranch foreman spun around and headed toward the barn, giving his boss no time to argue.

By the time Burke had saddled his horse and bundled into heavy winter gear, Yancy Martin, the ranch cook, stepped inside the barn to hand him several wrapped packages.

"You could be trapped up there a few days. Some roast beef sandwiches. Reed's favorites. And a bottle of whiskey for you. To keep from freezing, and hopefully to keep you from throttling that little spitfire when you find him."

"Thanks, Yancy." Burke shoved the supplies into his saddlebags before pulling himself onto the back of his trusty mount, Major.

The cook put a hand on the reins. "I know Reed's done a stupid thing, but he's been missing his folks something awful. It's a heavy load for a kid to bear." He paused.

"I know he's a handful, but that ornery kid has a way of sneaking into my heart. You bring Reed home safe, you hear?"

Burke nodded and pulled his wide-brimmed hat low on his head. Reed might be rebellious and reckless as hell, but he had that same effect on all of them. Despite all the trouble he could cause, they couldn't help but love him. He had a kind heart, and as his grandmother, Grace Malloy, was fond of saying, he was like an old man in a boy's body. In so many ways, Reed was wise beyond his years.

"You know I will, Yancy. The good Lord willin'."

As horse and rider faced into the storm and started across a high, sloping meadow, the old man found himself thinking about the terrible crash that had happened weeks ago on a night like this. The death of Patrick and Bernadette had left a void that would never be filled. Not for the Malloy family, and especially for Patrick and Bernadette's three sons, twelve-year-old Matt, ten-year-old Luke, and nine-year-old Reed, who were floundering in a world rocked by the sudden, shocking loss of their parents.

"Stay safe, Reed," the old man whispered fiercely. "At least until I can find you and tan your miserable hide."

For hours Major plodded through drifts that were now waist-high, before the outline of a mountain cabin loomed up in the darkness.

Burke unsaddled his horse in the shed behind the range shack, grateful to see Nell, Reed's favorite mare, contentedly dozing. Tossing the saddlebags over his shoulder, he trudged around and let himself into the cabin, bracing for the encounter to come.

Reed Malloy sat huddled in front of the fireplace, where a couple of stingy tree branches gave off a thin flame. He'd shed his boots, which now lay in a puddle of melted snow by the door.

The boy's head came up sharply. Seeing the fire in those eyes, Burke bit back the oath that sprang to his lips. The last thing the kid needed right now was any more fuel poured on the flame that was burning so hotly in his soul.

Without a word, Burke draped the saddlebags over the back of a wooden chair before heading outside, returning with an armload of logs.

"What're you doing here?" Reed's jaw jutted like a prizefighter.

"Getting out of the cold." Burke deposited the logs beside the fireplace and set the biggest one over the flame.

Crossing to the table, he tossed aside his parka and began removing the packages from his saddlebags.

When he saw the boy's gaze dart to the wrapped sandwiches, he took his sweet time unwrapping them. He walked to the tiny kitchen counter and filled a coffeemaker before placing it on a wire rack over the open fire. Within minutes the little cabin was filled with the rich fragrance of coffee boiling.

"Good place to sit out a storm." Burke glanced over. "You hungry?"

Still frowning, Reed shrugged.

Taking that for an answer, the old man placed the sandwiches on plates and handed one to Reed before settling into a rocker in front of the fire and easing off his boots with a sigh.

For long minutes the two ate without speaking, listening to the hiss and snap of the fire on the grate and the howling of the storm as the wind and snow buffeted the walls of the cabin.

"They sent you here, didn't they?" Reed set aside his empty plate.

"I volunteered. Everyone back home is worried sick." Burke calmly continued eating.

"I don't want you here. I came up here to be alone."

"You could have skipped the drama and just gone up to your room."

"Right. Where I'd have to listen to Matt and Luke jabbering all night long. Luke telling us to just suck it up. Matt telling us we have to put on a good face so we don't add to Grandpop Frank and Gram Gracie's pain. Easy for him to say." Reed hissed in a breath. "But what about us? What about our pain?" He turned away, but not before the old man saw the look of abject misery in his eyes.

"It's tough that you had to learn the lesson so young. Life's not fair. Never has been. Never will be."

"Gee. Thanks for nothing." Every word sizzled with hot anger.

"I'm not going to sugarcoat things, boy. I won't bother to tell you that pain will go away soon. It won't." Burke heaved a sigh. "But I will tell you that one day you'll wake up thinking about something besides the loss of your ma and pa. Not tomorrow. Not the next day. But one day it will happen. It's the same with all the tears that right now are sticking in your throat, threatening to choke you every time you swallow. One day, out of the blue, you'll find yourself chuckling. Or laughing right out loud. It'll catch you by surprise, but it'll feel good, and you'll do it again. That's the way life is. One day your heart is so broken, you can barely breathe. And the next day, you find a reason to smile. Maybe just a little reason, but it'll be enough to lift you up. And before you know it, you've gone more days smiling than crying."

"I've got no reason to smile. Not now. Not ever."

"You say that now. But you're one of the lucky ones, Reed." Burke turned to the boy. "You've got a powerful love of this ranch, this land, and especially the cattle. I've seen it since you were no bigger'n a pup."

Reed couldn't deny it. He loved this ranch with an all-consuming passion. He loved the land, the cattle, the wildness of this place. And he had dreams. Dreams he'd shared with his parents of making their herds the healthiest, and demanding the highest price ever. The Malloy Ranch would be a name respected around the world. He wasn't sure just how he would make that dream come true, but this much he knew: If being willing to work harder than anybody, if giving up everything others took for granted counted for anything, he would make it all happen.

And the key was the cattle. He didn't know the how or why of it, but the feeling was so strong, he was nearly consumed by it.

But the loss of his parents left him feeling alone and crushed by the weight of his loss.

The boy turned to the old man. "Did you ever lose someone you loved, Burke?"

The foreman stared into the flames, his eyes shrouded in secrets. "I have. I've been where you are now, son."

Something in the quiet tone of his voice had the boy holding back any more questions. Instead he sat, absorbing the heat of the fire and the warmth of understanding he could feel vibrating from the tough old man beside him.

Burke Cowley was the man every wrangler on the Malloy Ranch turned to in time of need, whether it was doctoring a sick cow or calming a cowboy during a crisis. He could be as tender as a new mother when treating a wrangler's injuries and as vicious as a wounded bear when crossed by some drunken fool who didn't follow orders. Burke could work circles around every wrangler on the Malloy Ranch and still tend a herd all night in a raging storm. If this tough old cowboy could survive a powerful loss, Reed felt the first tiny flicker of hope that he'd make it through the raw pain that burned like the fires of hell in his heart.

Like the man said, maybe not tomorrow. But one day.

Still, Reed sensed a storm raging inside him. Bigger, stronger than the one raging outside the walls of this cabin. Pa used to say he'd been born with it; it had been there simmering inside him from the moment he gave his first lusty birth cry. Unlike his older brothers—Matt, who was always in control, and Luke, a rolling stone who loved nothing more than a challenge—there was just something inside Reed, the tough, determined youngest of the family, that set him apart.

But first he would have to learn to put aside this terrible grief and tame the temper lurking inside him. He sensed that if he didn't learn to tame it, this emotion could take control, and that he would never allow. If anything, he wanted to be in control of his own destiny.

He knew one thing. Nothing would ever take him from this place and the cattle. Not even the loss of the two people he cherished more than any in the world.

CHAPTER ONE

Malloy Ranch—Present Day

After more than a month in the hills that circled the ranch, Reed Malloy looked more like a trail bum than a member of a successful ranch family. His hair hung to his shoulders. His face was covered in a rough beard. His clothes were filthy.

He unsaddled his mount, tossing the saddle over the rail of the stall before filling troughs with feed and water. In the stall alongside him, his uncle, Colin Malloy, did the same.

That done, the two men trudged toward the house, noting the line of trucks.

"As usual," Colin said with a laugh, "I see Matt and Luke and their wives manage to never miss a meal."

Both of Reed's older brothers were building homes on Malloy land, and they currently divided their time between the new construction and the family ranch. The bulk of their time was still spent here, but because of its size, nobody felt crowded.

Reed was grinning at the noise level as he scraped his boots before stepping into the mudroom. He hung his jacket and hat on hooks by the door and rolled his sleeves before pausing to wash up at the big sink.

In the doorway he stood watching as the familiar scene unfolded. Yancy Martin, the ranch cook, was lifting a pan of cinnamon biscuits from the oven. The wonderful fragrance filled the room.

Reed's grandparents, Frank and Gracie, were seated on a sofa across the room, sipping coffee. His great-grand-father, Nelson LaRou, a once-famous Hollywood director now retired, who was called the Great One by all the family, seemed to be enjoying the heated conversation between Matt and Luke, who were standing nose to nose while arguing over the best grazing lands. Matt's wife, Vanessa, and Luke's recent bride, Ingrid, along with Ingrid's little sister, Lily, continued setting platters on the big trestle table, oblivious to the noise. Burke Cowley stood to one side, grinning and sipping his coffee, without saying a word.

Matt turned to Reed. "Finally, somebody with a brain. Tell Luke what you told me about the South Ridge pasture."

Reed crossed the room and helped himself to a mug of steaming coffee. "Sorry. It's been a long morning. While you guys were still thinking about getting out of bed, Colin and I made the long trek from the hills after riding herd on a bunch of ornery cows for the past month. My backside aches, my stomach is grumbling, and I'm not getting dragged into a family feud."

"We're not feuding. Hell," Luke muttered, "if we were, fists would be flying."

"Not in my kitchen." Yancy drained a platter of crisp bacon and handed it to Ingrid.

The others chuckled.

"We're having a…lively discussion." Matt set down his mug with a clatter.

"And I'm having breakfast before I starve." Reed turned to Yancy. "Is it ready?"

"All ready." Yancy began tossing flapjacks onto a huge plate. "Get it while it's hot."

As one, the family began gathering around the big table, with Frank and Gracie at one end and the Great One at the other. Matt, Vanessa, Luke, and Ingrid sat on one side, and Lily, Reed, and Yancy sat on the other.

Ingrid's sister, nine-year-old Lily Larsen, had adopted the Great One as her very own grandfather, and she glowed whenever she looked at him. The old man accepted her hero worship as a sacred trust, and he had completely lost his heart to this tough little tomboy.

As they passed the platters of bacon, scrambled eggs, flapjacks and syrup, as well as toast and cinnamon biscuits, the conversation turned, as always, to the family business.

Frank turned to Reed. "I'm surprised you'd leave the herd in the middle of the season. How did Colin pry you away?"

Reed took a moment to savor Yancy's light-as-air pancakes before turning toward the ranch foreman. "Burke sent word that if I didn't take a break soon he'd hog-tie me and haul my—" A glance at his grandmother had him pausing to remember where he was. He might swear like a wrangler when up in the hills, but here at home, he was respectful. He added lamely, "He'd haul my hide down the mountain himself."

Frank turned to Burke. "What's this about? You know it's do-or-die time for Reed."

"True," the foreman said. "But even a dedicated cattleman needs time away from his herd so he doesn't forget how to be civilized."

Luke looked up. "Are you saying our little brother is going caveman on us?"

At his remark, the others laughed.

Burke nodded. "Take a look at him. Hair to his shoulders. Beard longer than Father Time's. He's been spending so much time in the hills, I wasn't sure he was even human. So I suggested he take a few days here. I'm sure the wranglers can keep his precious herd safe that long."

Reed ducked his head and continued eating.

It was no secret that he was pinning a lot of hope on a herd he was raising on the North Ridge, using no antibiotics to enhance their growth and feeding them only range grass. Since he'd begun experimenting with his special herd back in his teens, he'd never once seen a profit. In fact, if it hadn't been for the family picking up the cost, he would have had to give up on his dream years ago.

But now he was feeling even greater pressure to succeed.

On his last trip to Italy, Matt, the family's designated business manager, had managed to swing a deal with Leone Industries, a successful, well-respected multinational conglomerate. They were willing to take a chance on the fledgling green industry, hoping to corner the market on all-natural beef. For the first time since he'd begun his project, all Reed's years of backbreaking work promised to pay off. Not only could he repay the debt he owed to his family, but he could also bring their already successful ranch business into the future.

"They're looking healthy." He turned to his uncle, who'd accompanied him on his predawn ride. "Wouldn't you say so?"

Colin nodded. "We did the usual weigh-in, to see if they're keeping up with the herd getting antibiotics and enhanced feed. So far, they're matching pound for pound."

"That's great." Frank turned to Matt. "Think they'll be ready for shipment after roundup?"

"If Reed says they'll be ready, they will be." Matt smiled at his wife. "Maybe Nessa and I will go along to make sure they arrive safely."

"Very noble of you, bro." Reed nudged Yancy, and the two shared a grin. "I'm sure while you're in Rome, you'll be forced to spend some time at Maria's villa and sip a few bottles of her family's wine."

"Just to be sociable," Matt deadpanned.

Around the table, everyone shared in the joke. Matt had been promising his wife a trip to Italy when their new house was completed. And in truth, no one else was willing to volunteer. Most of them preferred life on the ranch to international travel, even if that travel meant enjoying some exotic perks.

"I need someone to drive me into town today," the Great One announced.

"What time?" Reed helped himself to seconds.

"Noon. I have an appointment with"—the old man stared pointedly at Colin—"Dr. Anita Cross. She wants to check my heart."

"Did you tell her you don't have one?"

At Colin's comment, the others chuckled.

"This is your last chance to have an excuse to see the pretty doctor, sonny boy."

"Sorry, Great One." Colin shook his head. "You know I'll take any excuse to spend time with Anita, but it's my turn to take up the Cessna."

The family routinely flew across their land to check on herds, outbuildings, and far-flung wranglers, to assess anything that might need their attention.

Reed polished off the last of his eggs. "I don't mind driving you, Great One. While you're seeing the good doctor, I'll load up on supplies and maybe even stop by the Pig Sty and have a longneck with the locals." He shot a grin at Burke. "Is that civilized enough for you?"

"Just so you don't spoil your appetite for supper." Yancy circled the table topping off cups of coffee. "I'm planning on grilling steaks."

"With your special twice-baked potatoes, I hope." Frank reached for a pitcher of maple syrup.

"You bet." Yancy ruffled Lily's hair before adding, "And chocolate torte for the ladies."

Grace was all smiles. "You just said the magic word, Yancy."

"I thought that'd make you happy, Miss Grace."

Later, as breakfast wound down and the family members made ready for the day, Luke elbowed his younger brother. "I suggest you shave and have Yancy cut that hair before you go to town, or nobody will recognize you. But I'm glad you're the one stuck taking the Great One to town. I'd rather watch paint dry than have to spend hours twiddling my thumbs in Glacier Ridge." He shook his head as he turned away muttering, "Nothing ever happens in that place."

* * *

Reed halted the ranch truck next to the entrance of the Glacier Ridge Clinic and hopped out, circling around to the passenger side to assist his great-grandfather.

After breakfast he'd taken a seat in the yard while Yancy gave him a haircut, a chore the ranch cook had gladly taken on when Reed and his brothers were kids. Then Reed had shaved his beard before taking the longest shower of his life.

Burke had been right, he thought. He was feeling almost human again.

The minute they stepped inside the clinic, the medical assistant, Agnes, hurried over. "Hello, Mr. LaRou. Dr. Anita told me to take you into Exam Room One." She turned to Reed. "Are you staying in town?"

He nodded. "I'll either be at D & B's Diner or Clay's Pig Sty."

"I'll call you when Dr. Cross is finished here."

He patted the old man's shoulder. "Have fun."

The Great One gave him a slanted look. "Don't I always?"

Reed was grinning as he climbed into the truck and drove slowly through town. Knowing the Great One, he'd soon have the entire staff mesmerized with his inside stories of Hollywood's rich and famous.

He spotted a vacant parking slot halfway between the diner and Trudy Evans's shop, Anything Goes. Minutes later he started walking up the street, enjoying the sunny day as he glanced in the windows of all the buildings that made up the little town of Glacier Ridge.

He paused to wave a greeting at one of the customers in Snips and Dips, the local beauty and barbershop, and almost missed the blur of motion that dashed past him and darted into the street.

He was still grinning, but his smile was wiped away when he realized that the blur was a little red-haired boy wearing a superhero cape, his legs pumping and arms swinging as he raced headlong into the middle of Main Street.

"Hey. Hold on there." Reed dashed after the little guy and scooped him up just as a driver in a delivery truck leaned on his horn and veered to one side, barely missing the boy.

Reed's heart was thundering when he realized how close he'd come to witnessing a tragedy.

He carried the boy to the curb before kneeling down, still holding on to his wriggling bundle. "Didn't your mother teach you to stop and look both ways?"

"Mama?" The boy shoved round-framed owl glasses up the freckled bridge of his nose and looked around with a puzzled frown.

"Yes. Your mama. Where is she?"

Suddenly the sunny smile was wiped from the cherubic little face, and the boy looked close to tears. "I want my mama."

"Yeah. So do I." Now that the danger had passed, Reed's famous temper flared. What kind of mother let her kid run wild? "Now let's find her."

When the little guy tried to wrench his hand free, Reed picked him up to keep him from dashing back into the street. As he walked along the sidewalk, he was peering into the window of each shop.

Within minutes, a young woman sailed out of the doorway of a shop, her eyes wide with fear. "Kyle. Kyle. Where are—"

Seeing her son in the arms of a stranger had the words dying in her throat.

"What are you doing with my ... ? Where did you ... ?"

"In the middle of the street. Isn't he a bit young to be running loose without someone looking out for him?"

Reed hadn't meant to be so harsh, but the thought of what could have happened had the words spilling out in a much rougher tone than he intended.

"My fault completely." She held out her arms and Reed handed the boy over. Then she buried her face in the boy's hair. "Oh, Kyle. You scared the wits out of me."

Reed studied the mother and son. It was easy to see where the little boy got his hair. Hers was a tangle of wild copper curls, falling past her shoulders and framing a face so pretty, he couldn't stop staring.

"I was flying, Mama."

"Yes. I see. But you know better than to go in the street."

"Cars can't hurt me when I'm Super Kid."

She took in a deep, shaky breath. "That's what I get for going along with your game." Over his head, she met Reed's disapproving look. "Thank you. I'm grateful you were there to save him. I'm Allison Shaw ... Ally, and this is my son, Kyle. He's four."

"I'm almost five," the little boy corrected.

"He's almost five." She stuck out her hand and Reed was forced to accept her handshake, though he was still feeling less than cheerful about a mother who let her kid tempt Fate.

"I guess almost five can be an ... imaginative age," Reed said.

"If his imagination was any stronger, I'd have to clone myself to keep up."

That brought a grudging smile to Reed's lips. Or maybe it was the tingle along his arm when their hands met. The rush of heat caught him by surprise.

"I'm sure he keeps you on your toes." He released her hand. "I'm Reed Malloy. Are you and Kyle new in town?"

She nodded. "We moved here from Virginia. I'm opening a business"—she pointed to the sign over a tiny shop that read ALLY'S ATTIC—"and Kyle and I are staying with my uncle. Maybe you know him. Archer Stone."

"Yeah, I know Archer. Sheriff Graystoke's deputy. I didn't know the town's bachelor had family."

"I think we're his only family. I know he's all we have. He was my mother's brother."

Was. Reed didn't bother to ask more. He was well acquainted with family that was here and then gone in the blink of an eye.

"Come on, Kyle. Time to get back to work." She set down her son and kept his hand firmly in hers as she started toward the shop.

Reed moved along beside them. "What sort of business is Ally's Attic?"

"It's a consignment shop. People can bring in things they have that still work but they have no room or use for. They can set a price, or let me set what I think is a fair price. I get a percentage of each item I sell. It's also a swap shop. For a fee, I can arrange for folks to trade something they have for something they want in my shop."

They stepped inside, and Reed looked around at the neat shelves, the clever presentations of items already listed for sale or trade.

Ally pointed. "Like that piano in the window display. Clara McEvoy brought it in yesterday. Her husband and son-in-law delivered it, saying she was glad to be rid of it. No one's touched it since her daughter grew up and moved away. Just this morning, even though we don't officially open until Saturday, a woman knocked on the door and left her card with a promise to be back after school today to pay me. Besides teaching here at the school, she wants to teach music in her home, and this piano is the answer to her prayers. She wanted to lock in the sale before anybody else even had a chance to see it."

"Looks like you're doing the folks in town a service, and making money doing it."

She smiled. "That's the plan. I certainly hope so. I really need this to work out for us."

Us.

Reed cleared his throat. "So, is your husband helping?"

"I don't have a—"

Kyle tugged on his mother's leg. "I'm hungry."

She glanced at the clock on the wall. "Oh, honey, I'm sorry. I got so busy, I forgot all about lunch. Come on. I'll fix some peanut butter and jelly sandwiches."

Before she could catch his hand, Reed blurted, "I'm thinking about lunch, too. Have you eaten at D & B's Diner?"

The minute the words were out of his mouth, he regretted them. Apparently his mouth was working ahead of his brain. Or what little he had at the moment.

Ally shook her head. "We haven't had time to visit any of the businesses here in town yet. We've been too busy cleaning and stocking the store. It's easier and a lot cheaper to just catch a snack here."

He noted her flush of embarrassment. "Well then, it's time you met the town newspaper."

At her arched brow he explained, "Dot and Barb. The twin sisters who own D & B's. They know everything that happens around Glacier Ridge almost as soon as it happens, and they're more than happy to share the news with their eager customers. In fact, just as many folks come in for the gossip as for their famous sandwiches, pot roast, and pie."

Though she was laughing, she shook her head. "Thanks for the invitation, but I can't—"

"My treat." He stared pointedly at Kyle. "Besides, it saves you from having to fix lunch. You can save the peanut butter and jelly for tomorrow."

Kyle looked up. "Do they have grilled cheese?"

Reed nodded. "In fact, it's one of my favorites."

"Oh boy." He turned pleading eyes toward his mother. "Please, Mama."

She sighed. "All right." She took his hand and trailed Reed from the shop. As they started along the sidewalk, she added, "You had me at not having to fix lunch."

Reed grinned. "And here I thought it was my charm."

When Colin Malloy lost his beloved brother and sister-in-law years ago, he swore he'd always be there for their three strong sons. Now that the boys are grown and have found love, Colin wonders if the time for his own happily-ever-after has passed. But when a holiday storm leaves him stranded with the town's beautiful brunette doctor, he may experience a Christmas miracle—and find true love.

A preview of *A Cowboy's Christmas Eve* follows.

CHAPTER ONE

Colin Malloy urged his big bay gelding through snow-drifts that were belly-high in places along the trail. When the latest snowstorm had begun in earnest in the hills, he'd had half a mind to remain snug and warm in his mountain cabin retreat until it blew itself out. But he couldn't miss Christmas Eve supper at the ranch.

Colin peered through the curtain of snow toward the distant lights of the Malloy Ranch. He wasn't really bothered by the snowy trail or the bite in the wind. Having grown up on these thousand-plus acres here in Montana, he was as comfortable in a blizzard as he was sleeping under the stars on a warm summer night. And though he often enjoyed a quiet night up at the cabin, with a steak over the fire and a cold longneck, the thought of his family's special Christmas Eve guest had him thinking instead about maybe a bottle of champagne and some roast goose. But only if it came with a certain pretty, dark-haired woman, Anita Cross, who'd been sneaking into his thoughts lately.

The only time they'd ever spoken was when his wild-and-crazy nephews got themselves bloodied badly enough to require a doctor's care, since her full title was Dr. Anita Cross. She had come to Montana to join her uncle at the town's medical clinic.

Since their first meeting, when his nephew Matt was seriously injured, she'd impressed him with not only her skill as a doctor but also with her radiant personality. Just the thought of her filled him with a sort of quiet joy. She had a smile that could light up the darkest night. And a sweet nature that just made him want to treat her with the greatest of care. That is, when he wasn't thinking about taking her into his arms and tasting those perfect lips and ravishing her until they were both sated.

He hadn't felt like this about a woman since Shelby Ross, whose father owned a ranch in Rock Creek. They'd been barely past their teens, but it had felt a lot like love. Maybe it was because his older brother had married the great love of his life, Bernadette, when the two were just seventeen. Watching Patrick and Bernie had Colin believing in true love and happily-ever-after. But those beliefs were shattered when the two had been killed in an brutal accident on a snowy road one cold December night. Shortly after, Colin learned that Shelby had run off with one of her father's wranglers.

So much for true love and happy endings.

And now, all these years later, he was beginning to believe in such things all over again.

He swore softly.

Not that a doctor from a big city would ever give him a

second look. And if she did, he stood no chance of being alone with her. With his big, noisy family, they probably wouldn't get a single word in edgewise tonight.

"Come on, Buddy." He leaned over to run a big, work-roughened hand over his horse's snow-matted mane. "Time to get home and make sure Ma has her Merry Christmas. And, if I'm lucky, I can sit in the corner and stare to my heart's content at the prettiest girl in the whole world, even though she doesn't know I'm alive."

"Hey, Yancy." Reed Malloy shook snow from his hair as he looked around the kitchen of his family's ranch house, where the table was set with festive holiday plates, and the countertops were covered with serving dishes of every size and shape.

Yancy Martin, the short, boyish-looking cook for the Malloy family for more than thirty years, looked up to grin at the youngest of the Malloy men. "Hey, Reed." He returned his attention to the finishing touches on an elegant holiday torte, making swirls of dark chocolate in the creamy white frosting.

"Something smells amazing." Luke Malloy, Reed's older brother, trailed behind, his arm around the waist of his bride, Ingrid. "Looks like you're going all out on the menu for Christmas Eve supper."

Yancy's head came up. "Miss Grace told me she wanted it to be extra special, because of our guests."

"Guests?" Matt Malloy, oldest of the three brothers, walked into the kitchen hand in hand with his wife, Vanessa, and tried to dip a finger in the frosting. It was quickly slapped away by Yancy's wooden spoon. "Are we having more than family here tonight?"

Yancy gave a conspiratorial grin. "Your grandma invited old Doc Cross and his niece, Dr. Anita."

Luke shared a look with his brother. "All this fuss for two extra people?"

"One of them is extra special, according to Miss Grace."

At their puzzled looks, Yancy shook his head, sharing a knowing smile with Vanessa and Ingrid. "Where've you three been? Don't you know your grandmother has had her eye on Anita Cross as a potential wife for your uncle Colin ever since that pretty young doctor came to town?"

The two women nodded in agreement.

"Wife?" Reed started laughing. "Seems to me Gram Gracie's had every pretty girl in the town of Glacier Ridge paired with Colin since we were teenagers. And none of them worked out. What makes her think this will be any different?"

Yancy shrugged.

It was the boys' great-grandfather, Nelson LaRou, called the Great One by all of them, seated in his favorite chair across the room, who answered. "If I had to hazard a guess, I'd say it's the two family weddings this past year. First Matt to his Nessa, and then"—he turned to fix Luke with a pointed stare—"Luke and Ingrid." He paused to sip the martini Yancy had learned to fix to his exact specifications and gave a nod of approval. "Now Grace Anne hopes all that romance rubs off on your uncle Colin. I swear, my daughter's bound and determined to get that poor man married off before, as she says, it's too late."

Reed reached for a gingerbread cookie cooling on a wire rack, until Yancy stopped him with a hairy eyeball. "Too late for what?"

"Too late for him to give me more grandchildren."

Grace Malloy breezed into the kitchen, wearing her usual ankle-skimming denim skirt and a sky-blue blouse that matched her eyes, her white hair a cap of breeze-tossed curls.

She made a full circle in the room, staring around with satisfaction. "It all looks and smells wonderful, Yancy."

Reed put a hand on her arm. "Are you really setting up poor Colin on the pretext of a holiday dinner?"

"Setting up poor Colin?" Grace gave her grandson a withering look. "I'm merely being a good mother and a good neighbor. After all, Anita came to Glacier Ridge from Boston to give her aging uncle a hand at the clinic, and she hasn't had any time off since. She's young and beautiful and certainly deserves at least a bit of a social life. It's the same with Colin. He's spent so many years helping us with the ranch, not to mention helping your father and me with you three—a handful, I might add—he's forgotten there even is such a thing as a social life."

Reed merely shook his head. "Poor Colin. Being led to the slaughter like a lamb, without even a warning."

"Enough of that kind of talk. He'll thank me one day. And," Gracie added with a twinkle in her eye, "I'll expect you to be here to witness his eternal gratitude. Maybe, if you're lucky, I'll even steer you toward finding that one special woman for yourself."

Reed put his hand up to his ears and gave a mock shudder. "Now you're working overtime to ruin my Christmas, Gram Gracie. I've seen enough lovey-dovey stuff around here in the past year to give me a sugar buzz."

The others laughed as Reed rushed from the kitchen and up the stairs to shower and dress for Christmas Eve supper.

* * *

Dr. Leonard Cross poked his head into the examining room, where his niece was busy soothing the mother of a crying five-year-old girl.

Anita Cross put her hand on the mother's shoulder. "The rapid strep test confirmed that it's strep throat, Millie. I'll write a prescription. Agnes will have it at the reception area when you check out. Be sure to pick it up at Woodrow's Pharmacy before it closes tonight, and start Brittany on the medication right away. She won't be feeling a hundred percent by tomorrow, but she'll feel a lot better than she does right now."

"Oh, thank you, Dr. Anita. She's been so worried that Santa wouldn't find her here at the clinic if she had to be admitted."

Turning on the megawatt smile that always put her patients at ease, Anita closed her hand over the little girl's tightly clenched fist. "You'll be home in plenty of time for Santa to visit, Brittany. But you should know that Santa has no problem finding children who have to be in the clinic. He visits children on Christmas Eve no matter where they are."

Big blue eyes went even wider. "He does?"

"He does. Why, when I was working in the hospital in Boston, Santa visited every boy and girl there and left them exactly what they'd asked for."

"That's nice." The tears were replaced with a big smile. "But I'm glad I can go home."

"So am I. I can't think of a better place to be on Christmas Eve than with the people you love." As the mother and daughter walked out of the room and her uncle stepped inside, Anita called out, "Merry Christmas."

Seeing that he'd changed from his white lab coat to a suit jacket, she raised a brow. "Is Dr. Miller here from Rock Creek yet?"

Her uncle shook his head. "Not yet. But I expect he'll be here any minute. He's already half an hour late."

"Have you phoned him?"

"Twice. No service. But he gave me his word he'd take care of things here while we were at the Malloy Ranch. I'm sure he'll be along any minute now."

Anita gave a sigh. "Is that the last of the patients?"

"According to Agnes. I told her to duck out of here as soon as she finishes with Millie Davis so she doesn't get stuck for another hour or two."

He glanced out the window at an approaching truck bearing the Malloy logo on the side. "There's our limousine. I promise you, you're going to love Christmas Eve dinner at the Malloy Ranch. Nobody cooks like Yancy Martin. You're in for a fine feast."

Anita knew it wasn't the feast she was looking forward to as much as the chance to spend some time with a certain cowboy. From the first moment she'd met Colin Malloy, quietly taking charge of the chaos that always seemed to accompany his family during a crisis, he had become, in her mind, the personification of a real Montana cowboy. Tall and ruggedly handsome. A body sculpted with muscle from years of ranch chores. Dark hair always in need of a trim. A quiet man who didn't say much, but when he spoke in that low, easy drawl, she felt a hitch in her heart. And when he aimed those blue eyes her way and smiled, her whole world seemed to tilt.

She didn't need food. Colin Malloy was a feast for her eyes and heart and soul.

Until coming to Montana, she'd despaired of ever meeting a man who seemed to check off every item on her personal wish list.

Of course, she thought, there had been men in the past, and one in particular, who had tempted her to believe they were special. Not one had ever lived up to the promise.

She thought about the bitter tears she'd shed over Dr. Jason Trask. At the time, she'd thought her heart would never mend. Now she realized she'd been too young and foolish to recognize that while she'd been spinning dreams of love and marriage, he'd been concerned only with himself and his career. It was only later, hearing the whispers and rumors, that she learned she'd been one of many naïve med students who had fallen for his tired line. As she followed her uncle along the hallway, she paused to greet Burke Cowley, the Malloy Ranch foreman, who was heading toward them. "Hello, Burke."

"Miss Anita." The courtly old cowboy removed his wide-brimmed hat and gave her a smile.

"I'll just be a minute while I get my coat."

"I'll let you lock up." Her uncle picked up several handled bags, containing the cookies she'd lovingly baked, along with gifts she'd insisted on wrapping for the entire Malloy family.

With his hands filled, he indicated several more bags, and Burke picked them up.

Over his shoulder her uncle called, "We'll load these and wait for you in the truck. I'm sure Dr. Miller will be here any minute now."

Anita stepped into her office and was hanging up her lab coat when she heard voices calling from the reception area. She hurried out to find a rancher with his arm around a teen boy's shoulders.

The boy's arm was wrapped in a bloody towel.

"Ma'am." The rancher looked relieved. "I saw old Doc Cross getting into a truck outside. I called to him, but he couldn't hear me over the wind blowing, and I was afraid we were too late to get any help. My name's Huck Whitfield. This is my son Ben. He put his hand through a glass windowpane."

"Mr. Whitfield. Ben. I'm Dr. Anita Cross."

"I heard old Doc talked a niece into coming out from the big city to give him a hand with this place."

"That's me. And I assure you, I didn't need to be talked into coming. I'm loving this experience in your pretty town. Please come this way." She led them to an examining room and carefully removed the blood-soaked towel.

She looked up at the boy. "That's a nasty cut, Ben." She tried to put him at ease. "You must have been really mad at that window to hit it so hard."

Instead of the expected laugh, two bright spots of color bloomed on the boy's cheeks. "Oh no, ma'am. I was just giving my pa a hand trying to clear the snow."

His father nodded. "That's a fact."

"I was only teasing."

At that, the father and son realized her joke and grinned.

She indicated the table. "You can lie down here. I'll need to look at this closely under the lights, to remove any glass fragments. Then, from the looks of all that blood, you'll need a few stitches." She started toward the door. "I'll be right back."

Once in the hallway she punched in the number of Dr.

Rob Miller, praying he would tell her he'd be here any minute now. In reply, she got a no-service notice.

She retrieved her lab coat before going in search of her uncle and Burke. When she stepped outside, she was surprised to see that a heavy snow had begun falling. And even though it was early evening, the sky had grown as dark as night.

Burke lowered the window as she approached the truck.

"Sorry, Uncle Leonard. I tried Dr. Miller's number, with no response. I won't be able to go with you. This is an emergency. Huck Whitfield and his son, Ben, came in while you were loading up the truck. Ben put his hand through a window, and the cut looks deep. I'd hoped to pass them along to Rob Miller, but since he's still not here, I have to stay. From the looks of that boy's arm, I'll be another hour or more."

Old Dr. Cross gave a sigh. "That's what I was afraid of. Even on Christmas Eve, we always seem to get slammed with one emergency or another. That's why I arranged for a doctor here, just in case."

Anita gave him a gentle smile. "Please don't worry, Uncle Leonard. You go ahead and have a lovely dinner with the Malloy family. I'll stay here and take care of business."

The two men exchanged a look before Burke said, "We'll wait for you."

"There could be complications. I don't want to hold up the entire Malloy family on Christmas Eve."

Burke considered before nodding. "All right. But don't you worry, ma'am. I'll take Dr. Cross out to the ranch now, and I'll head right back for you."

"That's awfully generous of you, Burke. But you could end up missing dinner."

"Wouldn't be the first time, ma'am."

She gave him a grateful smile. "All right. But you'd better phone first. Like Uncle Leonard said, I could get slammed with more emergencies. And I can't leave unless my replacement arrives."

Burke nodded. "Yes, ma'am. I'll call, and no matter how late it is, someone will be here to drive you to the ranch. When Miss Gracie issues an invitation, it's like a royal command."

"Please give Miss Grace my apologies for this hitch in her plans." With a grin, Anita sprinted back to the door of the clinic.

As she stepped inside, she had to shake snow from her dark hair.

Squaring her shoulders, she headed toward the examining room. Even Christmas, she thought, couldn't stem the flow of emergencies. Hadn't she known, when she completed her medical studies, that this would be her life? Not that she regretted it. Not a bit of it. Nor did she regret her move from a bustling city hospital to this sleepy little small-town clinic. Here, finally, she was doing what she'd always dreamed of. Seeing to every sort of medical emergency possible, from setting broken bones to removing tonsils. From dealing with preschool illnesses to arranging end-of-life care. As her uncle had promised, this place offered her the chance to follow her patients from childhood into old age. These strangers were no longer patients but were slowly becoming her neighbors and friends. Her family. She couldn't think of a more rewarding gift than the chance to live out her life in this sleepy little town of Glacier Ridge, with its fascinating assortment of characters, and this homey little clinic, which had taken over her life.

And if she felt a twinge of regret at missing her chance to spend more time with a handsome cowboy, she reluctantly pushed it aside. For now, she would give all her attention to Ben Whitfield and get him home in time for Christmas with his family.

Fall in Love with Forever Romance

TOO HOT TO HANDLE
By Tessa Bailey

Having already flambéed her culinary career beyond recognition, Rita Clarkson is now stranded in God-Knows-Where, New Mexico, with a busted-ass car and her three temperamental siblings. When rescue shows up—six-feet-plus of hot, charming sex on a motorcycle—Rita's pretty certain she's gone from the frying pan right into the fire...The first book in an all-new series from *New York Times* bestselling author Tessa Bailey!

SIZE MATTERS
By Alison Bliss

Fans of romantic comedies such as *Good in Bed* will eat up this delightful new series from Alison Bliss! Leah Martin has spent her life trying to avoid temptation, but she's sick of counting calories. Fortunately, her popular new bakery keeps her good and distracted. But there aren't enough éclairs in the world to distract Leah from the hotness that is Sam Cooper—or the fact that he just told her mother that they're engaged...which is a big, fat lie.

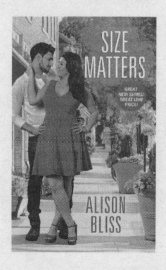

Fall in Love with Forever Romance

MAYBE THIS TIME
By Jennifer Snow

All through high school, talented hockey player Jackson Westmore had a crush on Abby Jansen, but he would never make a move on his best friend's girl. He gave her the cold shoulder out of self-preservation and worked out his frustrations on the ice. So when Abby returns, newly divorced and still sexy as hell, Jackson knows he's in trouble. Now even the best defensive skills might not keep him from losing his heart...

LUKE
By R. C. Ryan

When Ingrid Larsen discovers rancher Luke Malloy trapped in a ravine, she brings him to her family ranch and nurses him back to health. As he heals, he begins to fall for the tough independent woman who saved him, but a mysterious attacker threatens their love—and their lives. Fans of Linda Lael Miller and Diana Palmer will love the latest contemporary western in R. C. Ryan's Malloys of Montana series.

Fall in Love with Forever Romance

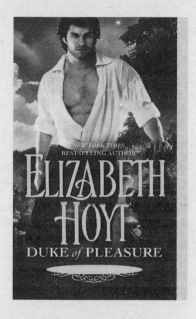

DUKE OF PLEASURE
By Elizabeth Hoyt

Sent to defeat the notorious Lords of Chaos, Hugh Fitzroy, the Duke of Kyle, is ambushed in a London alley—and rescued by an unlikely ally: a masked stranger with the unmistakable curves of a woman. Alf has survived on the streets of St. Giles by disguising her sex, but when Hugh hires her to help his investigation, will she find the courage to become the woman she needs to be—before the Lords of Chaos destroy them both?